TRANSFIXED BY HIS GAZE

She found herself mute, a most unusual experience, as she watched him come closer. He stretched out a hand and cupped her chin, lifting it slightly. Then his lips lightly brushed hers and her skin tingled. When she made no move, he slid his other hand around her waist, drawing her close against him.

When his lips pressed against hers, warm, pliable and yet firm with a hint of demand, she gave herself up to the tactile whirl of feeling, her eyes closing her into a world of pure physical sensation. His body was hard against hers, his arm warm and strong around her waist, the taste and scent of him a heady mélange of woodsmoke from the fire and the sweetness of butter and honey with an underlay of lemon, fresh and sharp on his skin.

When finally his mouth left hers, her eyes opened, looking straight into the piercing blue intensity of his gaze. "I enjoyed that," he said softly, brushing a loose strand of hair from her cheek.

She found her voice at last. "Yes," she murmured. "I did too."

"When can we do it again?" he said, a glint of humor in his eyes.

"Now?"

He drew her against him again, and this time the kiss was harder, fiercer, more demanding, and Fenella found herself responding with the same fierce demand, her body pressing against his as his hands moved down her back. . . .

Also by Jane Feather

Tempt Me With Diamonds

Love's Charade

Smuggler's Lady

Beloved Enemy

Reckless Seduction

SEDUCE ME
With SAPPHIRES

JANE
FEATHER

ZEBRA BOOKS
KENSINGTON PUBLISHING CORP.
www.kensingtonbooks.com

ZEBRA BOOKS are published by

Kensington Publishing Corp.
119 West 40th Street
New York, NY 10018

All Kensington titles, imprints, and distributed lines are available at special quantity discounts for bulk purchases for sales promotion, premiums, fund-raising, educational, or institutional use.

Special book excerpts or customized printings can also be created to fit specific needs. For details, write or phone the office of the Kensington Sales Manager: Attn.: Sales Department. Kensington Publishing Corp., 119 West 40th Street, New York, NY 10018. Phone: 1-800-221-2647.

Zebra and the Z logo Reg. U.S. Pat. & TM Off.

First Printing: February 2020
ISBN-13: 978-1-4201-4362-1
ISBN-10: 1-4201-4362-X

ISBN-13: 978-1-4201-4363-8 (eBook)
ISBN-10: 1-4201-4363-8 (eBook)

10 9 8 7 6 5 4 3 2 1

Printed in the United States of America

Chapter One

The Honorable Fenella Grantley glanced quickly along the corridor before she tiptoed past her mother's sitting room. Lady Grantley's avid curiosity about her only child's plans for the day was inconvenient at best. Fenella loved her mother dearly, but she found it difficult to turn aside the questions without appearing uncivil. And her mother was bound to want to know how her evening with George had gone. Lord George Headington was rapidly becoming a thorn in Fenella's side, but her mother's hopes in that direction were, if not openly expressed, obvious to the dullest intelligence.

She hurried down the horseshoe staircase and across the hall to the front door. To her relief, none of the servants were around and, most importantly, Collins, the butler, was nowhere to be seen. Collins had an uncanny ability to get information without appearing to ask for it, and Fenella was in no mood for questions from anyone.

She stepped out of the house onto a frigid Albemarle Street. It was not quite midmorning and the street, normally busy with hackney carriages and delivery carts, was unusually quiet. The winter had been vicious, and on freezing days like this one, the residential streets of Mayfair tended to be almost deserted.

She turned up the collar of her sable coat against a violent gust of icy wind and quickened her step, looking for a hackney, but she had reached Piccadilly before she saw one. The wide, shop-lined thoroughfare was busy with foot and carriage traffic and she waved down a hackney with little trouble.

"Gower Street," Fenella told the cabbie as she climbed in, grateful to be out of the wind for a minute. Alone in the musty interior she felt her spirits lift. She always felt this heady sense of freedom once she was on her way to Bloomsbury. She reveled in the sense that no one knew where she was, not even her dearest friends and certainly not her mother. No one knew where she was going or how she would spend her morning. Apart from the time she spent with Diana and Petra, life seemed, these days, to have a monotony to it. There was no sense of expectation or the possibility of surprise. She knew she had no right to feel this way; she should be thankful for her life of privilege and comfort. But somehow it didn't seem to be enough, and however often she chided herself for being ungrateful and spoiled, she couldn't shake off the grayness of her mood. And whenever she thought of Lord George Headington, the grayness grew darker and thicker.

The carriage turned the corner from Bloomsbury Square onto Gower Street, and Fenella fumbled in her change purse for the fare, her spirits lifting anew as she opened the door and jumped to the pavement, reaching up to the cabbie with the coins. He took them with a nod before taking a swig from a hip flask, clearing his throat and spitting phlegm onto the far pavement. Even in the bitter cold, the air was thick with the foul-smelling smoke from the sea coal fires of the poor and the heavy smoke from the anthracite heating of the houses of the rich. A day spent on London streets produced labored breathing and phlegm-filled lungs.

But Fenella was unaware of the polluted air; in her present uplifted mood, it smelled crisp, redolent of freedom. Bloomsbury was a respectable if unfashionable part of London, and one that had become familiar ground in her weekly forays over the last year. She went up the steps of a narrow, terraced house halfway along Gower Street and let herself in through a front door badly in need of repainting. The narrow hallway was equally in need of redecorating, the skirting boards scuffed, the linoleum on the floor scratched and lifting at the edges. The air was chilly despite the rattling huff from a steam radiator and the gaslight showed only dimly through its dust-coated sconce on the dingy, gray wall.

A narrow staircase rose to the upper floor from which the sounds of scales on a piano drifted down. Fenella hurried up the stairs to the first-floor landing. The piano was louder, coming from behind one of the closed, badly painted doors along the corridor. The chill light of the February morning showed through a grimy window at the far end of the corridor. Fenella opened a door halfway along.

"Good morning, everyone," she greeted the small group of people gathered around a long table in the large room. They were all huddled in coats, gloved fingers fumbling with sheaves of paper in front of them. Another steam radiator grumbled ineffectually from beneath a window, which looked out onto the street.

"Oh, good, you're here at last," commented an elderly man with a distinguished mane of silver hair sitting at the head of the table. His threadbare frock coat, fingerless gloves and stringy woolen muffler did nothing to diminish the power of his presence.

Fenella refrained from pointing out that she was actually five minutes early. "My apologies, Cedric, I didn't realize I was keeping everyone waiting." She offered a general smile, remarking, "It's bitter out there," as she took a spare seat at the table, drawing her coat closer around her.

"It's bitter in here," a young man muttered through his muffler. "If we're to continue meeting like this through the winter, Cedric, we need a kerosene stove or something."

Cedric Hardcastle, an irascible man at the best of times, ran his little drama school out of this run-down Bloomsbury house on a shoestring and glared at the speaker. "If you can pay for the fuel, Robert?"

Robert muttered something and chewed the tip of a pencil, staring down at the scratched tabletop. Fenella winced. She was the only member of this troupe who could afford to supply both stove and fuel, but she tried not to draw attention to her privileged world. They were all here for one reason: a passion for drama and a longing to tread the boards themselves. Cedric had been a well-known classical actor until alcohol and memory loss had rendered him incapable of taking the stage, so he'd set up his acting school, the only one of its kind, in the hopes of making some kind of a living. It was a paltry one at best.

Fenella picked up the sheaf of papers in front of her. It was an unfamiliar script; in general, their readings were from various forms of classical drama.

"We're reading a new play today," Cedric announced. "And we're very fortunate to have the playwright with us to interpret any complexities in the script. Edward, do you have anything to say before we start?" He nodded toward the shadows at the far side of the room.

Fenella looked up from the papers, wondering why she hadn't noticed the stranger sitting on the high stool when she'd first entered the room. When he stood up and stepped forward out of the shadows, she wondered even more at her initial failure to notice him. His physical presence was significant. He was a tall man with broad, powerful shoulders and square, competent hands. Fenella had always been drawn to a man's hands. She liked them well-manicured and capable-looking. This Edward's certainly fit that bill. She offered him a curious and friendly smile and was rather put off to encounter something akin to a scowl. The effect of the scowl was somewhat diminished by his eyes, which were of the most penetrating, startling blue Fenella had ever come across. Thick, unruly black eyebrows matched the equally untidy thatch of black hair flopping on his forehead and curling over his collar. It gave him a rakish air. It was a pity about the scowl, she thought.

She glanced down again at the script. "Edward Tremayne" was written boldly on the title page, and beneath it, *Sapphire*. The only Tremaynes she knew socially, Viscount Grayling and Lady Julia, were the children of the Earl of Pendleton, but this morose individual couldn't possibly be associated with that family. He reminded her of an ill-tempered, scruffy mongrel, with his black, overlong hair much in need of a brush. Which, of course, was most uncharitable of her, and Fenella was not, in general, uncharitable.

"*Sapphire*?" she queried pleasantly. "Is that the title of the play?"

"It's a working title," Edward Tremayne declared with a dismissive flick of his hand. His voice was attractive, deep and well-modulated. "If you read the script, you might understand the point."

Fenella felt her initial prickle of irritation blossom into an active dislike. She and Mr. Tremayne were not going to get along well if matters continued in this fashion. His arrogance was palpable. But perhaps he was nervous at the prospect of hearing his play read by strangers, or even perhaps for the first time ever. With an effort, she accepted the charitable explanation and swallowed her annoyance, removing her attention from him by deliberately turning her head away and asking Cedric, "Do we have specific parts for the reading, or are we going around the table?"

"You're reading Rose," Edward Tremayne declared. "I don't mind who else reads what. Cedric, you decide."

"Why am I to play this Rose character?" Fenella asked, genuinely puzzled at such a definite statement. "You don't know me. You haven't heard me read. How can you be so sure I'll be right for it?"

"I can't. Call it instinct," he responded.

Fenella frowned, a strange feeling of déjà vu prickling the nape of her neck. There was something familiar about him, a sense that she'd caught an image of him in her peripheral vision at some point. A glancing familiarity. She stared at him as the memory crystallized. She *had* seen him before, she realized. Several times, in fact. She remembered one of the innumerable dances she'd attended during an occasion as boring and unproductive as most of them except that she'd been acutely aware of a man standing, arms folded, against the wall, glaring at the dancing couples. She'd been struck by the glare, which rather mirrored her own feelings hidden beneath the polite smile and cheerful inconsequential chatter.

She'd forgotten all about him once the dance was over, but now she remembered that once she'd thought he'd been outside her house, just hovering across the street when she'd come down the front steps. If he hadn't been such a large and imposing figure, she probably wouldn't have noticed him at all among the ambling pedestrians on Albemarle Street.

And once, walking down Park Lane, she'd had the unmistakable sensation of being followed. She'd cast an involuntary glance over her shoulder just as a tall man disappeared into an alley. At the time, the glimpses had not struck her as strange. He was a member of the privileged society inhabiting the streets of Mayfair; it was hardly surprising she would catch sight of him now and then. Now the extraordinary thought struck her that perhaps these occasional appearances had been intentional.

Ridiculous idea. She was just being fanciful. What possible reason could he have had to follow her? Anyway, she was far too interested in the idea of the reading to continue pointless speculation. She shuffled the pages of the script and quickly saw that Rose appeared on almost every page. Well, she was always up for a challenge; this whole acting project had started as a challenge, one she kept very much to herself. Lord and Lady Grantley would have forty fits if they knew of it; it was hardly a suitable activity for a baron's daughter. For some reason she hadn't even confided in her oldest and closest friends. Fenella wondered if she was embarrassed or ashamed of this weird passion but decided that she was neither. It was just something very personal and private . . . a welcome distraction from the restless malaise that for some reason hovered over her these days.

However, it occurred to her now that it was definitely time to confide in Diana and Petra. The secret was getting too demanding to keep to herself. The whole business was taking up too much of her time to continue pretending to herself that it was just a hobby, of no more significance than Diana and her racehorse, or Petra and her passion for eccentric and colorful clothes and all things related to the music hall.

"Shall we begin?" Cedric said after allocating the remaining parts around the table.

Fenella, as usual, quickly lost herself in the drama of the reading. It was one of the things she loved so much about the activity, the way it took her out of herself. But she wasn't sure about her character. She seemed more a cipher than a real person and it was hard to get a handle on how to play her. Once or twice she became aware of Edward Tremayne looming behind her, seeming even larger on his feet than he had on his stool. And he made her nervous, which annoyed her even more.

She stumbled over a line and heard an audible sigh of exasperation behind her. She slapped her hand on the papers in front of her and turned to look over her shoulder. "Could you possibly stand somewhere else, Mr. Tremayne? You're putting me off."

The blue eyes narrowed, and for a second, a pop of fire illuminated their sapphire depths. Edward offered a mock bow. "Forgive me, Miss Grantley. I have no intention of disturbing your delicate sensibilities. In my experience, amateur actors can't afford to be too sensitive."

"I am not in the least sensitive *or* delicate," Fenella retorted, wondering what she could have done to arouse such hostility from a stranger. "But when all I can hear is your heavy breathing down the back of my neck, I find it impossible to concentrate." Her gray eyes snapped at him.

He stepped back, raising his hands in a defensive posture. "The lady has a temper, I see. Where should I put myself, ma'am, so that I don't disturb your concentration?"

"I couldn't care less," she stated. "Just don't stand behind me." Fenella was aware of the interested, amused eyes of her companions. This completely unnecessary spat was proving entertaining to everyone but herself.

"This Rose character has no stuffing to her," she declared, now more than ready to do battle. "She's just flat words on a page. There's no fire, no emotion, no hint of complexity, nothing to work with." She ordered the papers in a neat pile in front of her. "I have no interest in this reading, Cedric. I apologize to you all." She stood up abruptly, for the moment not caring what bridges she was burning. Drawing on her gloves, she left the room, an astounded silence in her wake.

She marched down the stairs to the sounds of the piano scales repeating endlessly behind her and let herself out onto Gower Street, hugging her anger and frustration to her against the February cold. She rarely lost her temper; it tended to do no good, and more often did the opposite, not to mention leading to a loss of dignity, and she was angry with herself now for letting Tremayne's arrogance and contempt to provoke her into abandoning an activity that was becoming essential to her sense of well-being, one that gave her so much satisfaction. She turned the corner toward Bloomsbury Square.

"Hey, hold on a minute, Miss Grantley."

The voice behind her made her increase her speed. She heard his steps coming up fast at her back. "Obviously I didn't make myself clear, Mr. Tremayne. I have no interest in your company and even less in your play." She spoke without slowing, but he caught up with her easily and fell into step beside her. He'd followed her in haste judging by his unbuttoned coat and gloveless hands.

"Allow me to buy you a cup of coffee, Fenella . . . I may call you Fenella? We have some fences to mend, it would seem."

She stopped and looked up at him, exasperated that she had to look up so far to meet his eye. "No, you may not call me Fenella. And no, I don't wish for coffee. Also, I have no interest in mending fences of any kind. Good day to you, Mr. Tremayne." Spinning on her booted heel, she stalked off toward Bloomsbury Square.

Edward hesitated for only a moment. He couldn't afford to let her go. The last thing he had thought he wanted was a pampered, privileged Society lady to play his Rose, and yet against every instinct, when he thought of Rose, he couldn't get the image of the Honorable Fenella Grantley out of his mind. It had been like that from the moment he first saw her at some dance on his one and only foray into Society's brittle playground. *Sapphire* and its main character were becoming solid, taking shape on the page, and for some extraordinary reason, the moment he laid eyes on Fenella Grantley, she became inseparable from Rose.

He moved swiftly after Fenella, drawing level with her again, putting a hand on her arm. "Please, just listen to me, just for a minute."

His tone was so different from the mocking sarcasm of earlier that she slowed almost involuntarily, glancing up at him again. Those blue eyes were different, warm, amused and most definitely penitent. "I was horrid, I know. Please forgive me. Sometimes, when I'm particularly anxious about something important, I can't seem to help myself. I become most unpleasant to people."

"I see," Fenella said dryly. "And is this unfortunate change of character a frequent occurrence, Mr. Tremayne?"

He ran a hand through the disordered thatch of hair, pushing it off his forehead. "I deserve it, I know. But could we go somewhere warmer while you excoriate me?" A violent gust of wind whistled around the corner of Bloomsbury Square as if in punctuation.

Fenella felt an absurd urge to laugh. Not for one minute did she believe the humble penitent side of Edward Tremayne, but she found herself both intrigued and amused by it. A sufficiently novel feeling these days for her to want to indulge it.

"You may buy me a cup of hot chocolate, Mr. Tremayne. There's a café on the far side of the square."

He bowed with a flourish. "You do me too much honor, ma'am." He offered his arm with an air of scrupulous formality.

Fenella slipped her gloved hand inside his arm

and, feeling very much as if she was acting a part in some comedy sketch, directed her step to the café in the square.

Edward pushed open the door onto a warm fug of well-wrapped bodies, cigarette smoke and steaming cups. Fenella stepped in ahead of him and he swiftly closed the door before anyone could complain at the blast of cold air.

"At least it's warm," she observed, loosening her scarf. It was hard to breathe and she waved a hand in front of her face, trying to clear the air.

"You'll get used to it in a minute," Edward told her, guiding her with a hand at her back toward a spare table by the far wall.

Fenella felt that prickle of irritation again. His tone was brusque, dismissive, and that guiding hand was far too familiar a gesture from a near stranger. Nevertheless, she sat down in the chair he pulled out for her and drew off her gloves, picking up the menu in front of her.

"You should undo your coat," he said, glancing at his own menu. "If you don't, you won't feel the benefit when you go outside again."

Fenella regarded him in astonishment and saw that he was laughing, or at least his eyes were; his mouth had a slightly humorous twist that against her better judgment she found rather attractive.

"At least that was what my nanny used to tell me," he said, pushing the menu aside.

"So did mine," Fenella responded, unable to keep the responding amusement from her voice. What was it about him? He could be so off-putting one minute, then the epitome of humor and charm the next.

A harried waitress hurried over to them. "What can I get you?"

"Hot chocolate, please," Fenella replied.

"Coffee," Edward stated. He glanced at Fenella. "Anything to eat?"

Fenella considered while the waitress tapped her pencil against her notepad. "Yes. I'd like a toasted tea cake," she decided.

"Two, then," Edward told the waitress, who sniffed and hurried away. "I don't think she's happy in her work," he observed drily.

Fenella gave a wry smile. "I can't imagine why she would be. It must be exhausting, on your feet all day carrying heavy trays, and not everyone's polite or appreciative."

"So, the Honorable Miss Grantley has a social conscience," he said, raising his thick eyebrows.

She frowned. "Must you always sound so unpleasant?"

"Oh, not always, surely," he protested, eyebrows still raised in a sardonic arch.

Fenella pushed back her chair, setting her hands on the table as she prepared to get to her feet. "I cannot think of a single reason why I should stay here as the butt of your ill-temper."

He moved, lightning fast, his hand shooting out to seize her wrist. "Forgive me, Fenella, please. Sometimes I just can't help myself. Please stay and let me redeem myself."

She regarded him for a moment in exasperation. "Why on earth should I?"

He kept hold of her wrist, although the clasp was light and she could easily free herself. "Because I am truly sorry, and because I want to talk to you about my play, and because I find you . . ." He hesitated, as if looking for words. "Because I find you compelling. I want to get to know you, Fenella. No, I *need* to get to know you. Please sit down again."

Every instinct told her to walk away, put him out of her mind, forget about him and his wretched play. And yet she sat down again as his fingers released her wrist. The waitress set their drinks and hot, buttery tea cakes on the table.

"Anything else?"

"No, thank you," Fenella said swiftly, stirring the thick, dark liquid in her cup with a show of concentration such a simple action didn't warrant.

Edward said nothing for a moment, cutting his tea cake in half, spooning sugar into his coffee. Finally he said softly, "Thank you."

"What for?" She took a sip of her chocolate, regarding him through the curling steam.

"For forgiving my rudeness . . . for staying."

"I may be staying, but I'm not sure I've forgiven," she retorted, turning her attention to her tea cake.

He gave her a rueful half-smile. "Fair enough."

"We've never actually met before, but I've seen you several times," Fenella stated abruptly.

Chapter Two

"Yes, we've encountered each other before, but as we weren't introduced, I'm surprised you remember." He raised a quizzical eyebrow.

Fenella frowned. "Tremayne?" she mused. "The only Tremaynes I know are Carlton and Julia. Their father is the Earl of Pendleton, but we don't move in the same circles."

"That doesn't surprise me," he responded with his sardonic smile. "I myself find my half siblings thoroughly unpleasant."

"Half siblings?"

"Yes. I'm what I think is generally known as a by-blow." His tone was caustic, but he was watching her closely for her reaction.

"Ah, born on the wrong side of the blanket, in other words," she responded matter-of-factly.

"Precisely. My mother was an actress. Elizabeth Austel—you may have heard of her." He sipped his coffee.

"Not just heard of her. I saw her Desdemona at the Theatre Royal several years ago. She's a fine actress."

"Was," he corrected. "She died last year."

"Oh, I'm sorry. That must have been hard for you." Her smile was warmly sympathetic. "Were you very close?"

He shrugged, but there was something unconvincing about the casually dismissive gesture, Fenella thought. "I wasn't able to spend much time with her," he said. "My father insisted I live at Tremayne Court most of the year and went to Eton with Carlton. A second-class citizen, perhaps, but no one could fault my father for his insistence on treating me the same way he treated his legitimate offspring. On the surface, at least," he added.

Fenella absorbed this in silence. No wonder he was so moody, she reflected, having to play second fiddle to Carlton and Julia. From what she knew of them, neither could lay claim to an empathetic bone.

Again, she thought back to her first Season, when she'd been caught up in the whirlwind of the debutante dance for a husband. A dance in which she and her two oldest friends had engaged with a degree of scorn for its rituals and even more for the desired culmination of a Society wedding. She clearly remembered now seeing Edward several times during that frenzied social rigmarole. Something about his physical presence had attracted her, those amazing blue eyes for a start, and his loose-limbed, somewhat disordered appearance. Nothing you could put your finger on as out of place precisely, but an overall impression of raffish nonconformity. She had been struck by the fact that whenever she saw him, he was always on the outskirts of any gathering:

aloof, not given to conversation, and definitely not one for the dance floor. She had noticed him, registered that it was clearly not his first Season because he seemed rather older than her own set of friends, and then as quickly, she had put him out of her mind. He made no effort to participate in the social proceedings and she was far too busy to cultivate someone who made it clear he'd rather be anywhere else.

"During my first Season, I saw you at several of the events. But you didn't seem to be enjoying yourself," she added, lifting an eyebrow.

He laughed a little. "No, I wasn't. Nothing but empty-headed girls and equally empty-headed men prancing around in some matrimonial game."

"Harsh," Fenella observed wryly.

"Perhaps," he agreed, "but, forgive me if I'm wrong, I rather had the impression that you and your two friends—inseparable friends, as I recall—didn't seem particularly enthusiastic about any of it either."

She laughed. "How did you guess? I didn't think we made it that obvious."

"Maybe it takes one to know one."

"Well, you're certainly right. Diana, Petra and I heartily despised the whole business and we ended our Season triumphantly single . . . actually, that's not strictly true," she amended, pursing her lips. "Diana was secretly engaged to a childhood friend, but that would have happened with or without the Season."

"And you are still triumphantly single," he remarked with a slight questioning inflection.

"I'm certainly not married," Fenella replied somewhat evasively.

Edward merely raised an eyebrow and left it at that. "More chocolate?"

"No, thank you. I must go." Fenella buttoned her coat, getting to her feet as she drew on her gloves.

"When can we talk about the play?" he asked on a note of urgency. "I have to convince you that you're perfect for the part."

She hesitated, smoothing her kid gloves over her fingers. "If you have a copy with you, I'll read it at home and see what I think."

He shook his head. "No, I don't want you to read it alone. We need to read it together. I have to explain Rose to you or you might not understand her at first."

"If the character's that impenetrable, how do you expect an audience to understand her?" Fenella demanded, remembering how flat she had found the character on paper.

"I expect you to make Rose understandable to the most unsympathetic audience," he said simply.

Fenella stared at him. "You don't know anything about my acting abilities. I'm just an amateur who enjoys playreading in a group. It's a hobby."

"Cedric said you would be perfect for the part."

"*Cedric* said that?" She was incredulous. Cedric Hardcastle never complimented or praised anyone. Mostly he dismissed them all as rank amateurs, really beneath his attention except for the fees they paid.

Edward nodded. "When can we meet to read it together?"

Fenella wanted to resist the sense of being bulldozed into something she didn't want to do but found she couldn't, simply because, if she was totally honest with herself, she *was* interested. "Friday afternoon," she suggested.

"Come to my lodgings around three o'clock." He opened his wallet and took out a visiting card. "Praed Street."

She took the card, slipping it into her coat pocket. It was not a particularly fashionable address, on the fringes of Mayfair, but perfectly respectable. "Very well. Until then. Thank you for the chocolate." She raised a hand in farewell and left the tea shop on a blast of cold air.

Edward beckoned the waitress and asked for more coffee. He sat tapping his mouth with his fingertips, frowning. Ever since he'd first seen Fenella Grantley and her friends four years earlier, he had been struck by her perfect English Rose appearance, hair the color of summer wheat, clear gray eyes, perfect creamy complexion. He'd thought himself immune to physical appearances, particularly when it came to the spoiled, entitled debutantes who peopled the Society world, but something about Fenella and her friends had attracted him. They were different from their peers in some way, and Fenella's fair beauty stood out in any company. He was drawn first to her voice, clear and melodious, slightly deeper than customary, and her chiming laugh. She laughed frequently; she and her friends seemed to find much to amuse them in their lives. In contrast to his own, which at that point he had found dreary and unsatisfying.

He had found himself surreptitiously following

her if he saw her on the street, not really knowing why he did so, but it had become a compulsion. She seemed to embody sunshine, a fanciful thought but one he found hard to dismiss. He had almost finished writing *Sapphire* and found, as he wrote, that now the image of Fenella was superimposed on Rose. It had puzzled him because Rose was not all sunshine, not by any means; she had a much darker side. When he'd discovered Fenella's participation in Cedric's little drama school in Bloomsbury, his interest really had been piqued. The woman he had encountered today was not the unadulterated ray of sunshine she had been four years ago. He could sense unhappiness, or at least discontent, or was it disappointment, beneath her exquisite exterior, and now he was eager to see if Fenella as an actor could bring her own dark side to bear on that aspect of Rose.

He finished his coffee and went out into the cold, making his way to King's College, and his work as research assistant to a professor of literature. It was work he enjoyed, as much as he enjoyed the intellectual company of the professor and his academic colleagues. It was a world he understood and that fitted Edward Tremayne like a glove.

Fenella hailed a passing hackney on the corner of the square. "Albemarle Street," she called to the cabbie as she climbed inside, relieved to get out of the cold wind. She needed to think, or rather to clear her thoughts. Her mind was full of conflicting ideas, impressions. She couldn't even decide if she liked Edward Tremayne enough to spend another minute in his company. But the thought of not seeing him again, of putting Rose and the play out of her mind for good was not possible. Its promise of creative stimulation, of the excitement of exploring new, imaginative territory was too heady to ignore.

The hackney drew up outside Lord and Lady Grantley's elegant town house and she jumped down, handing the cabbie his fare before hurrying up the steps to the front door.

"Fenella . . . Fenella, wait for us."

At the familiar voice, she spun around in the act of putting her key in the lock. "Diana . . . Petra, oh I am so pleased to see you. I have so much to tell you both." She held out her hands in welcome to her friends as they came up the steps. "Let's get inside, it's freezing."

She opened the door and the three women stepped into the marble-floored hall, embracing one another in turn. "Let's go into the yellow drawing room. We won't be disturbed there. Collins," she addressed the butler, who stood patiently waiting to take their outer garments once the flurry of greeting was finished. "Could you bring coffee for us?"

"At once, Miss Fenella." He bowed and signaled a footman, who hurried forward to take their coats before disappearing through the baize door that led into the kitchen and servants' quarters.

"I'm intrigued," Diana Lacey said, adjusting the

folds of her paisley silk scarf as she followed Fenella to the stairs.

"Yes, we came to see if you were intending to go to the Warehams' masked ball. We can't make up our minds about it," Petra Rutherford added. "But it can wait until you've unburdened yourself."

Fenella flung open the door to a pleasant salon, furnished in various sunny shades of yellow. A fire burned brightly in the Adams fireplace and heavy, deep yellow velvet curtains hung at the long windows overlooking the street below. "Come in and get warm," she invited, going to the fire to warm her own hands.

Her friends followed suit. "So, speak," Diana demanded. "What's the big secret?"

"Well, for the last year I've been going to acting classes in Bloomsbury . . . oh, thank you, Collins," she broke off as the butler set the tray of coffee on the sideboard. "Leave it. I'll pour."

"Very well, ma'am." He bowed and left them alone.

"Acting classes?" Petra said, taking up the coffee-pot. "Why on earth would you do that?"

Fenella shrugged. "Because I'd always wanted to. I saw an advertisement in the *Gazette* for drama classes run by Cedric Hardcastle . . . d'you know the name?" When her friends looked blank, she said, "He was a very well-known actor about ten years ago, classical for the most part. But I think he took to the bottle with too much enthusiasm."

She shook her head. "I don't really know the details, but anyway, the idea of drama lessons intrigued me.

He's a miserable curmudgeon for the most part, but now I've started, I don't seem able to stop . . . except for this morning." She took the cup Petra handed her and sat down on a yellow brocade sofa. For a moment she was silent, gathering her thoughts, and her friends waited with growing impatience.

"Do you know Edward Tremayne?" She decided to abandon the preliminaries and start in the middle of the story.

"Is he anything to do with that loathsome Julia and her unpleasant brother?" Petra asked, wrinkling her nose. "They're the only Tremaynes I know."

"Half brother."

"The plot thickens," Diana murmured, leaning forward in her chair. "Start at the beginning, Fenella."

They listened attentively as she told them about the dramatic entrance of Edward Tremayne into what had seemed like a regular, weekly drama class.

"Just to be clear," Petra said when Fenella had finished her narrative. "You're actually intending to act on the stage . . . the public stage."

"Well, perhaps," Fenella replied, chewing her lip. "I don't think I ever really thought seriously about that. I was just enjoying the weekly classes with Cedric . . . they've become something of a bright spot in the week," she added after an instant's hesitation. "But I didn't think it would become a reality."

Diana regarded her with a slight frown. She hadn't missed the hesitation or the significance of what came after. She wondered if Petra had noticed it too. However, now was not the moment to probe. "It seems a logical conclusion, though," she said. "I mean, why take classes if you're not intending to do anything with them?" She chuckled. "Strutting the boards . . . you really will put the cat among the pigeons, my dear. I'm proud of you."

"But what about this Edward?" Petra jumped in. "You don't seem to like him much. Won't that make a difference to whether you play the part or not?"

"But Fenella doesn't *know* whether she likes him or not," Diana objected. "Or at least that's the impression I'm getting."

Fenella jumped up and went to the sideboard. "We need something more interesting than coffee. Sherry?" She lifted the cut-glass decanter in invitation before pouring three glasses.

"Thank you." Diana took hers. "So, do you or don't you?"

"Do I or don't I what?"

"*Like* him," she said impatiently. "You're being very fuzzy-headed, darling, and it's not like you."

"I feel fuzzy-headed," Fenella admitted, sipping her sherry. "Can one be attracted to someone one doesn't like?"

"Ask Diana," Petra said with a grin. "She and Rupert were at daggers drawn for ages, even while they were making mad, passionate love."

"I suppose that's true, but it does sound rather trite," Diana protested. "And it was as true for Rupert as for me. He detested me."

"I don't think he ever fell out of love with you," Petra stated. "It was all for show. No one was at all surprised when you eloped."

"Well, I only really met Edward Tremayne for the

first time today," Fenella declared. "So it's a bit premature to start talking of making mad, passionate love. He confuses me. He can be charming, funny and sympathetic one minute, and scornful, arrogant and detestable the next."

"Well, given his background, it's not surprising he's got an ax to grind," Petra said. "Can you imagine being forced to grow up at a disadvantage to Carlton and Julia? They must have made his life hell."

"Not to mention living with the stigma of his birth," Diana said. "Not that I would give a damn about it myself," she added hastily, "but you know perfectly well how some members of Society would look upon illegitimacy . . . unless, of course, it's a royal bastard," she added. "A Fitz-something is welcome anywhere."

"I suppose so," Fenella agreed. "But am I going to keep this rendezvous on Friday at his lodgings or not?"

"You said you would," Petra pointed out.

"Yes, and it would be very impolite to leave him in the lurch," Diana put in.

Fenella laughed suddenly. "Of course you're right. I have no intention of not keeping the appointment. I never did. Now, what about the Warehams' masked ball? It's next month, isn't it?"

"Yes, and it'll be the official start of the Season. Has George said anything about escorting you?"

"He mentioned it," Fenella answered rather vaguely. Lord George Headington was the most ardent of her many admirers. He was clearly assuming that he held precedence over all her other suitors and was beginning to act accordingly. She knew she had only herself to blame. Sheer inertia had allowed him to continue in his assumptions, and now it seemed a foregone conclusion that he was her permanent escort. Her mother certainly was all encouragement, another complication that she should have foreseen and prevented.

Diana regarded her with narrowed eyes. "Rupert said White's has opened a book on when he's going to pop the question, and what your answer will be."

"That's so vulgar. It's nobody's business but mine," Fenella said crossly. "I hope Rupert hasn't placed any bets."

Diana laughed. "Of course he hasn't. That's not my husband's style at all. On which subject, I am supposed to meet him at the Trocadero for lunch. He hates being kept waiting." She stood up, kissing Fenella on both cheeks. "Let's ride tomorrow in the park. Petra, are you up for a freezing winter canter?"

"No, definitely not. I'm not as mad a horsewoman as you two, and I definitely don't like being out in this weather if I can avoid it. But I'll share a hackney with you now. You can drop me off on the corner of Stanhope Gardens. I can walk home from there."

Fenella saw her two friends down to the hall to retrieve their coats. She was going back upstairs when Lady Grantley appeared at the head.

"Oh, there you are, darling." She greeted her daughter with a kiss. "Did I hear Petra and Diana?"

"Yes, they've just left."

"Good, then get your coat, I want you to come to

Madame Delaney's with me. I need your opinion on a hat. We'll have lunch in the Savoy afterward."

Fenella allowed herself to be swept on the tide of her mother's plans. Lady Grantley was hard to resist at the best of times, and at this moment, her daughter was too full of her own thoughts to summon sufficient energy to try.

Chapter Three

Fenella looked at the card in her hand, verifying the street number as she stepped out of the hackney. Twenty-Four, Praed Street. She looked up at the tall, narrow row house, identical to every other on the busy street. It looked neither down-at-heel nor well-to-do, which was a fair description of the area in general.

She approached the front door, which was flush to the pavement, and banged the knocker. After a few minutes, she heard the sound of bolts being drawn and the door opened. A thin woman in black bombazine, her gray hair drawn into a severe bun, regarded the visitor through pince-nez.

"Mr. Tremayne is expecting me." Fenella smiled, trying not to bristle at the scrutiny.

"He said." The woman opened the door wider in wordless invitation.

Fenella stepped into a narrow hallway. The smell of furniture polish and carbolic soap assailed her nostrils. Everything was spotless, including the rag rug thrown over the highly polished linoleum under her feet. "Thank you, Mrs. . . . ?" she offered rather tentatively.

"Hammond," the woman said. "If you'll follow me."

Fenella followed her up a narrow flight of stairs to a first-floor landing with three doors, and another narrower staircase continued to the upper floors. The landlady, as Fenella assumed she was, knocked on one of the doors.

It opened immediately. Edward Tremayne, in a threadbare, velvet smoking jacket, greeted Fenella with a somewhat distracted nod. "Good of you to come, Miss Grantley."

It struck Fenella as a less-than-enthusiastic welcome, and she felt the familiar bristling. She had better things to do on a Friday afternoon than stand on a drafty landing with a clearly censorious landlady and a host who seemed unprepared for her visit. She was about to say something to that effect when Edward smiled suddenly and those blue eyes danced like sunlight on the Aegean.

"Thank you, Mrs. Hammond." He reached for Fenella's hand. "Come in. I've a good fire going and tea and crumpets. You must be freezing." He drew her into a cozy parlor overlooking the street, closing the door quietly behind him. "I'm sorry about Mrs. Hammond. She's a dragon, but she keeps an impeccable house, and somewhere under that iron exterior I have a feeling there's a warm heart."

"I'd need some convincing of that," Fenella said, drawing off her gloves and looking around the room. There were books everywhere: towers of them on the floor, against the walls, all in imminent danger of toppling. They lined the bookshelves in higgledy-piggledy fashion. On a writing table beneath the window lay papers covered in an untidy scrawl.

"I'm sorry if it looks a mess to you; it's the only way I can work," Edward said, taking her coat and laying it over the back of a chair. "Sit down by the fire." He gestured to a cracked leather armchair and turned to a small table. "I hope you can toast crumpets." He speared a crumpet on a three-pronged toasting fork, handing it to her.

"I haven't done this since my schoolroom days," Fenella observed, sliding to the floor in front of the fire, the chair at her back. "In my experience, you can't get the right proximity to the fire from a chair."

"My experience too." Edward joined her on the floor, spearing a crumpet on his own toasting fork. "So, have you had any further thoughts on the subject of the play?"

"Not really," Fenella responded, gingerly pulling the hot crumpet off the tines to turn it to the other side. "Without seeing it properly, I don't know what to think. Why have you called it *Sapphire*?"

"Rose is the sapphire," Edward said slowly. "I know you thought there was no substance to her, that she was flat on the page." He sounded rather disgruntled. "But that was too hasty a judgment."

"Was it?" Fenella leaned back against the chair behind her, idly twirling her toasting fork. "Well, if you'll forgive me for saying so, you didn't exactly create an atmosphere conducive to an in-depth reading." She turned her gray eyes full on him. "It seems to me, Mr. Tremayne, that at times you're your own worst enemy."

For a moment, his eyes flashed, and she braced herself for a sarcastic tirade, but the flash lasted only a second. "That, to my shame, is absolutely true." He leaned forward and took the crumpet off her fork, tossing it between his fingers until it was cool enough to handle. "Honey or jam?"

"Honey, please." She watched as he spread butter liberally so that it dripped through the holes in the bread to make a buttery puddle on the plate beneath. Then he spread golden honey thickly on top, licked his fingers and passed her the plate.

"There you are, Miss Grantley. How do you like your tea?"

"Milk, no sugar," Fenella mumbled through a dripping but luscious mouthful.

For a moment, they ate in a silence broken only by the hiss and crackle of the fire, and Fenella was content to wait. Edward finished his crumpet and licked his fingers again. "Another one?"

"Yes, please. If you're going to answer my question, that is?" She raised an inquiring brow, holding a fresh crumpet ready to spike on her toasting fork.

"Have you ever heard of a color-change sapphire? They're very rare."

Fenella considered. She was no stranger to gems of all kinds; Diana's family had diamond mines in South Africa and her own mother had a wealth of jewels, mostly locked away in the bank for safekeeping. But a color-change sapphire? She shook her head. "No. I know there are many different kinds of sapphires, but color change?"

"To put it simply, they're stones that change color according to the light. There's an interaction between the light source and the stone itself," he explained. "It's something to do with the particular bedrock where they're found. A deep blue stone could change in a moment to a rose pink, or even almost black, depending on the light it's exposed to." He reached over to refill her teacup and leaned back against his own chair, his long legs extended in front of him. A lock of hair flopped over his brow, but he didn't seem to notice, and Fenella had to resist the absurd urge to brush it back with her fingers.

"And this Rose character has the same characteristics, she changes mood instantly?"

"Mood, and to a certain extent personality . . . angel one minute, devil the next."

He regarded Fenella carefully for a moment from beneath the flop of hair. "It's a very fine line you'll have to draw. It's imperative that you don't lose the sympathy of the audience even when you're at your most malevolent."

"It sounds impossible," Fenella stated. "At least for someone with no experience. I am a complete novice, Edward."

"I know that," he said with a touch of impatience. "But Cedric says you can do it and I trust his judgment."

"What's her background? Does she have a dark secret?" She instantly regretted the slightly cynical, almost mocking note to the question, but it did seem too obvious.

To her surprise, Edward didn't seem offended. "She's a changeling."

"Oh, what, a fairy substituted for a baby spirited out of its cradle by other fairies?" Now she made no attempt to hide her incredulous amusement.

"Not exactly," he said with a patience that surprised her. "She was found—"

"Not in a handbag!" Fenella interrupted on a bubble of laughter. The line from Oscar Wilde's most successful play was too apposite to resist and she was too busy laughing to realize at first how insulting she was being.

Edward's expression closed, his eyes losing the laughing glint they'd held a moment before. "This was clearly a mistake. Obviously, there's no point discussing this with you if you won't hear me out," he said stiffly. "I'll show you downstairs." He stood up in one easy, agile movement. "Let me get your coat."

Fenella finally realized what she'd done. She scrambled to her feet with a lot less elegance than Edward had shown. "No . . . no, please. How abominably rude of me. Please, Edward, forgive me. It was outrageous; I don't know what I was thinking. The words just came out of my mouth."

He stood looking at her, his hands resting lightly on his hips, his expression as dark as ever.

Inspiration hit her. "Is that something that Rose might do in one of her black incarnations? Find herself saying something appalling to someone, hurting them without thinking about it?"

He frowned. "It wouldn't be by accident. She does nothing without intention."

Fenella grimaced slightly. "So she's actually *evil*?"

"Some of the time."

They were still standing, as if poised on the brink of something. Fenella knew she didn't want to leave. It would mean the abrupt end of something that she now realized she wanted to pursue. Whether it was the play or Edward Tremayne himself she wanted to pursue was not entirely clear to her, but she knew it wouldn't become so if she allowed him to compel her departure.

Edward let his ready anger fade as he regarded her steadily. She was lovely, he reflected abstractedly. There was something almost ethereal about her appearance, but nothing ethereal at all about her personality. That was razor-sharp. He thought once again that she was the embodiment of Rose.

"You haven't finished toasting your crumpet." He returned to his place on the floor, sprawled against the chair at his back, his legs stretched in front of him.

Relieved, Fenella returned to her own position and took up the toasting fork. "Can we do a read-through? It might help me to see the character more roundly."

"I wanted to explain my thinking first," he responded. "But that doesn't seem to be a working strategy, so, yes, we'll do a read-through. On one condition . . ."

"Which is?"

"That we read it once, straight through, no stopping, no questions until we've come to the end.

You'll read Rose and I'll read the other parts." He reached for her toasting fork, snatching it from the fire just as the crumpet was about to burn. "Pay attention, Fenella. You'll burn the house down in a minute."

She flushed with annoyance at her carelessness, but also at his peremptory tone. "Sorry, I wasn't concentrating, but there's no need to sound like a schoolmaster."

He spread his hands in acknowledgment. "Mea culpa. May we continue?"

Fenella swallowed her irritation and picked up where they'd left off. "I agree, a straight read-through makes the best sense. I need to get a feel for the whole, even if I don't understand every aspect of the character." She took up the delicate bone-china teacup and drank the last of her tea while Edward buttered her crumpet.

She glanced at the clock as she ate. It was past four o'clock. A full reading would take at least two hours, even without breaks. She needed to be home for a dinner party her mother was giving. Her mother had invited several eligible bachelors, not to mention Lord George Headington. Lady Grantley was far from ready to give up on her efforts to get her only daughter suitably, if not spectacularly married, and Lord George was her first choice. Fenella needed to be home in time to make herself ready enough to satisfy her mother's exacting tastes. It would take nearly an hour just to do her hair.

"What's the matter? You look as if you've swallowed a worm."

With annoyance, she felt herself flush yet again. Was she going to compound her earlier offenses by telling him she couldn't stay long enough to complete the reading?

"It's awkward," she said finally. "I have to be home by seven at the latest. My mother's giving a dinner party and—"

"And you need to be looking your best before the first guests arrive," he interrupted. "Believe me, I understand the imperative. We'll do the reading another time, when there's nothing pressing to cut it short."

"Thank you. I was afraid . . ." Uncomfortable, Fenella let her sentence fade as she got to her feet.

"Afraid of what?" Edward asked, standing up, brushing crumbs from his faded corduroy trousers. "Afraid I wouldn't understand about dinner parties? Believe me, I've suffered through more than any man should in a lifetime."

Fenella put her head to one side, regarding him quizzically. "Aren't you too young to make such a definitive statement?"

"Maybe, if I was not who I am," he returned somewhat obliquely.

"And exactly who are you, Mr. Tremayne?" Fenella found herself very interested in the answer.

"You know enough about me to answer that question yourself." He turned to pick up her coat from the chair where it lay.

It wasn't the answer Fenella wanted. She understood, of course, that he was a Tremayne, even if a second-class one, and he would have experienced the tyranny of Society's demands. But he was much more than that. A playwright with a fascination for the dark side, a quick-tempered, easily insulted man who, nevertheless, had a stunning smile when he chose and the most amazing eyes that, when fixed upon one, seemed to exclude the rest of the world from his attention.

"I know enough to answer it superficially," she said, shrugging into her coat as he held it for her. "But I'd like to know more."

"Would you, indeed?" There was a hint of mockery in his tone, and Fenella sucked in her lower lip, feeling that with her own honesty, she had somehow made herself vulnerable to his sarcasm.

She walked to the door without responding. Edward moved quickly ahead of her, his hand on the doorknob, his back to the door, facing her with a quite different expression. "I've done it again," he stated with a rueful shake of his head. "Forgive me?" He took a half step toward her, though still blocking the door with his body.

Fenella was suddenly transfixed by his gaze. She found herself mute, a most unusual experience, as she watched him come closer. He stretched out a hand and cupped her chin, lifting it slightly. Then his lips lightly brushed hers and her skin tingled. When she made no move, he slid his other hand around her waist, drawing her close against him. He looked down into her upturned face and raised his eyebrows a fraction in question.

She had no difficulty reading the question and offered a half-smile in response, feeling as if everything was happening in a mist, in slow motion, her responses seeming to come without reference to her own will. When his lips pressed against hers, warm, pliable and yet firm with a hint of demand, Fenella gave herself up to the tactile whirl of feeling, her eyes closing her into a world of pure physical sensation. His body was hard against hers, his arm warm and strong around her waist, the taste and scent of him a heady mélange of woodsmoke from the fire and the sweetness of butter and honey with an underlay of lemon, fresh and sharp on his skin.

When finally his mouth left hers, her eyes opened, looking straight into the piercing blue intensity of his gaze. "I enjoyed that," he said softly, brushing a loose strand of hair from her cheek.

She found her voice at last. "Yes," she murmured. "I did too."

"When can we do it again?" he said softly, but now with a glint of humor behind the intensity of his gaze.

"Now?"

"If you like." He drew her against him again, and this time the kiss was harder, fiercer, more demanding, and Fenella found herself responding with the same fierce demand, her body pressing against his as his hands moved down her back, caressing her hips, the round curve of her bottom, and she felt the hard thrust of his penis against her belly.

It seemed a long time before they broke apart. Fenella's breath came rapidly, her cheeks flushed and her lips tingling. Edward kissed her again lightly, then released his hold. "Will you come tomorrow?

In the morning, so we have more time?" he asked, moving away from the door.

More time for what? Fenella wondered distractedly, but she kept the question to herself. "Yes," she answered simply. "Around ten?" And then she remembered she had promised to ride with Diana in the morning. But Diana would understand her reason for canceling, no one better, given her own history of impulsive imperatives.

"Until then, Fenella." A fingertip stroked the curve of her cheek in a fleeting caress, then he opened the door and bowed her out onto the landing before moving ahead of her down the stairs to open the front door. "Tomorrow, then."

"Tomorrow," she agreed, stepping out onto the pavement. The cold air of late afternoon seemed to wake her up, bring her back to a full awareness of the world in motion around her, and of what she had just done.

What kind of madness had propelled her into that intimacy with a man she didn't even know if she liked? Certainly some of the time she came close to detesting him. But there was no denying the thrill of excitement at the anticipation of meeting him tomorrow. It seemed to have been a long time since she'd felt that thrill of anticipation, and she hugged the feeling to her, enjoying the uplifting sense of future promise.

She walked almost blindly to the corner and looked around for a hackney. Her mind didn't seem to be properly ordered and she didn't feel in the least like herself. It wasn't as if she'd never been kissed before. She'd had several careless flirtations, all of which had led to some kind of physical touching, most recently with Lord George, who now seemed a rather pale and shadowy figure. He was nice enough, not in the least clumsy when it came to more intimate familiarities, but *enough* no longer seemed sufficient. Not when compared with the mercurial passions of Edward Tremayne. He was all scarlet and black compared with Lord George's pastel steadiness.

Of course, Lord George, second son of the Duke of Wellborough, was an eminently suitable suitor, one Lady Grantley had set her sights on as the perfect son-in-law. Edward Tremayne, an illegitimate son of an earl, could hardly compete in her mother's eyes, Fenella reflected as she flagged down a passing cab.

And in truth, Fenella herself couldn't picture Edward as husband material, not with the rosiest of spectacles. He intrigued her, though.

Resolutely, she turned her thoughts to the evening's dinner party, where Lord George would be an honored guest.

Chapter Four

"Oh, that's very nice, darling. You look lovely," Lady Grantley declared with an approving smile as her daughter entered the drawing room. "That deep blue brocade really suits you." She hurried across to make some minute adjustments to the pale blue chiffon shawl draped over her daughter's elbows. "A perfect choice, goes so well with the gown." She stood back to examine Fenella's appearance for any hidden flaws. "I do wish you would wear a corset," she said, sighing. "However perfect your figure, gowns these days need the right underpinning to sit properly."

"I won't wear one, Mama. They're horrifically uncomfortable. You know that yourself," Fenella responded. "Some doctors say they're actually dangerous, squashing all our inner organs."

"Really, darling, you mustn't talk about such things; it's quite vulgar," Lady Grantley scolded. "And what do doctors know about such matters? They're all men, after all." She shook her head, and the lamplight set the sapphires of her tiara alight with the movement. "Besides," she added with firm conviction, "one must suffer for fashion."

Fenella couldn't help laughing. She turned to her father, who stood in front of the fire, a large whisky in hand, his expression that of a man firmly excluding himself from the conversation between his womenfolk. "Will I do, Papa, even without a corset?"

"Look fine to me," he stated, waving a hand in dismissal. "What do I know about such frippery? That's your mother's business."

Fenella laughed and kissed him on the cheek before accepting a glass of sherry from the hovering footman's tray. "So, who else have you invited, Mother, apart from George?"

"Let me think. Lord and Lady Dalton—Everard will keep your father company; they can talk racehorses—Sir Peter and Lady Mortby—one must have a politician at the table these days—Sarah Gilbert and her fiancé . . . what's his name . . . ?"

"Geoffrey Maitland," Fenella reminded her.

"Oh, yes, that's right, and the Tremaynes."

"Carlton, Viscount Grayling, and Julia?" Fenella couldn't help the note of shocked surprise.

"Yes. Why, do you not care for them, Fenella?"

"Not much," her daughter responded. "I don't move in the same set as a general rule."

"No, well, they were both at Serena Mortby's at home the other day, and as I was inviting Serena, I thought it might appear unfriendly to exclude them. And they are very well connected, my dear."

Fenella contented herself with a small nod.

"With George and you, your father and me, we'll be a round dozen," her mother finished with a satisfied smile.

"I can always trust you to set a fine table, m'dear," Lord Grantley said with a fond smile. "No guest ever has a complaint about your hospitality."

"I should hope not," his wife stated. "Ah, I hear the door. It'll be George; he's always the first."

Lord George Headington was announced a minute or two later, and after punctiliously greeting his host and hostess, he turned to Fenella. "How lovely you look, as always." He bowed over her hand, his lips brushing her knuckles.

"Flattery will get you anywhere, George," she responded with a light laugh. "You look remarkably handsome yourself this evening, if I may return the compliment."

It was only the truth, she reflected. Lord George was blessed with a thick head of curly dark hair, soulful brown eyes, and the lean, strong physique of a sportsman. And he wore clothes very well, his evening dress perfect to the last detail, the tailcoat fitting snugly across his broad shoulders, his white waistcoat pristine.

He smiled the intimate smile he reserved for when they were alone and took her hand, kissing it again even as his smile told her that he would much prefer to be kissing her mouth.

Gently, she withdrew her hand as the butler announced Viscount Grayling and Lady Julia Tremayne.

Fenella moved beside her mother to greet the new arrivals. She had considered the brother and sister to be mere nodding acquaintances but now regarded them with more interest than hitherto. They shared some features with Edward—the well-shaped nose and wide brow—but their eyes were a muddy hazel, she decided, and their chins were receding and rather weak, quite unlike their half brother's square jaw. She had a sudden image of the deep cleft in his chin and the most absurd desire arose to touch it with the tip of her tongue. She felt her cheeks warm.

Hastily, she forced herself to concentrate on the guests, shaking hands and murmuring pleasantries. She drew George into their company as drinks were offered. For the next half hour, she was engaged at her mother's side, greeting the other guests as they arrived, and when it was time to go in to dinner, George was instantly beside her, offering his arm to take her in. She'd had little opportunity to observe the Tremayne siblings after that first moment, but her mother had placed the viscount on her left. George was on her right, and during the first course she concentrated only on him, but when the first cover was removed and the second replaced it, she turned with everyone else to her companion on her left.

"Been hunting this season, Miss Grantley?" the viscount asked through a mouthful of turtle soup.

"I've been in London since Christmas, Viscount," Fenella answered. "I should think the ground's too hard, isn't it?"

"Yes, frozen solid. I tried my hunter on it last month and the animal strained a tendon. Had to give it a rest. Damn nuisance . . . begging your pardon, Miss Grantley."

Fenella smiled faintly. "I hope you're amusing yourself with Town pleasures instead."

"Oh, yes, can't grumble. Won a few hands at White's the other night."

"Do you ever go to the theatre, Viscount?" Fenella watched his reaction out of the corner of her eye.

"Good God, no," he exclaimed, turning to help himself to quail from the platter held by a footman. "Can't be doing with that nonsense. Downright disreputable, in my opinion." He nibbled a leg of the bird, which seemed even tinier in his large, rather meaty hands. Fenella had a sudden vivid image of Edward's hands and his long, slim fingers. There was an ink stain on his right forefinger, she recalled.

"You're in the minority in that opinion, sir," she returned, delicately separating a leg from the body of the quail on her plate. "Many people love the theatre. I myself find it riveting entertainment."

"Oh, well, I daresay. More a female thing, really."

"So, how do you amuse yourself in Town, then?" she asked, ice tipping her tone.

"Oh, cards, Tattersalls, riding when the ground's not so hard. Parties, soirees, the usual thing." He waved a hand in a vaguely encompassing gesture before dropping the quail leg, picked clean, onto his plate again. "How about you, Miss Grantley?" He rinsed his fingers in the finger bowl beside his plate.

"Much the same," she said, ceasing to have any interest in furthering this uninspiring conversation. "I enjoy reading. D'you perhaps find pleasure in books?"

"Lord, no. Can't abide 'em. Had enough of that at school. Got sent down from Oxford in my second year and m'father saw no reason to send me back after rustication. Waste of time and money, he called it. I felt the same."

Fenella smiled a smile that would make those who knew her well very uneasy. "You're not a bookish family, then. Is there no member of your family interested in the more literary side of life?"

He looked sharply at her, then, his muddy eyes narrowing. "Only my half brother. But he's a by-blow, if you'll pardon the expression. Doesn't show much of the Tremayne spirit at all."

"Do you see much of him?" She helped herself from a dish of scalloped oysters.

"No. Good riddance to bad rubbish, if you ask me. He knows better than to come knocking on our door."

Fenella let the subject rest, but when her mother rose to signal the ladies' withdrawal from the dining room, she maneuvered herself onto a sofa in the drawing room beside Julia Tremayne. "How are you enjoying Town, Julia?"

Julia took a cup of coffee from the footman. "Oh, it's been quite entertaining. The Season hasn't begun properly, of course, but I still find plenty to amuse myself." She took an almond biscuit. "Card parties and luncheons and, of course, the high point of the Season will be the masked ball at the Warehams'. I do so love masked balls, don't you?"

Fenella had never seen the point of partially concealing one's features for an evening of dancing; no one was ever in doubt as to anyone's identity, but she merely said, "They can be diverting."

"Immensely so," Julia declared. "I just wish it was warm enough to walk in the park. One can always be sure of seeing friends there at five o'clock, but no one goes out in this freezing cold. But I do enjoy visiting, and I have my own at home on Tuesdays at four. You must come to Hanover Square one of these days," she said with a smile Fenella found irritatingly complacent.

"Thank you," she murmured without much enthusiasm and briskly changed the subject. "I enjoy the theatre at this time of year." She set aside her empty cup. "I remember when *Lady Windermere's Fan* was playing at the St. James's. The theatre was quite different in those days. Wilde was so wonderfully witty. Nothing's been the same since they stopped performing his work."

Julia looked at her in astonishment. "But the man was in prison for being a . . . a—" She came to a faltering halt.

"A sodomite, you mean? Yes, it would appear so. But that doesn't mean he was incapable of wit and beautiful writing."

Julia gave an exaggerated shudder. "I don't know how you could say such things. The theatre is a den of iniquity and anyone who is involved in it is not fit for decent society."

"That seems a rather sweeping condemnation," Fenella demurred without apparent heat. "What about Shakespeare, Marlowe, Congreve . . . and Bernard Shaw? His plays are becoming very popular."

"He's a socialist," Julia stated flatly, as if pronouncing the coup de grâce on the subject.

Poor Edward, Fenella thought. What appalling soil for a playwright to grow in. She considered her next conversational move. She desperately wanted to bring Edward into the conversation but was afraid it would seem too direct a sequitur. She didn't want Julia to know how much she knew about her illegitimate brother.

"I never see your brother around Town anymore," she said. "I used to see him often during my first Season."

Julia frowned, puzzled. "Carlton? But he's right over there. He's just come into the drawing room with the rest of the gentlemen."

"Yes, of course I know *Carlton, Viscount Grayling*." Fenella managed what she hoped was a convincing laugh. "But I thought you had another brother . . . maybe I misunderstood. He's a cousin, perhaps. I know his name is Tremayne."

"Edward. You must mean Edward," Julia said, wrinkling her nose. "He's only a half brother, and he's persona non grata in the family. We don't see him."

"Oh." Fenella said nothing else for a minute as she tried to think of a way to continue the subject without seeming too eager. "That must be rather awkward if you find yourselves at the same party," she remarked finally.

"Edward doesn't go to parties anymore. I imagine he can't afford to move in Society circles now. Our father cut him off when he refused the chance he offered him."

"I'm intrigued," Fenella said with perfect truth. Julia loved to gossip and she seemed willing to chat about the black sheep in her own family.

Julia leaned toward her, lowering her voice. "Edward is illegitimate, you see." She glanced around the drawing room to make sure no one was close enough to hear this shocking family secret. "My father acknowledged him and did everything for him. He wanted him to be accepted in Society despite the bar sinister, so he sent him to Eton with Carlton, and then to Oxford. When Edward came down from Oxford with a first-class degree—he was always clever, too clever for his own good," she added, taking another almond biscuit. "My father naturally expected him to contribute to the family, to pay back some of what he'd been given."

Fenella was now fascinated. This was new ground. "More coffee?" She picked up the silver coffeepot.

"Thank you." Julia passed her empty cup. "Edward refused the job my father offered him. Considered it beneath him, I suspect. He always did have ideas above his station."

Fenella felt the familiar bristling and bit her lip to keep from saying anything that would offend Julia and cause her to abandon the present subject. "What was the job?" she asked as casually as she could.

"Estate manager . . . and he turned it down. Can you believe it?"

Fenella could believe it all too well, but she contented herself with an air of wide-eyed interest. "At Tremayne Court in Cornwall?"

"Yes, there, and also the town house on Hanover Square and the tenant farms. It's a very important job, and Edward would have been part of the family. He could still move in Society circles, and Father was hoping he'd find a suitable match. Of course, it would have to be with a girl who had no real social aspirations, some respectable but not prominent family, only too happy for a daughter to marry into the Tremayne family despite the unfortunate circumstances of Edward's birth."

Julia's smile was smugly satisfied as she finished her coffee and set down her cup. "But now, of course, he can have no such aspirations. He has some job at London University, secretary to someone, I believe. Fairly menial anyway. So, the family doesn't have anything to do with him anymore."

Lucky Edward, Fenella thought even as she kept the smile glued to her lips. "Well, no wonder I haven't seen him for such a long time. Will you excuse me? I should talk to Lady Mortby. I haven't spoken to her all evening." She rose gracefully and gratefully and made her way across the drawing room.

George waylaid her before she could reach Lady Mortby. "There you are at last. I've been trying to catch your eye for five minutes."

"Why didn't you come over and join us?"

"I cannot stand Julia Tremayne. She puts on such

airs, you'd think she was royalty. Her father's only an earl, after all."

Fenella went into a peal of laughter. "George, listen to you. Just because your father's a duke . . . it doesn't make you any better than anyone else."

"I didn't say it did," Lord George protested, flushing. "I'm only a younger son, after all. And I don't go around throwing my ducal lineage in everyone's faces."

"No," agreed Fenella gravely. "That would be vulgar."

"Are you mocking me, Fenella?" George demanded with more than a touch of annoyance.

Fenella bit her lip on a depressingly familiar wave of disappointment. She'd noticed all too often George's lack of humor and his touchiness if he thought someone might be laughing at him, however gently. It was hard sometimes to keep a bridle on her own quick tongue, and she yearned for a sparring partner. But George was too self-conscious, too aware of his own social consequence to enjoy any mutual teasing.

"No, of course I'm not," she said, laying a smooth, white hand on his sleeve. She managed a smile, aware of Lady Grantley's eyes upon her. It would not do for George to take umbrage in her mother's drawing room. "I'm sorry you should think that."

"Perhaps you should prove it," he said, his eyes narrowing. He drew her arm through his and moved her expertly through the crowded room toward a curtained window embrasure.

"My mother will not approve," she pointed out as the curtain fell into place behind them.

"Just a quick kiss. I've been fantasizing all evening about having you to myself." He cupped her face between both hands and kissed her mouth hard.

It wasn't the first time he'd kissed her, but as before, it left Fenella unaroused. She didn't want to cause a scene by pulling herself away so instead found herself exploring with curious detachment the differences between this kiss and Edward Tremayne's. There was no comparison. George was not unskilled, but he could elicit only a lackluster response from her. Not for the first time, Fenella knew she could not possibly marry George, however suitable the match would be and however many of her nearest and dearest it would please.

He moved his mouth from hers eventually, looking down at her with an air of satisfaction. "There, that's better."

Fenella wondered if he didn't expect any real response from her. Perhaps he assumed women weren't supposed to feel any arousal. It made her feel rather empty. She gave him another fleeting smile and slipped discreetly through the curtain, moving across the drawing room to her mother's side.

Lady Grantley was organizing tables for whist. "Ah, there you are, darling. I've put you and George to play with Sarah and Geoffrey; young people should play with one another . . . where is George?" She looked around the salon.

"He can't be far," her daughter responded easily.

"No, I'm sure." Lady Grantley accepted this with a

brisk nod. "Now, Arthur, you cannot sit at the same table as Everard; you'll talk racing the whole time and drive your partners insane. You shall play with Carlton and the Mortbys. Julia, I shall put you at the same table as dear Eleanor."

Fenella took her place as George, who had discreetly emerged from behind the curtain, pulled out her chair for her. "Strictly by the rules, we should cut for partners," she remarked, shuffling the pack. "Shall we play by the rules?"

"No," George protested. "You're my partner; you always are."

"But that's the point," Fenella said. "We know each other too well for an exciting game. I think we should add a little unpredictability." She glanced at Sarah, then at Geoffrey. "Are you game?"

"Yes," declared Sarah. "Definitely. Let's stir things up a little. Two highest play against two lowest. Aces high."

"As you wish," George said, and Geoffrey merely shrugged. Fenella cut the pack, then passed it to George. She had drawn the ace of spades. George drew a two of hearts and grimaced. Sarah drew a ten of diamonds and Geoffrey drew a six of clubs.

"Looks like women against men," Fenella said with some satisfaction. She knew that Sarah was a good player and she was not exactly shabby herself. A battle of the sexes added a certain frisson to an all-too-familiar game, and when she and Sarah won the final trick, giving them the rubber, she was hardpressed to keep from a whoop of triumph.

"Why wouldn't you partner me, Fenella?" George

demanded as he stood in the hall with the rest of the departing guests.

She considered before deciding to give him a straightforward, honest answer. "As Sarah said, I wanted to stir things up a bit. We always do everything the same way, not just us but everyone. There are set rules and routines and woe betide anyone who steps outside the boundaries. But why shouldn't we cut for partners? It's a perfectly good formality and it adds some excitement."

"That sounds very radical, Fenella," he stated with a disapproving frown. "There's all too much of that around these days, all these factions agitating for change. What's wrong with the way things have always been? On my way over, I met a parade of those suffragists on their way to Parliament with their banners. I can't imagine what they hope to achieve by appealing to the prime minister. Balfour's made his views clear on the matter."

"Oh, I forgot you don't think women should have the vote." Her voice held a note of challenge.

George's frown deepened. "Of course I don't, Fenella. What on earth would women do with it? They don't know anything about politics or affairs of state. It's not appropriate and I wish you'd realize that."

Fenella sighed and shook her head. "Very well, George. Let's leave it at that before we both say something we'll regret."

"I don't understand you," he stated. "Sometimes I think you're not at all like other women."

"Do you want me to be?" she asked with interest.

"Of course I do. Why wouldn't I? My wife must honor her position."

She smiled. "But I'm not your wife, George."

"Not yet," he said firmly. "Now, kiss me good night like a good girl. You're tired, that's all." He leaned down and kissed her cheek, before turning to make his punctilious farewells to his host and hostess. He stepped out into the frigid night and Fenella closed the door softly behind him, shutting her eyes on a wash of dismay, wondering how she had allowed matters with George to drift into such dangerous waters. Somehow, she had to extricate herself without causing too much of an uproar.

She went up to bed, reflecting that while it had been an evening as uninspiring as most these days, it had given her some interesting insights into someone she did not find in the least uninspiring.

Chapter Five

Fenella awoke the next morning filled with an anticipatory excitement she associated with the mornings of childhood birthdays. It took her a few moments to clear her head sufficiently to look for the cause. This childish excitement couldn't simply be that she was spending the morning with Edward Tremayne? Or could it?

"Good morning, Miss Fenella." Her maid drew back the heavy brocade curtains at the long windows overlooking the slice of walled garden at the side of the house. A thin ray of sun poked its way into the room.

"Good morning, Alice. I didn't hear you come in." She propped herself on an elbow and pushed back her hair with her free hand. "I'm still half asleep."

"You asked me to call you at half past eight," Alice reminded her, turning to the tea tray she had set on the dresser. She took the cozy off the white Sèvres teapot and poured the steaming, fragrant liquid into a delicate matching cup, added a little milk and brought the cup over to Fenella, setting it down on the bedside table. "That'll help wake you, ma'am. It's good and strong." She propped pillows against the carved headboard and Fenella hauled herself into a sitting position, leaning against the pillows.

She reached sideways for the tea and took a deep draught. "Ah, that's better." She inhaled the fragrant steam gratefully.

"Will I draw your bath now?" Alice asked.

"Yes, please. I'm going out in just over an hour."

"What clothes should I lay out?"

Fenella considered the question. What impression did she want to give? Something casual, suggesting an artistic personality, or something smart, implying efficiency and control? She pictured Edward's apartment, the piles of books, the shabby furniture, his own careless, almost disheveled appearance. And made her decision. "The dark green skirt and the cream shirt with the big floppy green bow at the collar," she said. "Oh, and the wide leather belt." That was a good compromise, she felt. The bow gave the outfit a somewhat bohemian touch.

"I'll lay them out while you're having your bath." The maid disappeared into the small adjoining bathroom.

Fenella sipped her tea, listening to the sound of water running. How would Edward greet her? They had parted on that passionate kiss; would he be that man when she arrived, or the sarcastic, impatient, generally discourteous playwright who irritated her so much? He was a regular Dr. Jekyll and Mr. Hyde, she reflected, pushing aside the covers and getting out of bed.

She stretched, yawned and went to the window, her bare feet sinking into the heavy pile of the Axminster carpet. The lawn glittered under the pale sunlight catching the remnants of the night's heavy frost. A needle of icy air crept through a crack in the window frame, making her shiver. She turned back to the room, looking forward to the hot bath awaiting her.

"It's all ready for you, Miss Fenella." Alice came back into the bedroom. "You'd best get a move on if you're to have breakfast before you leave." She glanced at the pretty enamel clock on the mantel. "It's almost nine already."

"I only have time for coffee and toast, Alice. I'll have it here rather than in the breakfast room, if you don't mind bringing it up." She hurried into the bathroom, undoing the little pearl buttons of her nightdress as she did so. The air was heavy with scented steam from the perfumed water and Fenella slid into the bath with a sigh of pleasure. Life was good, she decided, reaching for the soap. Her hand hovered over the fragrant bar, arrested by the thought. It had been a long time since she'd acknowledged how good life could be, even the simple pleasures of a hot bath and strong tea in the morning. And it wasn't hard to find the reason for this suddenly bright outlook. She had something to look forward to. The drabness of everyday life had vanished beneath a sense of anticipation about what the morning would hold. Certainly, she was looking forward to reading Edward's play, and that was partly responsible for her present mood, but it was not the only factor. She was looking forward to being with Edward.

At nine forty-five, she was climbing into a hackney outside the front door. The footman who had summoned it for her closed the door firmly, calling up the address to the cabbie. Inside, Fenella huddled into her sable coat, her hands deep in a matching muff. Her fair hair was braided and twisted into a coronet around her head, leaving her ears unprotected from the cold, and she wished she'd bothered with a hat, but the monstrous concoctions that were fashionable at the moment didn't suit her; they obscured her face and made her feel like a forest mushroom, stunted and almost invisible among the undergrowth. She was vain enough to sacrifice warmth for visibility.

She pulled her purple, green and white scarf up over her ears as a compromise. She'd hesitated over wearing the scarf, which bore the distinctive colors of the suffrage movement. George's dismissal of the political movement had made her quietly angry and displaying that allegiance up front to Edward seemed somehow necessary. She was very curious to see how he would react, or, indeed, if he would react at all. Perhaps he lived so much in the world of his own writing he wasn't aware of the quiet movement for women's suffrage gaining momentum on the streets of this city and many others.

She jumped down from the hackney as soon as it pulled up outside the house on Praed Street, aware that her heart was beating faster than usual, and mingled with eager anticipation was a degree of apprehension. What mood was he going to be in this morning? And how would he react if he didn't like the way she read Rose?

Fenella was not accustomed to feeling at a disadvantage. Far from it. She expected to be in control of whatever situation in which she found herself. Now here she was, shaking in her shoes in case Edward Tremayne was in one of his bad moods. It occurred to her that perhaps that uncertainty contributed to her recaptured enthusiasm for life's twists and turns. Maybe a little danger was what she needed to spice things up. She wasn't sure how she felt about that as she marched up to the door and boldly banged the knocker.

It opened almost immediately, and instead of the monosyllabic Mrs. Hammond, Edward stood there, smiling. "I was watching for you from the window. How wonderfully punctual you are. Come in out of the cold." He threw an arm around her shoulders and guided her into the hall, kicking the door shut behind them.

So far, so good, Fenella thought, drawing her hands free of her muff. He looked tidier today than he had yesterday, she noticed. It seemed he had even combed his hair, although that undisciplined lock persisted in falling over his forehead. His eyes were almost luminous as they seemed to absorb her in a long gaze, his hands resting lightly on her shoulders. For a breathless moment she waited, immobile, then slowly, he leaned down and very lightly kissed her lips, murmuring, "I am so happy to see you, Fenella."

Before she could respond, he turned and led the way upstairs, his long legs taking the steps two at a time.

She followed him into his sitting room, which looked just the same as it had the previous day and was just as warm and inviting, with a bright fire and lamplight softening the harsh glare of the sunlit frost outside. "Let me take your coat and muff." He helped her out of her fur coat and took her muff, examining it closely, observing, "It looks remarkably like a dead rabbit."

"You're too kind," she murmured. "But for your information, it's not rabbit. If it's a dead anything, it's a sable—well, several actually."

"Ah, forgive me. I'm not very well up on furs. I should have known, of course, that a lady of your social standing wouldn't be seen dead in rabbit fur." He tossed the muff into the air, caught it and threw it onto the chair where he'd deposited her coat.

"And to think, I hoped I'd caught you in a good mood." Fenella shook her head as she unwrapped her scarf, throwing it on top of her coat. "Maybe I should leave; we're not going to get anywhere if you insist upon sniping at me at every turn."

Edward ignored the latter statement. Instead, he lightly brushed his fingers over her discarded scarf. "How involved are you?" he asked, regarding her closely.

"I go to meetings when I can, sign petitions, distribute leaflets when I can," she replied. "I've been on two marches so far. Petitioning Parliament is a long and frustrating business."

"Mmm." He nodded. "But women *will* get the vote eventually."

"Do you think they should?" she asked.

"Of course," he said simply.

She smiled, absurdly relieved. "Then perhaps I'll stay, if you promise not to snipe at me again."

"I don't know why I did. I was in such a good mood," Edward protested, running his hands through his dark hair in a gesture of frustration. "I've been looking forward to this moment since five o'clock this morning."

Fenella perched on the arm of the shabby sofa, re-membering her conversations the previous evening with Julia and Carlton. Perhaps it wasn't surprising that Edward's goblins sometimes showed themselves at inopportune moments; they seemed rooted in a deep dislike of the privileged society in which his half brother and sister were so at home. She still didn't think she should have to put up with it without protest, though. It wasn't reasonable to tar her with the same brush. She wasn't remotely like his half siblings.

"Can we start the morning again?" he asked, raising an eyebrow.

"Do you always get up before dawn?" Fenella asked, letting his question stand. She had regained her customary composure, feeling for the moment that she had the upper hand.

"I don't sleep well, never have. And I seem to be at my most creative in the dawn hours."

"Perhaps that explains your rudeness and irascibil-ity," she responded with a matter-of-fact nod.

"Probably," he agreed, still watching her closely with those piercing blue eyes. "You haven't answered my question."

Fenella shrugged. "I'm willing to try. But my patience is not unlimited."

"I don't expect it to be. I am very sorry we got off on the wrong foot, Fenella. I will do everything possible to keep us on the right one from now on."

Fenella stood up and extended her hand. "Good morning, Edward. I trust you passed a pleasant evening since we last met."

He took her hand and enclosed it in both of his. "I have missed you."

The simple statement sent a warm shiver down her back. With anyone else, she would have laughed it off as a move in a flattering, flirtatious game, but somehow she was convinced that Edward Tremayne did not indulge in games of flirtation. And her body was responding to the intensity of the gaze, the warm pressure of his hands around hers.

She managed a small smile in response and gently withdrew her hand. Matters were moving too fast. "Shall we begin the reading?"

A slight smile touched the corners of his mouth as if he had read her mind. He certainly didn't seem put out by her refusal to respond to his declaration.

"First a mug of mulled wine to chase the morning chill," he announced, moving away from her to the fire, where a saucepan stood on a trivet over the glowing coals. He knelt on the rug and reached for a long spoon with which he stirred the contents of the pan.

Fenella wondered why she hadn't noticed the rich

aroma of spice and wine in the room before. She sank into the depths of the cracked leather armchair and watched with salivating interest as he poured the steaming liquid into two china mugs, dropped a large knob of butter into each one and then handed her one before perching on the wide arm of her chair, raising his own mug in a toast.

"To Rose and good humor."

"To Rose and good humor." Fenella took a careful sip of the steaming liquid and gave a little sigh of pleasure. "It's a bit early in the morning for this; don't blame me if I'm woozy by noon." She took another sip, then leaned her head against the back of her chair and closed her eyes as the hot, spicy wine slipped down her throat.

She was barely aware that he had changed position on the arm of her chair until she felt his breath on her cheek, then his lips on hers, the warm sweetness of the mulled wine a lingering taste. She didn't open her eyes, didn't resist when Edward took the mug from her hand. But every inch of her skin seemed to come alive, every muscle poised, suspended, waiting for whatever would come next. Her lips parted involuntarily for his seeking tongue and her own partnered with his in a delicate dance of shared taste and sensation. His mouth was warm and sweet when her tongue explored the contours of his cheeks, stroked the roof of his mouth.

"You are so lovely, Miss Grantley," he whispered into the side of her neck before his tongue traced circles around her ear, probed within, tantalizing with little, darting movements that made her squirm with exquisite sensation. The moist caress moved to her throat, his hands now cupping her head, holding her face steady for a succession of tiny kisses that reminded her of the way a hummingbird sipped on a flower.

She felt his fingers on the buttons of her shirt, felt the warm air on her bared flesh as he spread the sides apart. His tongue dipped into the hollow of her throat and then moved down, lingering in the cleft of her breasts before his mouth slid sideways to kiss the firm upswell of each breast above the lacy edge of her camisole.

"Open your eyes," he directed softly, and she did so, looking into the intense blue gaze hovering above her. He smiled, stroking a strand of hair from her cheek, twisting it around his finger. "I'm afraid to rush things."

He was kneeling on the floor now, his body leaning over hers, and Fenella reached to touch his mouth fleetingly with a fingertip, tracing the sensual curve of his lips, lips she could still feel pressed against her own. "Deferred gratification?" she questioned, dipping her fingertip into the deep cleft of his chin.

"Not really; more a matter of enjoying a leisurely progress to the inevitable."

A jolt of sensual excitement set her blood running fast and hot. She couldn't pretend not to know what the inevitable would mean. It was as if such a consummation had somehow been decreed by some fate or destiny from the inauspicious moment of their first encounter. If she wanted to prevent the inevitable, it had to be now. Instead, she heard herself ask, "Which would you rather?"

For answer, he bent to kiss her breasts in turn, pushing the lace edge of her camisole lower with an insistent finger. Wordlessly, she arched her back, lifting her breasts to his mouth, her eyes closing involuntarily once again. He lifted her breasts free of the camisole and Fenella groaned softly as his teeth grazed the acutely sensitive nipples, now erect and wanting. His tongue drew small circles around them, his lips suckling, nuzzling, his mouth enclosing.

Slowly, he drew back, leaving her bared flesh suddenly cold and needy. Matter-of-factly, he tucked her breasts back into her camisole and buttoned her shirt, adjusting the big, floppy bow with deft fingers. "I think I'd enjoy deferring the gratification," he said, leaning forward to kiss her, this time a firm, definitive kiss. "We'll move a little farther next time."

Fenella told herself she was not disappointed, but she did feel somehow suspended, cheated, as if a promise had been abruptly broken. And yet, at the same time, the prospect of *next time* filled her with a thrill of anticipation.

She stood up, shaking out her skirts, adjusting the broad leather belt that accentuated her small waist. Then she turned to the gilt mirror above the fireplace, checking that her hair was still in its neat coronet, straightening the floppy bow at her throat. The movements all served to return her to reality, to slow her speeding heart. "So, shall we do the reading now?"

"I don't think so." Edward handed her the now-cooling mug of mulled wine. "I don't think it will go well at this juncture. Sit down again and drink your wine."

Fenella did so but said with a frown, "Why won't it go well? You've been so anxious to get on with it."

He sighed. "I know, and as a result, I'm afraid I'll probably snap at you, or say something offensive if it doesn't work out the way I want it to. And I don't want us to fall out again. At least not today."

Fenella smiled, shaking her head. "But another day it won't matter if we fall out?"

He shrugged, kneeling before the fire to recharge the saucepan on the trivet and grating nutmeg onto the contents. "It's a foregone conclusion, dear girl. I have a vile temper and I'm shockingly oversensitive about my work. It's a positive recipe for offense. And I daren't hope that you'll just ignore it. You have too quick a tongue of your own." He stirred the aromatic contents of the saucepan.

"Oh." Fenella was somewhat taken aback. "I always considered myself to be of a remarkably even temper."

He grinned at her over his shoulder. "I'm sure in the right company you are. But not in my company, and I can't say I blame you . . . pass me your mug."

She did so, debating a suitable riposte but not finding one. It seemed beyond strange that a man who could arouse in her such sensual passion could also arouse the desire to hit him over the head with a coal shovel.

"If I drink this, I'll be good for nothing for the rest of the morning," she said, taking the refilled mug as he handed it to her.

"You can always take a nap on the sofa. It's quite

comfortable." Sitting on the floor, he leaned back against her chair, his legs sprawled, his head resting against her knees. "Now, isn't this comfortable?"

It was a little too comfortable, Fenella reflected, resisting the urge to trawl her fingers through the thick mass of his black hair. "At the risk of ruining the moment, can we talk a little about the play?"

He seemed to stiffen, but he kept his gaze on the fire. "You really want to talk about the play?"

"Yes. We started to talk about it yesterday, but I ruined the conversation, so I'd like to begin again." She set aside her mug, sat upright, her hands folded in her lap, her expression one of utter concentration. "You said Rose was *found*. What does that mean?"

Edward shook his head. "Not in the sense that she was lost. When she was ten years old, she was found not guilty of murdering her sister."

Fenella inhaled sharply. Whatever she had expected, it wasn't that. "Did she do it?"

"That's something the audience will have to answer for themselves. Their answer will depend on how they see Rose as you portray her."

"But then I have to decide for myself whether she was a murderess or not," Fenella said slowly. "I can't play her if I don't know within myself whether she did it, and if so why."

"Very true," Edward agreed, and she could feel his satisfied smile in the sudden relaxation of his body against her knees.

"But you must know whether she did or not . . . you couldn't have written a character with such ambiguity yourself. You have to know in your heart of hearts whether she was guilty," Fenella protested.

"Ah, but do I?" he murmured, toeing a fallen log back into the hearth.

"Of course you do," Fenella stated with a touch of impatience. "I can see the appeal in writing a character with an ambiguous history, but it's inconceivable that you, the author, wouldn't know the truth of that history."

Edward laughed softly. "Maybe I have an opinion," he said. "But it's one I'm keeping to myself. When we've read the play together, I'll be most interested to hear yours."

"I think that's a very bad idea." She shook her head vigorously.

"Why?" He turned his head against her knees to look up at her, a sly grin on his face.

"Because if my opinion annoys you, you'll turn into Mr. Hyde again."

He laughed outright. "Oh, my dear girl, is that how you see me?"

"You can't deny I've had good reason," she retorted, sounding as cross as she was beginning to feel.

Edward swiveled until he was kneeling in front of her. As he looked at her, his eyes glowed with an almost predatory hunger. He leaned forward, his mouth hovering over hers for a breathless moment before joining with it in a kiss so deep and powerful and possessive that Fenella felt as if she was melting into him, yielding her mouth to his demanding tongue, to the insistent pressure of his lips.

His hands moved to her waist with warm, firm

pressure as he stood up, bringing her with him without releasing her mouth. He clasped her face between his hands as he kissed her ever more deeply. She leaned into him, feeling the lines of his long, lean body hard against her softness. He lifted her off her feet and moved them both to the sofa, coming down with her as he let her slip to the cushions.

He pushed her skirt over her thighs, his fingers slipping inside her drawers. Her own hands now fumbled for the buttons of his trousers. She bit his lip and tasted blood, hearing her own low moan as he found her sex, moist and wanting. As his mouth plundered hers, he parted her lower lips, his fingers reaching deep inside her. Her hips lifted, thrust against the hot, probing hand that was bringing her closer and closer to the peak. She could feel his penis pressing against her belly and she used one hand to caress and stroke, feeling the moisture at the tip, the pressure of her fingers increasing as his response strengthened, his breathing quickened.

Fenella moved against him, following the insistent rhythm of his knowing fingers, bringing her inexorably to dissolution. She could not have held back her climax if her life had depended upon it, and in the moment she fell, she held his sex tight in the palm of her hand, aware even through her own rush of pleasure of the firm, even pulsing against her palm.

She heard Edward cry out in orgasmic completion and his head dropped heavily against her breast, his hand now still but warm in the cleft of her thighs, the hot gush of his seed on her belly. For a long time neither of them moved until Edward slowly raised his head from her breast and smiled at her, pushing his disheveled hair from his eyes.

"All right?" he murmured, kissing the corner of her mouth.

"Better than all right," she responded, lightly touching his lip where she had bitten it. "I'm sorry about that."

He shook his head with a chuckle. "A wound I bear with pride." Pushing back from the chair, he sat on his heels regarding Fenella with an almost quizzical smile. "I hadn't intended that to happen."

"No," she agreed, sounding as dazed as she felt. "Neither had I."

"But it did."

"But it did." Fenella smiled slowly. "How smug and complacent we sound."

"That's rather how I feel." Edward stood, buttoning his trousers. He held out his hands to her, pulling her to her feet, her skirt falling back around her.

"Is there somewhere I could straighten myself up a bit?" she asked, aware of her disheveled undergarments and the stickiness on her belly.

"Through the bedroom. But you'll need hot water." He lifted a kettle off a hook where it hung above the fire. "Come with me."

She followed him through a bedroom, too conscious of her own state of disarray to pay much attention to the room itself. He opened a door in the far wall to reveal a small washroom, with a washstand, ewer and basin, a hip bath and a commode.

"Rather primitive, I'm afraid. Mrs. Hammond doesn't run to all modern conveniences," Edward said, opening a cupboard and taking out a towel and washcloth. "There's soap on the washstand." He poured hot water into the ewer. "Is there anything else I can get you, ma'am?"

Fenella shook her head. "No, this is perfect. I won't be long."

"Take as long as it takes, dear girl." He kissed the tip of her nose and left her, closing the door quietly behind him.

Fenella poured hot water into the basin, then unbuckled her belt and took off her skirt and drawers. She dipped the washcloth in the basin and set about making herself respectable again. She might as well be a whore in a brothel, she thought, wondering why instead of shocking her the reflection merely produced a self-satisfied grin.

Chapter Six

Fenella felt oddly shy as she reentered the sitting room. Edward was standing at the window but turned instantly. "Better?"

"Tidier," she responded. "Thank you."

He smiled and held out his hands, reaching for hers. He drew her closer to him, looking down into her face with a searching expression. "Regrets?" he asked, a slight frown drawing his thick black brows together.

Fenella considered, finally shaking her head. "No, none at all. But I have to admit I feel a bit . . ." She searched for the word she wanted. "A bit unfinished," she said, frowning, wondering if it was just her inexperience that made her feel that way. "It feels as if something's been left out."

Edward looked at her with some incredulity. "But it has," he said. "There's a difference between pleasuring each other and truly making love. We haven't yet made love. The best is yet to come."

Relief at his instant understanding chased away the shyness. "I enjoyed what we did, nevertheless."

Laughing, he kissed her full on the mouth, a warm, firmly declarative kiss. "Are you hungry? I'm ravenous after such an energetic morning."

Fenella realized she was starving; her breakfast toast seemed a very long time ago. "It must be nearly time for lunch."

"Almost noon." He stepped away from her to pick up her suffragist's scarf and wrapped it around her neck before helping her on with her coat and handing her the fur muff. "There's a little French restaurant on Spring Street that does an excellent cassoulet on Saturday. Just the thing for a freezing day. I'll be back in a minute." He disappeared into the bedroom.

Fenella buried her hands in her muff. She still felt very strange, as if her world had turned an unexpected corner. She had no comparison to what had just happened, although she didn't consider herself naïve or completely ignorant of matters of passion. She and her friends had read *The Pearl* while they were still at school and had not shied away from experimentation when the opportunity arose, but she had not until this morning experienced the full glory of sensual fulfillment. It occurred to her that she was probably very fortunate to enter that world hand in hand with Edward Tremayne. There was nothing callow or unpracticed about him. And she suspected that, unlike George, he would notice immediately if he was not drawing a responding passion from his partner.

"Ready?" He came in from the bedroom, tying a plaid muffler around his neck.

Her cheeks warmed at the ridiculous notion that he might have read her mind. She turned quickly toward him. "Yes, quite ready. I could eat a horse."

"I don't think Marcel puts horsemeat in his cassoulet, but it's not beyond the realms of possibility." Edward opened the door to the hall. "After you, madam." He swept an ironic bow in invitation.

They walked quickly, Fenella's hands tucked into her muff, Edward's right hand tucked into her elbow, guiding her through the busy foot traffic. "It's a lively part of Town," he remarked, steering her around a corner.

"Yes," agreed Fenella, taking an involuntary step sideways on the narrow pavement as a brewer's dray passed in the middle of the street pulled by two enormous cart horses. It was certainly a lot busier than her own part of Town.

"Most people who live in these parts work for a living," he commented.

Fenella looked swiftly across at him, expecting to see a curled lip and the always readily derisive glint in his eyes, but his expression remained neutral. Even his voice was still light and conversational.

"Here we are." He stopped outside a small restaurant, two shallow steps leading to the front door. The window to the side was foggy with steam and impossible to see through. The sign above the door proclaimed "Chez Marcel." "It's not the Trocadero or the Criterion," Edward said, "but what it lacks in pretension it makes up for in quality."

And there it was, the derision and the curled lip. Fenella chose not to respond, merely walked past him as he held open the door for her into a square room dominated by a long, wooden communal table with backless benches where people were jostled together, eating and talking against the background sounds of chinking glass and the scrape of cutlery against bowls. A few individual tables covered in red-and-white-checked tablecloths occupied the outskirts of the room.

"Ah, M'sieur Edward, *comment ça va?*" A man swathed in a none-too-clean white apron and a checkered scarf at his throat emerged from the back of the room, greeting them with a broad smile.

"*Ça va bien*, Marcel," Edward returned, submitting to a bear hug from the ruddy-cheeked, rotund Frenchman. He turned to Fenella, taking her hand and drawing her forward. "Fenella, this is Marcel, who makes the best cassoulet this side of the Channel. Marcel, Mademoiselle Grantley."

Fenella held out her hand to Marcel, who kissed it with great reverence. "Mademoiselle, my little bistro is honored indeed."

"I suspect, m'sieur, that you are too modest," she said, smiling.

He gave a booming laugh and gestured to a table in a nook beside the fireplace. "Your usual table, *mon ami*. I always keep it for M'sieur Edward on a Saturday, mademoiselle. He loves my cassoulet." He kissed his fingertips and Fenella had to stop herself from laughing. Marcel was playing the typical French chef with outrageously exaggerated comic gestures. She glanced at Edward and he winked, putting a hand to the small of her back and steering her across the noisy room to the fireplace nook.

"Let me take your coat." He took the fur as she slipped it off her shoulders and handed it to Marcel, together with her muff and scarf, then followed it with his own before pulling out her chair.

"*Un bon* bordeaux, M'sieur Edward?" Marcel asked with a knowing smile above the pile of coats in his arms.

"Please, Marcel. And the cassoulet for both of us."

"D'accord, m'sieur." Marcel went off with his burdens and Edward leaned back in his chair, regarding Fenella with a quizzical eye.

"Are you at ease?"

"Yes, of course. Why would you think I might not be?"

He shrugged. "As I said, it's not the Trocadero."

"Do you really think of me as a spoiled, over-privileged snob?" she demanded. "Have I ever given you reason to do so?"

"I don't need a reason, I'm afraid," he replied with a grimace. "I have a chip on my shoulder."

"Oh, is that what it is?" she inquired with a sardonically raised eyebrow. "I would never have guessed."

"You, my dear girl, are a very thorny rose," he declared.

"If by that you mean I give as good as I get, I won't argue with you," she retorted.

"Fair enough," he conceded with a twitch of his lips. "But let's not spoil our lunch." He reached across the table to take her hand, playing with her fingers. "When were you last in Paris?"

Fenella accepted the change of subject without argument. "Last summer. It was very hot, as I recall, but still lovely." She reached for a piece of crusty French bread from the basket a waiter had just placed on the table.

"*Ici, du vin,*" Marcel announced, flourishing a bottle and a corkscrew. He drew the cork, sniffed it critically, then nodded, poured a little into a glass the waiter handed him, swirled it and sipped. "*Bon.*" He poured the ruby liquid into Fenella's glass and then into Edward's. "Your good health, mademoiselle, m'sieur." He stood back, watching carefully as they each sipped. "*C'est bon, non?*"

"Delicious," Fenella said, reflecting that maybe Chez Marcel was not the Trocadero, but the service was every bit as attentive. She broke off a piece of the crust from the warm bread on her plate before taking a sip of wine. "There is nothing more perfect than plain French bread and good red wine." She sighed with satisfaction. "Why are you looking at me like that? Is something wrong?" Edward's blue gaze was fixed upon her with the intensity she found so unnerving.

"No, dear girl, nothing could be wrong. I just enjoy seeing how you enjoy simple sensations, the hunger you have for life's physical joys." He sipped his wine appreciatively, savoring its bouquet. His eyes narrowed suggestively as he murmured, "Indeed, I can hardly wait to explore such pleasures with you in rather more depth."

Fenella bit her lip, trying to conceal her reaction as pure lust sent a jolt of fire through her belly. She took an overhasty gulp of wine and coughed as it went down the wrong way. Burying her face in her napkin, she coughed and choked, her eyes streaming.

Edward pushed back his chair and came to her side of the table, patting her back vigorously until the fit had passed. She raised her head from the napkin, her cheeks scarlet, her eyes wet with cough-induced tears and saw that the table was surrounded by a circle of anxious waiters.

Marcel proffered a glass of amber liquid. "A sip of this, mademoiselle. This is what you need." Blindly, she reached for it, bringing it to her lips, assailed by the powerful fumes, but before she could sip, Edward took it from her nerveless fingers. "I don't think calvados is the right remedy, here, Marcel." He reached for a water glass. "Drink this, Fenella. Slowly."

She did so and felt the cool, clear liquid soothe her raw throat as the spasms finally ceased. "I'm so sorry; I don't know why that happened." She mumbled her apologies, dabbing at her streaming eyes. "How mortifying."

"Nonsense," Edward said briskly. "You drank the wine too quickly. It happens to us all. Drink the water and you'll be fine in a moment." He gestured to their audience with a dismissive wave and the circle of waiters melted away, the buzz of conversation resuming around the room, and Fenella felt her high color fade.

"That was really your fault, Edward," she accused after a minute.

"Oh, how so?" He raised his eyebrows.

"Making inappropriate remarks." She essayed another sip of wine, looking at him over the rim of the glass.

His eyes narrowed again. "You must forgive me, then. I certainly hadn't intended to induce such a dramatic response." He was laughing as he spoke and Fenella couldn't help an answering chuckle.

"Le cassoulet," Marcel announced, setting down a brown earthenware pot from which the most enticing smells arose. "I shall serve you."

Fenella leaned back from the table and the chef ladled the richly aromatic stew into a deep bowl, carefully adding the crispy crust of buttery breadcrumbs on top before placing the bowl in front of her. He did the same for Edward and then stepped back with a deep bow. "Bon appétit, *mes amis*."

Fenella dipped her fork into her bowl, finding pieces of duck, thick sausage and white beans. "I once had this in Toulouse," she said, savoring a particularly succulent piece of duck. "It seems strange to be eating it on Spring Street in London on a freezing winter's day."

"I can't think of a better place or occasion," Edward responded, dipping bread into his bowl. His eyes danced as he watched her hungry enjoyment of the rich peasant dish. "So, do you have siblings?"

"No, there's just me. I don't know whether my parents decided I was more than enough for them, or whether it just didn't happen." She dabbed at her mouth with her napkin. "I have cousins, though. My father's sister has a significant brood, so the title and property will go to Miles, her eldest."

His gaze sharpened, but he kept his attention on his food. "So you won't inherit anything from your father?"

Fenella shrugged, taking a sip of wine. "As it happens, I don't need to. My maternal grandmother made me her beneficiary. Apparently, she and my mother decided, as my mother was already well provided for by my father, that I shouldn't be left penniless." She laughed, shaking her head. "I rather think my grandmother suspected I wouldn't be very cooperative when it came to finding a suitable husband who could maintain me in the manner to which I was accustomed."

"That's very enlightened of them," he observed, setting down his fork in his now empty bowl.

"Of my grandmother," Fenella specified. "She was a most unconventional lady with very strong views, and she lived by her own rules. Fortunately, she inherited a fortune from her father, who was something of a nabob as I understand it . . . made a fortune in India . . . and that gave her the freedom to do as she pleased." She smiled reminiscently. "Apparently, I look rather like her. She didn't take much notice of me when I was young, but as soon as I was old enough to have a conversation, she took me under her wing. I loved spending time with her; she had some wonderfully outrageous views on the world. My darling mother, on the other hand, is not in the least enlightened about a woman's place. She really believes it is a man's duty to provide for his wife, and a wife's to submit to her lord and master in every arena."

She sighed, shaking her head. "I love her dearly, make no mistake, but when I once broached the subject of women's suffrage, she was utterly bewildered. She couldn't imagine *why* we would want to vote; our feeble brains couldn't possibly understand the intricacies of politics and governing. We should be content to stay home and support our husbands, who were doing the work to keep us safe and happy."

"Not an unusual viewpoint," Edward observed, leaning back as a waiter cleared away their empty dishes.

"No," Fenella agreed, thinking of George. Once again, she felt herself tense at the prospect of dashing his hopes. It would be a horrible conversation, but she would have to face it sooner rather than later. And her mother, while refraining from outright censure, would be unable to hide her disappointment. Familiar depression hovered.

Edward watched her face with a slight frown. She had the most expressive countenance and something was clearly troubling her. He announced briskly, "Now to an equally important subject: dessert. Marcel's wife makes an amazing tarte Tatin, and *oeufs à la neige*, if you'd prefer something smoother, more luscious."

His assertive voice broke her mood, reminded her of where she was and with whom she was. "The latter," she responded instantly. "It's one of my absolute favorite desserts."

"And after that we shall conclude with the calvados," he declared, nodding at the hovering Marcel. "More appropriate as a digestif than a cure for choking, I believe."

Fenella merely smiled. Once again, she was feeling sated, warm and slightly disconnected from the humming room around her. But she was not in the least disconnected from her companion. She was aware of Edward in all his solid reality. There was nothing in the least dreamlike about his presence, or the little streamers of desire flickering through her loins.

"Your floating island, mademoiselle." A waiter set in front of her a shallow dish where fluffy, lightly toasted islands of egg white swam in a rich, golden custard. "And tarte Tatin for m'sieur."

"I'm not in the least hungry, but who could resist this?" Fenella remarked, dipping her spoon into the custard, breaking into an island.

Edward, his mouth full of apple tart, merely nodded his agreement, and for the next ten minutes, they ate in silence. Around them, the buzz of conversation began to die down as other diners came to the end of their lunch. When Fenella sat back with a small groan of repletion, she noticed only a few customers remained.

"I hope we're not overstaying our welcome," she said, nodding her head to an offer of coffee with the calvados.

"Oh, don't worry about that. Often enough I've finished my meal in the kitchen with Marcel and the crew while they have their lunch." Edward looked around the almost empty restaurant before taking a sip of his apple brandy. "Ah, that's good."

Fenella followed suit with a tiny sip. It occurred to

her that this meal must have been expensive, even though it wasn't the Trocadero or the Criterion. For a man without a fortune to fall back on, it would be a considerable expense. She took another sip of her calvados and said somewhat hesitantly, "That was absolutely delicious. I hope that you'll let me p—"

"Let you *what*?" A white shade appeared around his lips, his blue eyes shooting angry fire at her.

Fenella realized her mistake too late. "I'm sorry. I just thought . . ."

"What did you think?" Nothing in his expression changed.

"That maybe you were enlightened enough to let me pay my share," she said, refusing to be intimidated. "Perhaps I should go now, because I seem to have ruined the moment." She began to get up, but his hands shot across the table, grasping hers and holding them flat on the table.

"Sit down, Miss Grantley."

For a moment, they glared at each other in a silent battle of wills. Finally, Fenella broke the furious silence. She tugged at her hands, and instantly, he relaxed his grip. "Hypocrite," she accused, resuming her seat.

"What on earth made you think that after I invited you for lunch you needed to reject my invitation with such an insult?" he demanded.

"I wasn't rejecting an invitation," she protested. "Or at least I didn't see it that way."

"No, well, we'll discuss our different interpretations somewhere less public. Would you excuse me for a moment?" He pushed back his chair and stalked off toward the door that led to the kitchen.

Fenella sat in silence, idly twirling her spoon in her coffee. She was no longer in the least detached from her surroundings; indeed, she was acutely conscious of every scrape of a chair, the jingle of cutlery, the sound of plates being cleared.

"Right, let's go." Edward appeared with their outer garments. He held her coat for her, then shrugged into his own. Fenella draped her scarf around her neck, drew on her gloves and pushed her hands into her muff as she followed him to the door and out into the still-freezing street. They walked back to Praed Street in an equally frozen silence.

Chapter Seven

As they reached the corner of Spring Street, Fenella caught sight of a hackney coming toward them. She took a half step to the edge of the pavement and raised a hand.

"What do you think you're doing?" Edward grabbed her hand, forcing it down.

"I'm a hailing a cab, of course. I'm going home. Let me go at once."

"Oh, no, we're going to set a few things straight, my dear Miss Grantley. And I have no desire to do that in the middle of the street." His hand closed around hers in what could have been a friendly clasp, but Fenella was under no such illusion.

"Let go of my hand."

"I'd rather not, if you don't mind," he replied, tucking her hand into the crook of his elbow and resuming the walk back to Praed Street.

Fenella could see little appeal in a public tug-of-war and fell into step beside him, her mind, as usual, playing its inconvenient trick of forcing her to see the other side of the argument. It would never have occurred to her to offer to pay her share of a meal with any of her other male friends and acquaintances, however easy she felt in their company. She could only imagine their astounded reaction if she did so. They would be completely bewildered at such an extraordinary flouting of protocol. Even among her more enlightened circle, it would still be considered a dreadful faux pas. So why should she be surprised and indignant at Edward's reaction?

They reached the house on Praed Street without having exchanged a word and Fenella walked past Edward into the house. "Ah, it's you, Mr. Tremayne. I heard the door. I hadn't realized you were out." Mrs. Hammond seemed to appear from nowhere, an expression of disapproval on her angular countenance. She surveyed her tenant's guest with a twitch of her nose.

"I'll remember to inform you of my movements next time I decide to leave the house, Mrs. Hammond," Edward said, his voice glacial. "Although I'm not aware of any house rules that make it a necessity."

He moved behind Fenella, gesturing she should precede him up the stairs. She did so, hiding her reluctant amusement at the way he had taken the wind from the disagreeable landlady's sails.

He unlocked the door to his rooms and eased Fenella inside with a hand at the small of her back. "Good, the fire's still in." He stirred the dying embers vigorously with the poker, then threw a handful of dry kindling on the renewed glow. It caught at once, and he followed it with a small log and then a larger one before straightening and turning to Fenella, who still stood by the door, her hands tucked into her muff.

"Let's see if we can disentangle this mess," he said, his tone entirely reasonable. "Take off your coat and sit by the fire. I'll make some tea." He took the kettle from its hook over the fire and disappeared into the washroom to fill it at the cold tap.

Fenella hesitated. If she wanted nothing more to do with this strange, infuriating and very complicated man, she could just walk away from him now. She knew he wouldn't try to stop her, however forceful he had been in preventing her getting a cab home. But she also knew that she didn't want to leave things unfinished between them. There was an unfulfilled promise there somewhere, and she found she wanted very much to redeem it.

So she discarded her outer garments, gave the fire an encouraging stir with the poker and sat in the old, leather armchair, stretching her feet to the andirons.

"I don't have any cake or crumpets, I'm afraid." Edward came back into the room and hung the filled kettle above the fire.

"I couldn't imagine eating another thing after that lunch," Fenella told him. "In fact, I can't imagine that I will ever be hungry again."

"For food . . . or something else?" he queried, raising an eloquent black brow.

She was angry with him, angry with herself, but none of that stopped the liquid surge of desire. She inhaled sharply and, to her increased annoyance, Edward laughed. But it wasn't unkind laughter.

"I know exactly how you feel," he said. "We have

far too much unfinished business between us, my thorny rose, to stalk off in high dudgeon." He opened a cupboard and took down a Brown Betty teapot and two bone china cups and saucers, glancing at her over his shoulder. "As I recall, milk, no sugar?"

"Yes, please." She watched him make the tea with deft efficiency, heating the pot before measuring tea leaves and pouring boiling water over them. He set the pot on the hearth and covered it with a thick, calico cozy. "We'll let it brew for a few minutes."

"Does Mrs. Hammond cook for you?" she asked, wondering why such a mundane question came to her lips when there was so much more of moment to discuss.

He shook his head. "If I'm too busy working to go out, Marcel will send one of his boys with dinner. Otherwise, I patronize one of the many small and simple cafés around here. They all know me well."

"I imagine so," she said, unable to think of anything else to say.

"So, explain to me why you thought it would be acceptable to offer to pay for your own lunch?" He asked the question as he went to the window, reaching behind the curtain for a half full bottle of milk.

"How do you keep it cold in the summer?" she asked, distracted by an issue that had nothing to do with his question.

"I throw away a lot," he said matter-of-factly, pouring tea, adding milk to her cup before setting it down on the small side table beside the chair. "Now, will you answer my question?"

Fenella blew on her tea to cool it as she considered

how best to reply. Edward sat down on the sofa and watched her cogitations without prompting. Finally, she said, "Julia and Carlton were guests last night at my mother's dinner party."

He sipped his tea, saying nothing as he continued to regard her calmly.

"I don't know them at all really, except for a social nod when we come across each other at some party or other, but my mother is very polite and she happened to be at an at home when they were there and felt she couldn't invite her hostess without inviting them too. She would see it as just common courtesy."

"Did you find their company . . . uh . . . interesting, shall we say?"

Now there was an edge to his voice, but his expression remained calm as he continued to sip his tea.

"Unpleasantly so," she responded. "But I think you're asking if I was probing them for information about you? Am I right?"

"Yes," he said, setting his teacup aside.

Fenella debated how best to proceed. She could see little point in prevarication in the face of Edward's straightforward answer. "Well, I didn't ask either of them about you directly."

"Of course you didn't," he responded. "I'm sure you're far too discreet."

Fenella winced at the bite in the statement. But she couldn't really blame him. She'd hate the idea herself of someone clandestinely trying to discover things about her. It just hadn't seemed like that was what she was doing at the time. "Your brother said little enough about you, except that you were persona non grata in the family, and you'd told me that yourself. Julia was a little more forthcoming, but essentially, she said the same thing, that your father had disowned you because you wouldn't work for him."

"'How sharper than a serpent's tooth it is to have a thankless child,'" Edward murmured.

"She didn't actually quote *Lear*," she said. "In fact, given how deeply Julia despises the theatre, I doubt she even knows the quote."

He laughed suddenly. "No, I'm sure you're right. My half siblings are philistines, the pair of them."

Fenella was relieved at his change of tone, but she felt she needed to put the whole subject of money to rest even if it meant he reverted to his previous anger. She replaced her teacup on the side table and persevered. "Anyway, to explain my unfortunate offer to share our lunch bill, I was given to understand that you were, as a result of being disowned, rather short of ready money. And because you've at least appeared somewhat enlightened on the subject of female emancipation, I didn't think you would feel insulted. So, there you have it." She folded her hands in her lap and regarded him with a challenge in her gray eyes.

Edward frowned, nodding slowly. "It is very strange how one can hold certain views quite fervently and yet those views crumble in the face of convention."

He sounded as if he was preparing to debate a philosophical point, and for a moment, Fenella was too surprised to respond. Was he apologizing for jumping at her? Or had he simply put that aside in favor of discussing the larger issue?

"To avoid any more unfortunate misunderstandings, let me explain my financial situation—"

"No, that's not necessary," Fenella protested, appalled at the idea. "I don't need to know anything so personal."

"Well, let me simply assure you that while I choose to live frugally . . ." he gestured at their surroundings, "I'm not financially obliged to do so. My mother was not poverty-stricken and I was her only child. But, as I just said, I choose to live well within my means. I like things simple. I have no time for extravagances or for spending just for the sake of appearances. So you need have no scruples about accepting my invitations."

"I can assure you, I won't make the same mistake twice," Fenella said uncomfortably. She hadn't forced this personal accounting from him, but she still felt as if she'd obliged him to reveal financial details that were no one's business but his. "I think it's time for me to go home."

"Oh, don't do *that*," Edward said. "I can think of a much pleasanter way to end the afternoon." The intensity of his gaze seemed to enfold her and the deep, penetrating blue occupied her vision, excluding the world around them so that the solid shapes of the furniture, the flame of the fire, receded.

He uncurled from the sofa and came over to her chair, resting his hands on the arms as he leaned over her. She felt paralyzed, held by his eyes, by the searching gaze, seeming to look deep into her thoughts. Her head rested against the chair back, her face upturned, waiting for what seemed an eternity before at last his mouth took hers and her eyes closed involuntarily.

"Shall we do this properly, sweetheart?" he whispered against her lips, and for answer, she reached a hand to caress his cheek.

He drew her to her feet, his mouth still on hers, and her arms went around his neck. She pressed herself against him, her blood running hot, her body on fire with a fierce wanting. Clarity of thought receded as this passionate physical need took control of her senses. She had never felt anything like it and blindly obeyed her body's demands, still pressed against him as he moved them both sideways into the bedroom. She fell backward onto the bed, her eyes opening to look up at him, passion mounting as she saw fire ignite the blue gaze. She was aware of him removing her shoes and then his fingers moved swiftly over her shirt buttons, opening her shirt as he had done earlier, but this time he slid a hand around her, lifting her slightly as he pushed the garment off her shoulders.

"Sit up a moment," he murmured, moving his hand from her back. She held herself upright, raising her arms as he lifted her chemise up over her head, baring her breasts to the cool air in the fireless room. She shivered a little, whether with the chill or desire she neither knew nor cared. Her nipples stood erect for his encompassing lips, for the moist, flickering caress of his tongue.

"You're getting cold," he murmured. "Stand up for me." He took her hands, drawing her off the bed. A few deft movements and she stood naked in a puddle of skirt and petticoat. Edward turned from her for a moment, swiftly pulling back the covers on the bed, then he half-lifted her away from the discarded garments. She fell back again onto the bed, momentarily aware of her gartered silk stockings before he made short work of them, and finally, she lay naked on the crisp white sheets of his bed.

"You'll be warm in a moment," he said, bending to cover her with the quilt. "Much as I'd like to look at you like that forever, you'll catch your death." He turned away to draw the curtains across the window and then undressed rapidly as Fenella watched him in hungry anticipation. Naked, he was as splendid a sight as Michelangelo's *David*, she thought. His lean, muscular body was perfectly proportioned, not an ounce of redundant flesh. And he moved with such ease, perfectly in tune with his perfect physique.

He lifted the coverlet and slipped between the sheets, gathering her tightly against him. "Now, let us concentrate on getting warm." His breath was warm against her cheek as he held her, sharing his own body heat. She stretched long against him, then, without conscious intent, she rolled on top of him, looking down into his momentarily startled expression.

"If this is what pleases you . . ." He laughed softly and his hands ran down her back, caressing, stroking, feeling, moving over the curve of her bottom, the length of her thighs, his hips lifting beneath hers in tantalizing invitation.

She had no idea whether it was what pleased her or not, but her body seemed to know what it wanted. His sex was hard, pressing against the top of her thighs, and she moved her legs apart, kneeling astride him, reveling in the feel of him as his penis pressed against the opening cleft of her body.

"Guide me inside," he whispered. Her hand closed over his penis as she raised her hips a little and gave a tiny gasp as he pushed against her tightness and then slowly eased inside her, filling her. "Move at your own pace," he whispered, holding her hips. "You control your own pleasure, my sweet. I'll follow your lead."

For a moment, Fenella was still, growing accustomed to the feel of him, of being somehow occupied in such a deeply intimate way. But then she felt his sex move within her. Something deep inside her responded with a surge of pure, lustful desire, and she circled her hips around him, relishing in the different sensations.

Edward lay beneath her, watching her face, loving the deep light of arousal in the gray eyes, the flush on her cheeks, the way her tongue darted over her lips, the moment she inhaled sharply, her teeth closing over her bottom lip. The moment when she was lost in the surging wave of delight as her body convulsed around his penis and he moved his hips, increasing the pressure as his own pleasure flooded through him.

And when it was over, she lay on top of him, her head nestled into the hollow of his shoulder, her damp skin pressed into his own as the sweat dried on their bodies. He rolled her gently onto the bed beside him, still holding her close as his other hand pulled the covers up over them. Fenella fell into a deep trance of fulfillment and Edward held her, smiling up at the ceiling as the winter light of late afternoon faded.

Chapter Eight

It was dark in the room when Fenella awoke. She felt instantly bereft as her hand moved sideways across the bed, finding the space empty. But it was still warm, still retained the shape of his body, and she relaxed into the deep feather bed. It hadn't been a dream after all.

Edward came in from the sitting room wearing a gray, woolen dressing gown. He paused for a moment, looking at the bed, a small smile on his lips. She was awake; he could sense it. The deep languor of fulfillment still held his body in thrall, but his mind was clear. He held a lit taper and crossed the room to light the gas lamp on the dresser. The soft, yellow glow spread across the room. He blew out the taper and turned back to the bed, bending to kiss Fenella's brow, brushing away a thick lock of fair hair falling over her eyes.

Her thin, blue-veined eyelids fluttered open and she stretched languidly, reaching a hand to run a caressing finger over the curve of his mouth. "How long did I sleep?"

"About an hour. What do you think about a hot bath in front of the fire?"

"I think I would like that," she replied with a lazy smile. "But you don't have hot water."

"Oh, it can be arranged," he responded. "The bathtub is already in front of the fire, waiting for water. Then after, a little supper, and after that . . . who knows?"

"But I have to go home," she protested weakly.

"Do you?" His gaze sharpened, searching her expression. "Must you really, Fenella?"

Must she? Fenella pondered the question from the depths of her utterly relaxed self. Edward's proposal for the evening was irresistible. "Perhaps not," she said. "I'll need to send two messages. Is there someone who can take them for me?"

"Certainly there is. Mrs. Hammond employs her nephew, for his sins, to do the heavy work. He's always glad of an extra shilling or so to run an errand." He turned to open the wardrobe, taking out a deep crimson velvet dressing gown. "This should do. It'll swamp you but keep you warm." He brought it to the bed and held it for her in invitation.

Fenella forced herself to relinquish the warmth of the bed and pushed aside the covers, standing up with an eloquent shiver before shoving her arms into the velvet sleeves and pulling the garment closely around her naked body. Curious, she stepped over to the long mirror by the dresser and examined her reflection. "It's certainly huge, but I can't somehow picture you in crimson velvet."

"No, neither can I," he replied with a flickering smile. "Which is why it's never been worn."

"Why would you have it, then?"

"It was a present. A somewhat misguided one."

"Oh, who from? Someone who didn't know you very well, obviously."

"I think she thought she did," he returned casually. "Come by the fire now. Harvey's bringing up hot water for the bath."

She? Fenella shrugged. Of course he had had other women in his life. It was ridiculous to imagine him living like a monk. Her hair was already falling in an untidy straggle from the loosened pins. She pulled them all out and, thinking of the bath to come, twisted the thick fall into a knot, pinning it roughly on top of her head. She followed him into the warm, well-lit sitting room, its curtains drawn against the encroaching night.

A sturdy youngster came in, struggling under the weight of two heavy, steaming kettles. He averted his eyes from Fenella, his cheeks blazing red, whether with effort or embarrassment was anyone's guess. He poured the water into the tin tub sitting on a sheet before the fire. "I'll bring two more, sir."

"Thank you, Harvey. That should do nicely." Edward nodded at him.

"Poor lad," Fenella said as the door closed behind him. "I should have stayed in the bedroom."

"I don't see why. He's old enough to know what goes on between men and women, and if he doesn't by now, he should."

"That's a little harsh," Fenella objected. "Look at

me in this absurd garment. It's obvious I've got no clothes on underneath and the poor boy can't be more than fifteen or so."

Edward shook his head. "An age that's ripe for the exploration of the infinite mysteries of the female sex."

"My point exactly."

"Why don't you sit in the chair and turn your back when he returns? That way he might be able to ignore you . . . although I doubt it," he added. "No red-blooded male could do so. Unless he was of Oscar Wilde's persuasion, of course."

Fenella didn't respond to this sally, instead taking his advice and curling up in the armchair, her eyes resolutely on the fire when Harvey returned with two more steaming kettles. She stayed as she was until she heard the door close behind him.

She turned back to the room as Edward mused, "I don't think it's big enough for both of us, I'm afraid."

"What's not?"

"The bath, my sweet. What else?" He sprinkled drops onto the water from a glass vial he held.

Fenella laughed. "We'd swamp the room if we tried . . . what's that you're putting in?"

"Lavender oil."

"Do you always put fragrance in your bath?"

"Not in general. It rather depends on the circumstances." He recapped the vial and set it aside.

What circumstances? Fenella wondered. But she knew the answer well enough. It was connected to the crimson velvet dressing gown.

"If we can't get in together, I suggest you get in

and I'll do the washing; then you can do the same for me." Edward rolled up the sleeves of his robe and gestured imperatively to the bathtub. "Don't let the water get cold."

His brisk tones were quite at odds with the deeply sensual gleam in his eyes. Fenella swallowed the sudden lump in her throat as the now-familiar rush of desire shot through her loins. Forcing herself to move slowly, she slipped the robe from her body, turning to lay it neatly over the chair. She could feel his eyes on her back, caressing the curves and straights of her nakedness. As slowly she turned to face him, stood for a moment so he could absorb the sight of her. He held out a hand to her and she placed her own in his and stepped daintily into the hot water, sliding slowly, inch by inch, below the surface.

Edward knelt by the tub, a bar of soap in his hand. "Put your head back and relax," he instructed, beginning to soap her breasts. She gave herself up to the sensation, the warm, fragrant water against her skin, the clever manipulation of his soapy hands moving over her, beneath her and, fleetingly, within her. But it became clear that this time he was not interested in bringing her to orgasm, only to a titillating anticipation, which in its own way was every bit as wonderful. When his hands left her skin, she felt a moment of disappointment. She opened her eyes, looking up into the blue gaze above her, and the moment vanished, replaced with a deep, sensual contentment.

"My turn," he said, sitting back on his heels,

reaching for a thick Turkish towel before getting to his feet.

He held the towel for her as she stood up slowly, scented water cascading from her body, which now felt amazingly invigorated, more alive than she could have imagined following the deep relaxation of a few minutes earlier. She gathered the towel around her and stood still as he dried her body with swift efficiency. She was about to put on the robe again and then decided against it; the room was warm and she relished the feeling of her bare skin in the soft air.

Edward stepped into the bath, sliding down into the water. He was too tall to immerse himself completely and his knees poked above the water. Fenella concentrated her attention on the deep vee made by his bent knees and his half-sitting body, her soapy fingers reaching beneath the water, tantalizing with an intimate caress that made him draw a sharp breath.

Fenella smiled to herself, reflecting that she had learned a lot in the last few hours. She ran soapy hands over his smooth, muscular chest, bending to kiss him in the warm, scented steam, running her tongue over his lips as her hands continued their work.

"Enough, sweetheart," he said, his voice a little hoarse. "Enough for the moment."

She made a little moue of disappointment but sat back on her heels, her wet hands dangling over the edge of the tub. "I was enjoying myself."

"So was I, dear girl. But sometimes the pleasure is all the greater for not rushing matters."

"Deferred gratification again?" she said with a chuckle, pushing back to stand up, passing him a fresh towel as he stood up out of the water.

"There's a time and place," Edward agreed, rubbing himself down as he stepped out of the bath. "If you want to write your notes, you'll find paper and pen on the table. Don't disturb any of the other papers, though."

Fenella, pulling on the velvet robe, walked across to the table, looking down at the piles of papers and books that littered it. Except, of course, that "littering" was not the right word. On closer inspection, some order became clear in the apparent chaos. Papers were stacked edge to edge, leather strips marking pages emerging from closed books.

"What are you working on?" she asked, peering at the titles of the books. Weighty tomes, they all seemed to concern the literature of medieval England and France.

"A research project for my employer at King's College," he answered, shrugging into his robe and coming across to her. "I enjoy doing his research. He's a good scholar." He shrugged easily. "Besides which, it keeps me busy and pays well . . . not that that's a particular consideration," he added deliberately.

"Oh." Fenella couldn't think of anything else to say. She picked up a pad of paper. "Is this what I should use?"

"Unless you want more formal writing paper. I have some sheets of vellum."

"No, this will do." She sat down, took up a pen, dipped it in the inkwell and began a note to Diana Lacey.

Dearest, I must beg a boon. I'm telling Mama that I'm spending the evening and night with you. Please, could you back me up should there be any inquiries? If you need to get hold of me for any reason, I'm at this address. F.

She wrote down the Praed Street address, blotted the sheet and folded it carefully.

"Here, you can seal it with this." Edward handed her a stick of wax that he'd softened over the gas lamp.

"Thank you." She dropped the wax on the folded paper, then took up the pen again and wrote a note to her mother, explaining that she was staying with Diana for the night and would be back around mid-morning. That done, she returned the pen to the inkstand, folded and sealed the sheet and turned to Edward. "Will Harvey take these for me?"

"I'll take them downstairs and give them to him. He's very reliable. "

"Could you tell him to take this one first? That's very important." She tapped the note to Diana.

Edward glanced at the addresses and nodded his comprehension. "You need to be that devious?"

"I may be beyond the age of consent, but I'm still a single woman . . . and sufficiently concerned with my mother's peace of mind to use the occasional white lie in my dealings with her."

He nodded again, saying lightly, "Of course, I

understand. I'll make sure Harvey delivers the truth first and the lie second."

He left the room and Fenella took a deep breath. Things seemed to be moving very fast, too fast almost; she wasn't sure how to catch up. She felt no guilt about lying to her mother, but she knew that her letter to Diana would lead to an inquisition. Diana would do as she asked, of course, but she would demand a price. And once she had openly acknowledged this relationship with the touchy and frequently disagreeable playwright, she would be admitting to herself that it was a fact of her life and not some fleeting experience to be easily dismissed.

"A note has just come for you. Looks like Fenella's writing to me." Rupert Lacey entered the bedroom where his wife, sitting before the dresser mirror, was screwing a pair of diamond drops into her earlobes.

"Oh? That's unusual." Diana turned on the dresser stool to take the letter. It was definitely her friend's writing. She slit the wax seal with a long fingernail, unfolded the single sheet and read it quickly. "Well, now," she murmured, a mischievous smile on her lips. "What is the darling girl up to?" She looked up at her husband. "Where's Praed Street?"

"Marylebone way," he responded. "What's Fenella up to?"

"I'm not entirely sure, but I'll find out soon enough. For the moment, as far as the world is concerned, she's spending the night with us."

"It's not like her to be devious," he observed,

selecting a diamond pendant from the jewel box on the dresser. "I assume you're wearing this with the earrings?" He didn't wait for an answer but fastened the pendant at her neck.

"Oh, I don't know," Diana said with a smile. "She may be milk and honey on the surface, but Fenella has a steely side. And she's very clever into the bargain." She adjusted the position of the pendant so that the diamond nestled into the hollow of her throat. "There. I'm ready for the fray."

"What fray? I thought we were having a quiet dinner and card party," Rupert protested.

His wife laughed. "Don't worry, we are. Just Petra, Anthony Sullivan, and the Duncans. I'll have to tell Petra about Fenella's fib so she doesn't get caught out with Lady Grantley at some point."

Fenella sat curled in the big armchair, still wrapped in the velvet robe, watching Edward open a bottle of wine. He had removed all evidence of their bath and the only sound in the room was the crackle of the fire, followed by the discreet pop of the cork as he pulled it. He filled two glasses and brought one to her.

"Now, as for supper, I can produce a very fine Cheddar, an excellent ham, a good loaf of bread and butter. Will that do you, do you think?"

"Amply," she replied lazily, taking a sip from her glass. "This is good."

"It's a decent claret. My provisions are stored in Mrs. Hammond's pantry. I'll only be a minute. You'll find plates and cutlery in the cupboard by the window." He gestured toward the window and left the room.

Reluctantly, Fenella uncurled herself from the chair and went to the cupboard. That moment of invigoration and energy had been fleeting at best; now she was once more wrapped in the warm languor of complete contentment. It seemed she required nothing to complete her pleasure in the present. She found plates and knives and some plain, linen table napkins, which she set out on the side table. One look at the desk table, which was the only other option, convinced her it was no option at all without sweeping away enough papers and books to free up a corner.

Edward returned, carrying a wicker basket. He looked at the arrangement she had made on the side table and said, "You didn't fancy making space on the table, then?"

"I wouldn't dream of touching anything there," she replied. "It looks chaotic at first, but I have the feeling it's all very well ordered."

"I can certainly find anything I need," he agreed, setting down his basket and moving a stack of papers and a pile of books to one side of the table. "That should be enough room for the food. We can help ourselves." He set out bread, butter, cheese and ham and turned to Fenella. "Ma'am, will you partake of this humble supper?"

"With pleasure." She took a plate to the table. "Who's the professor you work for at King's?"

"Dr. Robert Franklin. He's a scholar of medieval literature. One of my own particular interests. I read Medieval French at Oxford," Edward told her.

"Medieval English presented no challenges, I suppose?" she said with a grin, then was suddenly afraid he would take offense.

He shook his head with a half laugh. "It presented plenty, as I was studying that at the same time."

Fenella buttered a chunk of bread and laid a thick slice of ham on top. "Impressive . . . why didn't you go into academia? It would seem an obvious choice."

"Obvious to you and to me, and to my professors," he said, his tone suddenly bitter. "Unfortunately, my father had other plans. At that point, I was financially dependent upon him. My mother was very much alive. She would have helped if I'd asked, but . . ." He shrugged dismissively. "Long story short, one has to eat and keep a roof over one's head, so I turned to writing plays and doing research for someone else's work."

"I'm sorry," she said inadequately.

"Oh, I've never regretted it for an instant," he responded, no longer sounding distant and bitter. "I find the work and the companionship most congenial, and it was Robert who introduced me to Cedric and suggested I show him *Sapphire*. With Cedric as director, there's a good chance it will find a backer and a theatre. But first, I need my Rose." He turned away from the table, a piece of cheese in one hand. "And now, I believe, my dear girl, we have come full circle."

Chapter Nine

"So, as we have come full circle, are you ready to read through the play, Fenella?"

Edward was leaning his broad shoulders against the mantel, cradling his wineglass between both hands, his eyes seeming to look directly into her mind as if he could read the tumult within.

Fenella pulled her eyes free of that penetrating scrutiny and stared into the fire. *Was she ready?* Ready to do this, to read *Sapphire*. To become Rose? If she couldn't fulfill Edward's vision of her, that would be the end. The end of what exactly? A burgeoning friendship? A relationship, an affair? An affair with promise . . . a future even? What was she risking in this warm, firelit room with Edward, so intense and yet seemingly so relaxed. What was she prepared to risk? Could they have a deep, intimate connection without Rose?

And if the answer to that was no, she had nothing to lose by trying. If it didn't work, nothing else would work between them. The prospect of losing this wonderful sense of living life to the fullest again was suddenly insupportable. She could not lose whatever this relationship with Edward would bring, so she had no choice but to risk failure. However, perhaps she could at the very least dictate some of the terms to lessen that risk.

"I have to read it by myself first," she stated. "I can't commit to a cold reading. I have to form an opinion, a feel for the character, particularly in light of what you've told me about her."

Edward was silent, frowning, then he moved to the table and took up a folder. "Very well. Are you prepared to read it now?"

Fenella nodded. Edward dropped the folder onto her lap. "There you are, then. I have some work to do, so I'll leave you to it." He returned to the table, sat down and opened one of the volumes.

Fenella opened the folder and looked at the first sheet. She felt faintly nauseated, as if facing some tremendous trial on which everything depended. She could hear the scratch of his pen on paper from the table behind her. Otherwise, the room was utterly silent.

And the silence continued for over two hours. Fenella finally closed the file and leaned back in her chair, closing her eyes. She had read *Sapphire* twice, the second time concentrating only on Rose's lines, trying to picture her.

Edward set aside his pen and turned in his chair. "Well?"

"I don't know exactly . . . she's a cipher. What does she look like?"

"Like you," he replied simply.

"But there's no physical description of her anywhere, no inkling from anything anyone says to give even a hint about her appearance."

"In my mind's eye, she looks exactly like you. Pale, ethereal, fair. In no way dramatic; nothing about her stands out except for her pellucid beauty."

Fenella had never thought of her own appearance as "pellucid." She wasn't entirely sure it was a compliment. It seemed a bit wishy-washy to her. She frowned. "I suppose if she doesn't stand out in any way, that makes it easier for her to do the things she does," she said finally. "Her malice . . . evil, even . . . is so surprising coming from such an inoffensive creature. And yet," her frown deepened, "and yet in her other manifestation, she's such a thoughtful, considerate, *loving* person."

"That's the idea, certainly." Edward rose from his chair and came over to the fire, where he stood, one arm resting along the mantel, his eyes on Fenella. "Can you do it?"

Fenella considered before meeting his gaze. "Honestly?"

"Of course."

"I honestly don't know." She folded her hands in her lap on top of the closed folder and met his eyes. "I don't know whether I can make each aspect of her personality equally real, equally believable. The bad side could be quite fun as well as challenging to do, but I don't know how I could switch so completely to the angelic side. She's almost too good to be true in that form."

Edward pulled at his chin and Fenella could hear

her heart beating in her ears in the ensuing silence. Had she offended him? He was so touchy where his work was concerned. But finally, he said, "You won't really know what you think until we read it aloud and you have a chance to inhabit the character. Will you agree to do that before you make a final decision?"

His touchy side was obviously dormant for the moment, she thought with relief. And the only thing she knew for a fact was that she was not prepared to give up their growing intimacy without a fight. There was too much unfinished between them. If they worked on the play together, perhaps, even if in the end she had to throw in the towel, their relationship might have advanced beyond the point where it depended upon Rose.

"Yes, I'll do that," she said with a smile. "But not tonight. D'you mind if we do it tomorrow, or some other time very soon? I seem to be incredibly sleepy all of sudden." A deep yawn punctuated the declaration.

Edward bent down to take the folder from her lap, setting it aside. "Later, then," he agreed easily. "But I hope you're not too tired to indulge in a little play of another kind." Taking her hands, he pulled her to her feet. "I can promise you won't have to do anything, just lie back and enjoy yourself."

"Lie back and think of England?" she queried with a mischievous chuckle.

His lips twitched at the old expression, but he turned it around neatly. "By all means, my dear, if that enhances your pleasure."

"Touché." Fenella raised a hand in the gesture of a swordsman acknowledging a hit.

"You shouldn't try fencing with a master," Edward returned with a grin before bending to put the fire screen in front of the fading coals.

Fenella hesitated, trying to come up with a witty riposte, but she couldn't think of anything on the spur of the moment. However, she was not prepared to concede that when it came to wordplay, he was indeed her master.

Edward straightened, regarding her with a knowing smile, as if he could read her inner struggle. "There'll be other opportunities, I'm sure," he said consolingly.

"You are so infuriating," Fenella exclaimed, half-laughing. "How did you know what I was thinking?"

"You have remarkably expressive eyes, my sweet. And right now, I'd like them to be expressing a desire other than wanting to get the better of me."

Her exasperation ran away like water after a rainstorm as his eyes swept over her in a long, languid caress that seemed to strip her naked. Her skin tingled, and involuntarily, she lightly touched her lips with the tip of her tongue.

His own eyes took on a smoky hue. "Get into bed, Fenella. I'll be with you in a moment." He turned aside to extinguish the gas lamp, leaving the room lit only by the dying fire.

Fenella hurried into the bedroom. For a distracted moment, she wondered whether to tidy the disheveled bed before getting into it, then decided it was hardly worth the trouble. It wouldn't stay neat for long.

"What's so important you had to see me before I'd even finished my breakfast, Diana?" Petra Rutherford demanded, entering the breakfast room of the Laceys' Cavendish Square house the next morning in a flurry of ribbons and flounces, her cheeks flushed from the cold. "Good morning, Rupert . . . Hera, Hercules." She bent to stroke the two South African Ridgebacks who had left the fireside to greet her.

"I'm sorry, Petra darling, but I had to be sure to catch you before you went out. Sit down and have breakfast here." Diana took up the silver coffeepot, reaching for a clean cup.

"Good morning, Petra. I can vouch for the deviled kidneys." Colonel Rupert Lacey rose to his feet to greet the new arrival, kissing her lightly on the cheek. "I apologize for my wife's importunate summons, but I daresay she'll explain all in great detail, so if you'll excuse me, I'll leave you to it. I promised the dogs a run in the park." He snapped his fingers. "Hera, Hercules." The dogs instantly went to the door and with a small bow to the ladies, Rupert left the room, the hounds racing before him.

"You look very gypsylike this morning, Petra," Diana observed, examining her friend's attire with interest. Petra had her own style, somewhat flamboyant, and this morning was no exception. In fact, if anything, it seemed even more outré than usual. Her skirt was a patchwork of blues and greens, with a deeply ruffled hem. Her blue jacket fitted closely at her waist with ruffles that matched the skirt on the sleeves and hem. The high, ruched collar of her pale green blouse cradled her small chin. Her hat was an extravagant affair decorated with blue and green ribbons and a large blue flower.

"I decided it was spring," Petra declared, casting aside her hat, gloves and muff. "Mind over matter."

"Did it work?" Diana inquired, buttering a piece of toast.

"Not in the least," Petra replied cheerfully, pulling out a chair. "It's still brass monkey weather out there."

She spooned sugar into her coffee and stirred it, reaching for a piece of toast from the rack. "So, what's so urgent?"

"This came last night." Diana pushed across the table the note she had received from Fenella the previous evening. "It's so intriguing. Fenella's normally so straightforward."

"Yes, but she's been a bit, I don't know what the word is, distracted, perhaps, a bit gloomy, don't you think?"

"Yes, I had noticed. These last few months . . . She's seemed rather down, which isn't like her at all. She's normally so positive."

"Mmm," Petra agreed as she read the short note, spreading butter and marmalade on her toast. "Well," she said after a minute, looking up from the note. "That's very interesting. Was she with the playwright, d'you think?" She took a bite of her toast.

"It seems the obvious answer," Diana said. "But I hadn't realized it had gone this far."

"Spending the night with him, you mean?"

"Well, isn't that the obvious conclusion?"

"Yes, I suppose it must be." Petra sipped her coffee. "Things must have moved very fast, though. She wasn't even sure she liked him when we last saw her."

"Well, as we agreed, dislike doesn't always preclude passion," Diana pointed out with a rueful smile.

"True enough." Petra tapped her lips with a fingertip. "Spending the whole night, though? That's quite extreme passion. She only lives a short cab ride away."

"I'd never have thought of Edward Tremayne as a particularly passionate man," Diana mused. "Not that I've ever really met him properly, just a passing impression some time ago, but he never struck me as worth cultivating. Did he you?"

Petra shook her head. "I always thought he looked bored to tears all the time. But you know what they say about still waters."

"Running deep, you mean?" Diana frowned. "Fenella is very particular about the people she takes as friends. She doesn't have much patience with people she doesn't find interesting."

"And simply finding someone interesting doesn't in general lead to a night of illicit passion," Petra pointed out. "Therefore, there must be more to this Tremayne than he lets on."

"Certainly much more than his half brother and sister," Diana said. "I have no time for them at all . . . more coffee?"

"Yes, thanks." Petra pushed her cup toward the coffeepot. "What about George, though?"

"Yes, indeed. *What* about Lord George Headington?" Diana shook her head. "I just wonder whether Fenella has thought about how she's going to steer along that path."

"I have and I have no idea. But I'll be grateful for any ideas."

The two women at the table turned to the door where Fenella stood, sounding and looking somewhat put out.

"Fenella dearest, if you will creep up on people of course you're going to hear things that maybe you don't like. But Petra and I weren't saying anything about you that we wouldn't say to your face." Diana rose from the table and came over to Fenella, kissing her on both cheeks. "Don't be cross, now."

"I'm not really," Fenella said, giving her friend a hug and turning to embrace Petra. "I came to thank you for helping me out."

"So far, I haven't had to do anything," Diana said. "Sit down and have some coffee. There's breakfast if you're hungry." She gestured to the chafing dishes on the sideboard.

"No, thanks, I've had breakfast. But I'd love a cup of coffee." Fenella unwound her scarf and discarded the rest of her outer garments. Edward had gone out before she awoke and returned with hot rolls from the bakery on the corner. He'd produced butter, apricot jam and coffee. He didn't seem in the least hampered by a lack of a kitchen when it came to putting food on the table.

"That's a very wicked little smile on your face, Fenella," Diana said, pouring coffee. "Whatever you're thinking about it has to be something very pleasant."

"Yes, you have to tell all," Petra demanded. "From the beginning."

"I was going to anyway," Fenella protested. "I think I should begin with Mother's dinner party on the night before last . . ."

Her friends sat rapt as she told them everything that was fit for public consumption. "So that's it," she finished, leaning back in her chair. "And now it's imperative that I make matters clear to George." She sighed, "I don't know why I let things drift for so long."

"You can't just drop him like a hot brick," Petra pointed out. "You'd have to have a reason."

"And think how awkward it's going to be. You and George move in the same circles; you'll always be bumping into each other. What're people going to think?"

"But we're not engaged or anything," Fenella said, frowning. "It wouldn't be as if I was jilting him."

"As far as Society's concerned, you're as good as engaged, all but the notice in the *Gazette* and the ring on your finger."

Fenella looked at her friends in frustration. "I don't want to hurt George; it's not his fault we don't suit . . . well, it is a bit. He can be very stuffy and old-fashioned at times. His attitudes toward women are positively antediluvian."

"Talking of which," Petra said, "Did you hear about Poppy Chase?"

"No, what about her?" Fenella regarded her friend over her coffee cup.

Petra grinned. "I heard on the grapevine that she's having an affair with the prime minister at the same time she's entangled with that artist . . . what's his name? Sargent, isn't it? Judging by his portrait of her, they were *very* entangled."

"I'm not Poppy Chase," Fenella pointed out. "And you shouldn't listen to gossip, Petra."

"Don't be such a prude, Fenella."

"Besides," Diana put in, "you're intending to act on the stage . . . it's not that different from having a nude portrait painted by a renowned artist."

"Oh, Diana, of course it is. There's nothing in *Sapphire* that requires me to take off my clothes on stage," Fenella said, half-laughing. "At least," she added, "not as the play stands at the moment."

"What's that supposed to mean, darling?" Diana leaned forward, her eyes sharpening.

Fenella shrugged. "It just occurred to me that anything could change if Edward gets an idea for an improvement when we're rehearsing."

"You wouldn't do it, though, would you?" Petra asked, sounding slightly doubtful. She was beginning to sense that Fenella was no longer as predictable as she'd always seemed.

"No," Fenella said. "No, of course not." But she turned her head toward the window, averting her eyes from her friends. Was it possible Edward could demand something more from her as the play developed? Something she absolutely wouldn't do? And what would be the consequence if she refused?

She shook her head. "We're a long way from that. I haven't even read the play aloud yet. But I must go home. Mama is bound to be wondering why I stayed with you last night, Diana."

"Oh . . . tell her I asked you to make up a four at bridge when one of the players suddenly felt faint, and then you and I wanted to sit up late and gossip. That could easily have happened," Diana suggested.

"Plausible enough," Fenella agreed, wrapping her scarf around her neck before putting on her coat. "Lunch at Claridge's later?"

"Excellent. Around one o'clock."

"Are you going to the WSPU meeting tomorrow evening? It's at the Baker Street library," Petra asked, putting on her hat and adjusting the flyaway ribbons in the mirror above the fireplace.

Fenella grimaced. "I had planned to. I should go. But it's so cold and draughty in that hall, and the tea's always stewed."

Diana laughed. "All quite correct. But we should show our faces, even if it's only for an hour. I'll bring a flask to liven up the stewed tea."

"An irresistible inducement," Fenella said. "I'll be there."

"Your Lord George has very strong feelings about the Union," Petra observed. "I made the mistake of mentioning a meeting and he got very supercilious and said I shouldn't trouble my pretty head about matters that were way beyond my comprehension. I nearly threw the sherry decanter at his head."

"He's not *my* Lord George," Fenella protested. "And I wouldn't have blamed you if you had. He said much the same to me . . . Are you coming, Petra?"

"Yes, I'll walk with you as far as Stanhope Gardens. What does your playwright think of the Union, or have you been too busy doing other things to talk politics?"

"He's in favor of women's suffrage," Fenella responded shortly. "Come on, I must get home."

Chapter Ten

"Is George still going to escort you to the Warehams' masked ball?" Petra asked as they walked briskly toward Stanhope Gardens against the wintry wind gusting around street corners.

"I assume so," Fenella replied. "It's been tacitly agreed for weeks. Anyway, escorting someone to a ball doesn't mean anything important; it doesn't signify anything serious about their relationship, not if they're not engaged or anything. Everyone knows George and I are friends and we're often seen in the same company." *Methinks the lady doth protest too much.* Her inconvenient inner voice mocked her, but she tried to ignore it.

"Yes, and everyone assumes you'll be announcing your engagement any day now."

"Well, they can stop assuming," Fenella said crossly. "Poking their noses into other people's business."

"It's called Society, dearest," Petra pointed out with a laugh. "And nothing will still Society's tongue."

Fenella sighed. "You're right, of course. I have to put a stop to the gossip, or to the gossipy anticipation of a juicy engagement. I know George assumes it's as good as agreed and I haven't done anything definite about disabusing him." She sighed again. "I'm afraid he won't take it well."

"Will he be angry?" Petra asked.

"Probably," Fenella said with a grimace.

Petra wisely didn't venture any more questions on what was clearly a difficult subject. They walked in silence to the corner of Stanhope Gardens and Fenella turned with a rueful smile. "I'm sorry, Petra, I didn't mean to snap. Forgive me?"

"You didn't," her friend declared. "It's a wretched situation, but Diana and I will back you up however you need us."

"I know, dearest, and I know how lucky I am to have such good friends. Whatever you do, don't stop telling me the truth as you see it. I need your observations, and Diana's. How else am I going to steer some kind of a clear path through this morass?"

Petra hugged her in response. "I'll see you at Claridge's at one o'clock." She hurried off with a quick wave and Fenella made her own way home.

"Good morning, Miss Fenella." The butler greeted her with his usual equanimity, showing no surprise at her sudden appearance at an hour when she would ordinarily be taking breakfast with her parents.

Fenella assumed he was aware that she had not spent the night at home; Collins was always aware of anything toward or untoward that went on in the Grantley household. However, she contented herself with a smile and a cheerful "Good morning," then asked, "Is Lady Grantley still at breakfast?"

"No, Miss Fenella. She's in the morning room, I believe, discussing menus with Mrs. Bowden."

"I won't disturb them, then. Would you let Lady Grantley know that I'm back and I'll come to see her when I've changed? Oh, and ask Alice to come up, please."

She hurried upstairs to her own room, unwinding her scarf as she did so. Her bedroom was a large corner room with windows facing both the street and the side garden. A small sitting area was reached through an archway. The fire was already lit, the curtains drawn back to let in the pale wintry light, and Fenella wondered what Alice must have thought when she'd come to wake her at her usual nine o'clock and found the bed unslept in.

"Good morning, Miss Fenella." Alice greeted her as she bustled in with a tray. "I thought you'd like a cup of coffee as you've just come in from the cold." She set the tray on the dresser. "It's early to be out there on a freezing February morning."

"Yes," Fenella replied. "I spent last night with Mrs. Lacey in Cavendish Square. It was certainly a chilly walk back."

"Shall I draw you a bath?"

"Yes, please, and I'm going to lunch at Claridge's later. I think I'll wear the dark gray wool suit with the lavender silk blouse." She took a gulp of the hot coffee and choked, reminding herself of the previous day's lunch at Chez Marcel and all that it had led to. Hastily, she sat on the bed to kick off her shoes.

An hour later, respectable and ready for the day,

Fenella went in search of her mother. She found her alone in the morning room, writing letters.

"Oh, there you are, darling." Lady Grantley looked up with a smile. "Is everything all right with Diana? I was worried when I got your note. I was afraid she was ill or something."

"No, nothing like that, Mama." Fenella bent to kiss her mother's fragrant cheek. "Diana is in the pink, but she wanted me to make a fourth at bridge after one of her guests dropped out, and then we started talking and . . . well, it was just as if we were back at school, when we used to talk late into the night. We wanted to relive those days . . . our ill-spent youth," she added with a self-deprecating laugh. "I'm sorry if I worried you." She had never considered herself an accomplished liar, but it seemed she had hidden depths. It was not a particularly pleasant acknowledgment.

"Oh, I wasn't truly worried," Lady Grantley said with a vague gesture. "I knew that if it was really serious you would have told me. What are you doing today?"

"Lunch at Claridge's with Diana and Petra. Then maybe a little shopping."

"Do you have dinner plans?"

"Not at the moment," Fenella said. Edward had said nothing about meeting again when she'd left that morning. She'd thought nothing of it at the time but now felt somewhat adrift as she realized that until this moment she had fully expected to see him that evening. But now she wondered why she should have expected any such thing.

It was ridiculous. Her life did not depend upon Edward Tremayne and his whims. She was an independent woman, as far as it was possible to be while living under her father's roof. "There's a soiree at Audrey Jensen's house this evening, though. I might go to that after dinner."

"Very well, my dear. So I'll expect you to join your father and me at dinner."

"Yes, Mama." Fenella kissed her mother's cheek again. "I have some letters to write before I go to lunch." She left the morning room, returning upstairs to her own room. The pretty enameled clock on the mantel chimed eleven o'clock as she closed the door. She was restless and had an hour to kill before leaving for Claridge's. Ordinarily, she would have found plenty to occupy herself, writing letters, reading a book . . . or she could summon Alice and they could go through her wardrobe, discarding clothing she was tired of, getting them ready to donate to charity. But as so often these days, none of her usual pursuits appealed.

She stood at the window, staring down at the small side garden, where nothing seemed to move in the frosty air. A knock at the door was a welcome interruption. "Come in."

"Lord George Headington wishes to know if you're at home, Miss Grantley," the liveried footman inquired from the opened door.

George? He was the last person Fenella wanted to

see at this juncture, but the sooner she began her plan of disengagement the better for both of them. "Yes, thank you, Boris, please show him into the yellow salon. I'll be down in a minute."

The door closed again and Fenella turned to check her reflection in the mirror. Did she look different after that day and night of passionate love-making? On the whole, she didn't think so. There was nothing detectable, no visible marks, although beneath her impeccable outfit she hugged to herself the knowledge that her body showed some signs of a particularly rumbustious half hour in the early hours of this morning.

She could have expected her eyes to seem rather heavy after an almost sleepless night, but she could detect only an added sparkle to their cool gray and a slight rosy bloom on her cheeks. Almost a glow, she thought. And the lavender silk blouse enhanced that glow.

But George wouldn't notice such tiny things. He was hardly the most observant of men.

She went down one flight of stairs to the yellow drawing room, the small salon that was tacitly as-sumed to be her own private parlor. Her mother had her own suite of rooms adjoining her bedchamber if she wasn't using any of the more formal entertaining salons. Lord Grantley occupied the library and the smoking room when he was in the house and not at his club.

"Good morning, George. This is an unexpected

pleasure," Fenella said, more brightly than she felt, as she entered the salon.

George was standing before the fire, hands clasped at his back. His tweed frock coat and britches fitted him as if they had been made on him. His appearance was perfect in every detail, not so much as a stray hair in the carefully coiffed dark curls. His brown eyes lit up as soon as Fenella entered the room and he came forward, hands extended.

"Dear girl, how ravishing you are," he declared, taking her hands and raising them both to his lips. He stood back, still holding her hands, to run an admiring glance over her. "You grow more beautiful every day, my dear."

Nothing about pellucid or wishy-washy, Fenella thought. It was an unwise thought, and she had to stifle the urge to laugh. "As I've said before, George, flattery will get you everywhere," she said lightly, allowing him to kiss her cheek. "What brings you here on this frigid morning?" She moved away from him, going over to the decanter of sherry and glasses on the sideboard. "Sherry?"

"Please." He watched her pour two glasses, idly twisting his gold signet ring. "I wanted to know if you'd like to come to the Royal Opera House tonight. It's *Lucia di Lammermoor*."

"But George, you detest the opera, almost as much as you hate the theatre," Fenella exclaimed, half-laughing. George's dislike of London's cultural offerings was almost a joke. If he could be persuaded to patronize a comedy, or something equally light and undemanding, he still grumbled sotto voce throughout the performance. He much preferred social gatherings of any description. And, on such occasions, he was an impeccable escort, Fenella had to admit.

"Well, I daresay I could endure one performance," he said with an expression that belied the statement. "My aunt had tickets but couldn't go at the last minute, so she gave 'em to me."

That was hardly surprising, Fenella reflected. It would never occur to George to buy tickets for such a tedious form of entertainment himself. "I've never seen the opera, although of course I read Walter Scott's book, *The Bride of Lammermoor.* Actually," she confessed, "the melodramatic plot made me laugh. The idea of the hero drowning in quicksand after all that passionate drama."

George merely looked puzzled.

"So . . . who else will be in the party?" she asked

George took a large sip of his sherry. "Well, no one else. I thought we could go à deux. It's quite proper. We're often seen about Town together."

Fenella took a deep, internal breath. He'd served her the ball and it was the perfect opportunity to lob it back in a way that wouldn't hurt his feelings too badly but would make him rethink his assumptions. "Yes, I know, and I think we should be seen à deux a little less often, George. People are beginning to talk. And no lady in my position can afford to be the subject of gossip." She managed a careless laugh. "We should perhaps be seen more often in company than alone."

He looked at first confused and then put out. "This is very sudden, Fenella. You've never seemed worried about notions of propriety before."

"It's true that I've been careless of appearances," Fenella admitted carefully. "But I seem to be growing wiser as I grow older." *Oh, God*, she thought. *Listen to yourself.* She could almost see Diana and Petra's incredulous expressions at such an unlikely statement. And she could only imagine how Edward would react. "I think my mother is a little concerned about gossip too." *In for a penny, in for a pound.*

George looked at her, frowning. "Lady Grantley hasn't said anything to me . . . she's always most welcoming."

"Yes, Mama is never less than courteous," Fenella replied with perfect truth. "And she would never say such a thing outright, but she has dropped a few hints. I just think we should be seen a little less in public together . . . without being in a party," she concluded in a rush, desperate now to bring this awkward parcel of half-truths to an end before she was in too deep to extricate herself.

George looked solemn. "You know I want nothing more than for you to be my wife, Fenella—"

"No, no, George, don't say anything else," Fenella interrupted in horror, realizing that she should have anticipated this response from him. "I'm not ready for any such declaration. I . . . I really don't wish to be married yet."

Now he looked crestfallen and she immediately felt sorry for him. How in Hades was she to get herself out of this without hurting him more?

"I've wanted to declare myself for several months, Fenella, but my father insists that I not commit to marriage until I am thirty, when my inheritance from my uncle will no longer be held in trust. Once it's released, I'll be independent and well able to support a wife and children. At the moment, all I have is the allowance from my father. It's generous enough, and I would be willing to live on crumbs in a cottage if you would marry me now, but I couldn't ask that of you. But if you would agree to a long engagement, only three years until my thirtieth birthday . . ."

Fenella could see the chasm yawning at her feet. She stepped back from the brink. "No, George, that wouldn't be fair to either of us. Anything could happen in three years. You could meet someone else and—"

"There could never be anyone else," he interrupted, seizing her hands again in a passionate clasp. "My darling Fenella, you are all I want, all I could ever want." Kisses rained down on her imprisoned hands and she was for once speechless.

"Oh, George, no, please don't." She found her voice at last, pulling her hands free of his clasp. "I am very fond of you, my dear, but I'm not ready to commit to an engagement, long or otherwise. And I honestly don't think you would find living with me to be at all comfortable. I have very strong opinions . . . political opinions," she added in a flash of inspiration.

"How would you manage with a fiancée, let alone a wife, who marched with the WSPU and picketed Parliament, and—"

"Oh, you'll soon forget that nonsense when you're married. You'll be far too busy with the household, and children, and . . . and . . . well, all the things that occupy married women."

And thank you, George. Relieved to be given a genuine reason for rejecting him, Fenella moved away from him. "That's exactly my point, George. I will not change, I promise you. There's no way in which I could be a satisfactory wife to someone who didn't hold the same political opinions as I did."

Nonplussed, he stared at her. "You can't be serious, Fenella. Surely you can't. Women of your position don't march with a rabble of scullery maids and milliners' assistants and the like."

"I have news for you, my dear. Many of them do, and I have done so several times already and fully intend to do so again."

He shook his head, his full mouth tightening. "Then there's nothing more to be said."

"On the subject of marriage, no," she agreed. "But we are still friends, aren't we? We'll see each other at balls and parties once the weather gets better and the Season gets properly underway. We can still enjoy ourselves in company, George."

"I don't know," he said, sounding almost sullen. "I don't know whether I can spend time with someone who thinks as you do, Fenella." He picked up his discarded homburg and kid gloves from a table under the window. "I need to think things over, so I'll bid you good morning." He offered a stiff bow and marched from the room.

Fenella sighed, feeling drained. For all his misguided views, George had been a pleasant enough companion and a reliable escort over the last year or so. And as long as they kept away from difficult subjects, she had been able to enjoy his company. Now, she felt uncomfortably as if she had just been using him for the sheer convenience of having him at her beck and call. And it was all because of the malaise that had haunted her over the last months, a sense that nothing was worth getting excited about. Life seemed to have acquired a patina of pointlessness and, as a result, she had simply let matters with George take their course because she hadn't had the energy or will to direct them herself.

But it was different now; she looked at the world quite differently. And Edward Tremayne was responsible.

She glanced at the clock; it was time to go if she was not to be late for lunch. How awkward was it going to be, bumping into George? It was inevitable in the social circles they shared, and she knew Society well enough to know how quickly the gossips would pick up on something amiss between two people who for months had been considered a couple on the verge of engagement. Maybe Diana and Petra would have some suggestions as to how she could weave her way through this maze of her own making.

She hurried upstairs to fetch her coat. She slung a

fur stole around her shoulders that would keep her more elegantly warm than the striped scarf of the WSPU and would certainly not cause adverse comment. Gloves, muff and leather handbag completed the ensemble.

She was halfway down the stairs to the hall when Lady Grantley emerged from the dining room. "Oh, Fenella, is something wrong with George? He came running downstairs a few minutes ago as if he was escaping a fire. I barely got a good morning out of him." She came to the foot of the stairs as her daughter took the last steps. "Have you quarreled, dear?"

"Not exactly," Fenella answered. "We just had a difference of opinion."

"Oh, well, I hope it wasn't too serious," her mother said. "He knows he's dining here with us before the Warehams' ball. I trust your difference of opinion won't play havoc with my seating plan."

"No, Mama, I'm sure it won't," Fenella said, hoping that was true. "I'll send him a note later this afternoon to remind him."

"Yes, do that, dear," her ladyship said with a vague smile. "I'm going to order the flowers now. I know there'll be at least six other dinner parties that night before the ball and one can't order too soon to be sure of getting what one wants. I've decided on lavender and yellow freesias and blue and white hydrangeas. That'll be pretty, don't you think?"

"Very," Fenella assured her. "A harbinger of spring."

"Yes, and the colors will complement your new taffeta evening gown," her mother said.

"Actually, Mama, I don't think I'll be wearing that gown. I have another in mind."

"Oh?" Lady Grantley looked askance. "What color is it?"

Fenella grimaced, knowing what her mother's reaction would be. "Well, actually, it's black, with silver lace."

"Good heavens, Fenella. Young girls only wear black when they're in mourning," her mother exclaimed.

"I don't think anyone will mistake this gown for mourning dress," Fenella reassured her. "Wait until you see it. It's still at the dressmaker's; I have two more fittings next week."

Her mother's sigh was resigned. "Well, I'll reserve judgment until I see it, then." She turned back to the dining room. "I must ask Mrs. Bowden to make sure the Georgian silver urns are polished for the mantel in here." She disappeared, her words wafting behind her.

Fenella smiled, her mother's vagueness partly for show, she knew. When it came to throwing parties, Lady Grantley never missed a beat.

"Should I send someone to fetch a cab for you, Miss Fenella?" The butler moved to open the front door.

"Oh, yes, please, Collins. I'll wait here in the warm." She turned to knock on the library door, wondering if her father was at home.

Lord Grantley looked up from his book as his daughter put her head around the door. "Oh, hello,

Fenella my dear. I don't seem to have seen you for days."

"Not exactly days, Papa." She kissed his cheek. "I'm on my way out, but I thought I'd say hello if you were in."

"Gadabout," he accused. "But then, you young things are so restless these days. It's time you thought about settling down."

Fenella gave an exaggerated shake of her head. "Heaven forfend. Until later, Papa."

He raised a hand in farewell and returned to his book.

Chapter Eleven

"I'm going to have the lobster soufflé," Petra announced, looking up from her menu. "And then the grilled plaice. What about you two?"

"I'll join you in the soufflé," Fenella said, "but then I'll have the trout."

"I'll have the same." Diana handed her menu to the hovering waiter with a smile. "Oh, and a bottle of the Chablis. Is that good for everyone?"

"Fine," Fenella said. "I need something to fortify myself after a wretched interview with George."

"Tell," her friends demanded in unison.

They listened intently as she recited the events of the morning. "So did you really quarrel with George?" Petra asked. "Are you not friends anymore?"

"That's not entirely clear," Fenella responded. "He was certainly very put out when he left to 'think things over,' as he said. And I'm assuming we won't be going to the opera tonight."

"You'll have to come up with some story to explain a sudden estrangement," Diana said. "Otherwise, you'll be the talk of the Town. And George will have to have the same story. He won't say anything to make you look bad; he's far too much of a gentleman to do that, but it's bound to be awkward for him if you don't have an agreed explanation."

"I'll write to him this afternoon to see if I can placate him without somehow implying that anything's changed. I don't know how I could have been such an idiot as to let things get this far. Poor George, it's not his fault." She took up her fork and dug into the soufflé in front of her. "Oh, this is good."

"Delicious," Petra agreed. "But it's not all your fault. George has a very strong belief in his own importance, if you don't mind my saying so. It wouldn't occur to him that any woman wouldn't want to be Lady George Headington."

"True." Fenella took a sip of the pale gold liquid in her glass. "Even so, I don't want George to be cast as a jilted swain. It wouldn't be fair."

"Then you'll have to persuade him to let you be the jilted one," Diana pointed out.

"But then he'll look unchivalrous, and that wouldn't be fair either."

Petra was sitting facing the entrance to the dining room. "Talk of the devil . . . don't look now, but George has just come in with the Sullivan twins. Did he know you were meeting us here?"

Fenella shook her head. "Has he seen us?"

"I don't know, but we have to behave naturally." Petra raised a hand and waggled her fingers at the three men. "They know I can't possibly not have seen them."

Diana turned her head and raised a hand in greeting and Fenella followed suit, praying that the men wouldn't decide to weave their way through the tables toward them.

"It's all right, they're going to the upstairs dining room." Petra returned her attention to her soufflé. "Danger's over."

"It's only postponed," Fenella said. "But bless you for your quick reaction, my dear. I need time to compose myself before facing him again."

"Well, let's finish lunch," Diana said. "I want to go to Swan and Edgar. I saw the most fetching black-and-white-striped silk shirtwaist in the window, which would be perfect for the races with my new cream straw hat."

"Are you planning to race Kimberley Diamond in the spring, then?" Fenella asked, finally distracted from her own muddle.

"Cameron, her trainer—you've met him—wants to try her out at Newmarket in the Guinea Stakes in early April. We're going to get up a small party, and if she does well, it's on to Ascot in June. And for that, Rupert wants to throw a big race day party."

"I've always loved Ascot," Fenella said. "My problem is finding a hat for Ladies' Day that doesn't dwarf me."

"Straw won't swamp you if it doesn't have too many frills and furbelows," Diana suggested. "Anyway, there's plenty of time before June to find the perfect hat."

* * *

"I must congratulate you on winning over Miss Grantley," Cedric Hardcastle said, carefully collating the sheets of paper in front of him in the draughty room on Gower Street. "I hadn't realized she could be so fierce, I must admit."

Edward's smile was rueful. "I have a habit of riding roughshod over people when my mind is set on something. Miss Grantley gave me a short, sharp lesson on that score. But she's made it fairly clear that she's not completely won over. She has some doubts about whether she has the ability to play Rose."

"I'm certain she has, even though she has no real experience on the stage," Cedric maintained with a vigorous nod of his head. "She just has to learn to have confidence in herself."

"Maybe a full-cast reading will give her that confidence," Edward said, frowning.

"Maybe." Cedric reached for another sheet of paper. "I've been mulling over the casting. Obviously, we need to use my amateurs because they won't cost anything. They'll be so grateful for the opportunity to act on a real stage, we could almost get them to pay for the privilege." His laugh was a little unkind, expressing his general opinion of amateur actors, as he pushed the sheet of paper across the table to Edward. "Take a look at these names. They'll be coming in for my regular class next Wednesday and we could audition them then."

Edward ran his eyes down the list, but the names meant little to him. They were Cedric's pupils, and his last attempt to sit in on a reading had collapsed in chaos. However, he trusted the old actor's judgment. He'd been working with this group of budding actors for over a year and knew what they could do.

"I look forward to seeing them for myself," he said. "But I have no reason to doubt your judgment and instincts when it comes to aptitude and character."

"Good." Cedric nodded. "The only doubtful issue I can see is whether Miss Grantley will attend the class on Wednesday. She left the last class so abruptly."

"I'll make sure she's on board," Edward said, twisting his muffler around his neck as he prepared to depart.

"You'll be seeing her before then?" Cedric raised an eloquent eyebrow.

"I'm not sure," Edward returned vaguely. "I have no immediate plans, but I have her address, and if I don't happen to see her, I'll send her a message."

Cedric merely nodded again. "I'll leave it with you, then." He stood up from the table with his visitor. "Have you given any more thought about the financing of the production? We should begin looking for a suitable theatre for when we're ready to rehearse in good earnest."

"I have some irons in various fires," Edward said, again vaguely, pulling on his gloves. "I'll give you good day, Cedric. Until Wednesday."

"Until Wednesday." Cedric waved his visitor down the stairs and returned to the wheezing radiator in his classroom.

Edward turned up the collar of his coat when he reached the street and set off at a brisk pace toward

Bloomsbury Square. He wondered what Fenella had been doing since she'd left him that morning. He wasn't sure why, but before she'd left, he hadn't suggested a firm arrangement to meet again. Was he reluctant to say or do something that would make their so-far serendipitous connection more concrete? He had always ensured that his relationships with women never progressed beyond casual intimacy with no strings on either side, but there was something very different about Fenella. He didn't see her as a casual liaison. Of course, his need for her to play Rose had something to do with that, but he didn't have to make love to her for that to happen.

So why was he ignoring the warning signals to which he was usually particularly sensitive? She was getting under his skin and the idea didn't alarm him nearly as much as it ought to. Put simply, he needed to see her again. He wanted Fenella for herself; spending time with her was becoming an imperative in its own right. And that would take him dangerously close to resuming the one thing he had sworn never to countenance: a reentry into Society.

He suppressed a shudder at the prospect. That would inevitably mean renewed contact with his half brother and sister, however distant that contact would be. Despite his reclusive nature and the irregularity of his birth, nothing had happened to make him persona non grata in Society at large. He was still a Tremayne. He still received social invitations, which he always courteously declined, always careful to burn no bridges even while he kept a good distance between himself and his old world. The ingrained courtesies of a privileged upbringing died hard, even though he had renounced those privileges long before his family had withdrawn them from him.

He bought a copy of the *Evening Standard* from a newspaper boy standing on the corner of the square blowing on his hands, reddened with cold. "Get yourself a cup of tea," Edward said, adding a few extra coins to the price of the paper. He turned aside into the teashop he'd been in with Fenella and ordered coffee from the same waitress, who showed no sign of recognizing him.

He flipped through the paper as he drank his coffee and his eye fell on the page of theatre listings. Shaw's *Candida* was playing at Drury Lane theatre. It was one of the playwright's lesser-known works and rarely performed. Edward drummed his fingers on the table as he stared into the middle distance, wondering. Was it worth the risk to get two tickets for tonight and invite Fenella? What did he have to lose beyond the price of the tickets? It would mean taking the risk of being seen in public together, but as he'd just come to accept, it had to happen sometime if he was to continue seeing Fenella as he chose.

He left a shilling on the table and hurriedly left the café. He walked back to Gower Street and took an omnibus to Covent Garden. At the theatre, he hesitated between a box or orchestra seats and finally decided on the latter. A box could be seen as having clandestine connotations and besides, if Fenella for whatever reason didn't accompany him, he'd be part of the audience in the body of the theatre. There was nothing sadder than a lone man in a box.

Back at home, Edward wrote a formal invitation to the Honorable Fenella Grantley, attached his visiting card, and dispatched Harvey to Albemarle Street. Then he made himself a cup of tea and sat down to await a response.

Fenella returned home at four o'clock, a delivery boy from Swan & Edgar accompanying her, weighed down with bandboxes. She had bought far more than she'd intended, but her friends had egged her on and, in an unusually reckless mood, she now owned two new afternoon dresses, a silk wrap and a pair of bronze satin slippers.

"Good afternoon, Miss Fenella," Collins greeted her as she stepped into the hall. "Fred." He clicked his fingers at a hovering footman, who took the parcels from the delivery boy and headed upstairs with them.

"Good afternoon, Collins." Fenella gave the Swan & Edgar boy a coin. "Is Lady Grantley in?"

"I believe she's resting, Miss Fenella."

"Oh, then I won't disturb her." Fenella moved toward the stairs.

"Oh, a moment, miss, a card was left for you this afternoon. The lad wanted to wait for a reply, but I sent him off as you weren't here." Collins held out a silver tray.

"Oh?" She turned at the foot of the stairs and took the sealed envelope and visiting card. Her heart jumped as she recognized the writing on the envelope an instant before she made out *Edward Tremayne* on the visiting card. Without another word, she hurried upstairs to her own room, aware of her swiftly beating pulse.

Her bedroom was deserted and Fenella slit the envelope with a long fingernail, walking to the window as she did so. She unfolded the paper and read the brief message:

> *My dear Miss Grantley, would you do me the honor of accompanying me to the theatre this evening? I have tickets for Shaw's* Candida *and very much hope that appeals to you as much as it does to me. I will collect you from your house at seven o'clock, and I hope you'll agree to sup with me after the play. Yours very truly, Edward Tremayne.*

Fenella laughed at the absurdity of the formal language after all the deep intimacies they had shared together. The tone was so unlike anything she could have imagined on Edward's tongue, she could only think it was intended to make her laugh. She went to the engraved rosewood desk and sat down, selecting a piece of writing paper. For a moment, she stared at the wall, tapping the pen against her teeth as she considered the mode of her response. Then, smiling, she put pen to paper. She folded and sealed the sheet and reached for the bellpull.

Alice answered her ring within minutes. "I was waiting for your bell, Miss Fenella. I understand from Fred that you have some new purchases. I'll unpack them right now."

"No, they can wait just a minute, Alice. First, I need someone to take this for me at once. It's urgent.

And could you please inform Lady Grantley that I won't be dining at home after all? I'm going to the theatre."

Alice took the letter downstairs and Fenella went to the armoire, wondering what to wear. What seats had Edward bought, presumably on the spur of the moment, or he would have mentioned it that morning before she'd left him? Supposing they were the cheap seats in the balcony or at the rear of the orchestra? She'd look out of place in formal evening dress. She looked again at his invitation. The formality of the salutation and wording indicated a special occasion. Center orchestra or a box . . .

She'd made the mistake once before of assuming he was not exactly flush with money; it was not a mistake she would make again. The occasion warranted her best efforts, and when Alice returned, she was holding up against her an emerald-green taffeta gown with a dramatic décolletage.

"What do you think, Alice?"

"That gown has always looked very well on you, Miss Fenella."

"I bought a gorgeous green-and-gold silk wrap this afternoon. It will be perfect . . . oh, and my new slippers as well. It's a perfect opportunity to break them in."

Alice began to unpack the boxes on the bed. She shook out the wrap. "I'll just pop the flat iron over this, in that case. It is lovely. Will you wear the pearls? The choker goes particularly well with the neckline of the gown."

"Yes, perfect; thank you, Alice." Fenella struggled

to curb her excitement. She loved the theatre, and the idea of going with Edward increased her anticipation a hundredfold. She would enjoy discussing the play over supper in the Piazza, if that was what he had in mind, and after that . . . well, that was anyone's guess. But her skin prickled and her mouth was suddenly dry at a rush of pure lust. She wanted him, wanted to bury her face against his chest, inhaling his particular scent, lemony and yet earthy, wanted to feel him against her, inside her, his hands on her body, moving over her, bringing every inch of her skin to throbbing life.

Chapter Twelve

The hackney drew up outside the Grantley's house on Albemarle Street precisely at seven o'clock and Edward stepped down, his black evening cloak settling around him. He looked up at the double-fronted house, remembering the times in the past when he'd strolled with apparent nonchalance along the street looking out for a glimpse of Fenella, whose pale beauty had struck him so powerfully as the incarnation of his imagined Rose. He smiled now at the thought that "pale beauty" was accurate enough when applied to her appearance but bore no relation to the dramatic colors of her vibrant personality.

He approached the door and rang the bell, stepping back a little as the door was opened by a butler. "Good evening. Miss Grantley's expecting me."

"Yes, indeed, sir. Mr. Tremayne, I believe. Won't you come in?" Collins pulled the door wide with a small bow.

Edward glanced back at the waiting hackney. He raised five fingers and the driver nodded, huddling deeper into his muffler. Edward stepped into the hall and glanced around. It was as he'd expected, the elegant, substantial hall of a wealthy aristocrat. His experienced eye told him the tall case clock was Jacobean, and he was certain the painting on the far wall was a Vermeer.

He was about to look more closely when Fenella called from the top of the stairs, "Good evening, Edward." She came lightly downstairs in her bronze kid slippers, holding up the skirt of her evening gown, just glimpsed beneath the high-collared, ermine evening cloak. Her fair hair was caught up in an artful knot, secured by a circlet of very fine pearls.

Halfway down, she paused, a gloved hand resting on the banister as she took in his appearance. His evening dress was impeccable, the white waistcoat, starched collar and flat white tie adhering strictly to the uniform demands of the costume, but as always there was something slightly out of kilter in the way he wore them. A hint of carelessness that was hard to define when nothing obvious seemed out of place. Maybe it was his hair, she thought. A little too long, a touch ungroomed, that loose, dark lock flopping onto his wide forehead. She noticed that he wasn't wearing the de rigueur white gloves; maybe that was it. And where was his black silk hat? A gentleman did not go out on the Town in the evening hatless, and yet she couldn't imagine Edward wearing one.

"A snow maiden, how delightful." He swept her an elegant bow.

Fenella frowned, wondering if he was being sarcastic again, but she could detect no hint of mockery in his expression, only appreciation. She acknowledged his bow with a flourishing curtsy. "Mr. Tremayne, how lovely to see you again. And how very tidy you look," she couldn't resist adding.

The penetrating blue gaze sharpened as he ran his eyes over her. "What were you expecting, dear girl? A ragamuffin?"

"I wasn't sure what to expect," she said, continuing down the last few steps. "But now I'm very glad I made an effort to look my best."

He raised a quizzical eyebrow. "I'll refrain from empty compliments because you know full well how lovely you look and don't need me to say so." He offered his arm. "I have a hackney waiting."

Game, set and match, Fenella acknowledged ruefully, slipping her hand into his elbow. A little shiver of pleasure rippled through her as he drew her closer against his side.

"Enjoy your evening, Miss Fenella . . . Mr. Tremayne, sir." Collins saw them out to the street, closing the door behind them.

Edward handed Fenella up into the cab and stood for a moment, one foot on the step, one hand holding the door. "We have a little time before curtain up, if you're hungry. It'll be after ten o'clock by the time we have supper. I know where we could get oysters and a glass of champagne to keep us going."

"I've never said no to either of those," Fenella replied.

Edward gave directions to the cabbie, then stepped up into the carriage. A black silk top hat was on the bench opposite Fenella and he picked it up as he sat down, holding the hat on his lap. "I'm so glad you were free this evening."

"So am I." She smiled. The only light in the cab's interior came from the street lamps outside. Traffic in Covent Garden was always busy in the evening and they were making slow progress as the outside glow from the gas lamps alternated shadows with flashes of light.

"I'm looking forward to this play. It's so rarely produced." For an awful moment, she felt as if she needed to make small talk, as if they were distant acquaintances. It must be because of the formality of their clothing, which did nothing to encourage their usual casually intimate banter. There had been that moment in the house, but that moment of ease seemed to have vanished. How was it, she thought, that one could know someone so intimately, every inch of skin, every hair on their head, and yet feel as if they were a complete stranger?

"So, my sweet, what have you been doing with yourself today?" Edward sat back against the thread-bare cushions of the cab, regarding her with a knowing smile, as if he could read her mind.

And suddenly, everything between them was as it needed to be. The endearment, the casually personal question, and the space between them was no longer awkward. It was on the tip of her tongue to tell him about her quarrel with George, but she realized just in time that, intimate though they were with each other, sharing that particular thought process and its consequence was not politic.

"Oh, nothing much. I had lunch with my dearest

friends, Diana and Petra, and we went shopping," she said with a shrug. "A typical day in the life of a no-longer debutante. What about you? How was your day?"

"Ah, well, that is something we need to discuss at length," Edward said. "I spent the morning in Gower Street with Cedric."

"Oh?" She leaned forward, making no attempt to disguise her interest. "Tell me."

The carriage drew to a halt and Edward said, "Later, it'll keep. Let's find a little sustenance before the theatre." He opened the carriage door and stepped out, reaching his hand toward Fenella as she stepped out herself. They were in one of the smaller streets running off Covent Garden. It was quiet, but the noise and bustle of the Piazza carried clearly on the frosty air. Light spilled onto the cobbles from a small establishment with the sign of the King's Head.

"In here." Edward gestured to the door, before moving her toward it with a firm hand at the small of her back.

They walked directly from the street into a crowded, noisy saloon bar, the press of bodies, smoke from cigarettes and pipes, the low-timbered ceiling and blazing fire in the inglenook creating a heat and stuffiness that was almost overwhelming. Fenella was suddenly afraid she might start to sweat into her damask gown beneath the ermine cloak and gratefully allowed Edward to take it from her, folding the creamy fur over his arm. It was some relief, but not as much as she'd have liked. *Concentrate on the bitter cold outside on the street,* she told herself firmly.

"Ned . . . Ned . . . over here." A man waved vigorously from a long deal table in the bay window. "Where've you been these last weeks? No one's seen you in forever."

Ned? wondered Fenella to herself. It had a raffishness about it and somehow seemed to suit him better than Edward. She glanced up at her companion, who was smiling broadly, a hand raised in greeting.

"Come and meet my friends," he said, once more steering her with a hand at her back across the thronged room to the table. "Ladies and gentlemen, allow me to introduce the Honorable Miss Fenella Grantley." He presented her to the table, like a prize at a county fair, she thought, a little put out at being thrust into a social setting for which she'd had no preparation.

"Good evening," she said, smiling with practiced ease. The assembled group were not dressed for a formal evening of theatre or opera. For the most part, they wore slightly shabby street clothes, but she noticed that the two women among them had a touch of flamboyance about their dress, one with a purple feather in her hair, held in place by a crimson bandanna, the other wearing a brightly colored, ruffled scarf flung carelessly around her long throat. They were both striking: not beautiful, but you wouldn't pass them in the street without a second look. She began to feel a little "pellucid" beside their colorful presence.

"Sit . . . sit, m' dear, and welcome." An elderly man, much bewhiskered in a brightly checkered waistcoat, patted the long bench beside him. "If you're what this rascal's been up to since last we saw him, he's forgiven for his neglect."

The fulsome and somewhat inappropriate compliment ordinarily would have made Fenella uncomfortable, but here, in this company, it didn't. She returned the man's smile and perched on the bench beside him. The table was covered with platters of oysters and tankards of what she guessed from their foaming brims was Guinness.

"Oysters?" Edward asked, resting a hand lightly on her shoulder. "Or something else?"

"Oysters, definitely," she said. "It seems to be what everyone's eating."

"Best in London," a younger man declared from across the table. "None of us would dare to set foot on the stage without a dozen of the King's Head's best under our belts."

"Good-luck charms they are," one of the women responded with a chuckle. "A ritual, you might call it." She leaned across the table, extending her hand. "I'm Harriet Aldershot, Miss Grantley."

"Oh." Fenella's eyes widened as she shook the proffered hand. "I saw your Gwendolen in *The Importance of Being Earnest*. You were wonderful, Miss Aldershot. I laughed so much."

"I was wonderful, wasn't I?" the actor said with a complacent chuckle. "But nothing lasts forever," she added, sighing.

"That's the business for you," another man said.

The statement produced a moment of contemplative silence in which Fenella dwelt on the realization that she was sitting at a table in Covent Garden with a group of actors, some clearly well-known, others perhaps less so, but the atmosphere was rarified for anyone with even a slight interest in all things theatrical. For Fenella, it was breathtaking.

"Champagne to accompany the oysters?" Edward asked, catching her attention with a little flick of a finger against her ear.

She looked up at him quickly. "Oh, sorry, I wasn't listening."

"Not to me anyway," he responded with a knowing smile.

"No, not champagne, Guinness," she said firmly.

He laughed slightly and moved away toward the bar, returning in a few minutes with two foaming tankards. "Oysters are being shucked," he told her as he set down the tankards and slung a leg over the long bench, squeezing beside her, thigh to thigh.

"So, Ned, how's the play going? Weren't you going to talk old Hardcastle into directing it for you?" someone asked from the far end of the table.

Fenella stiffened slightly, eager for his answer. Edward felt her body tense against him; they were sitting so close together, he was aware of every twitch of a muscle. He turned to look at her with a flicker of an eyebrow before replying casually, "Cedric has agreed to direct and we begin auditions next week. But I already have my Rose." He picked up Fenella's hand. "Here she is, if she will agree. I'm still trying to persuade her."

"Why the doubt, Miss Grantley?" Harriet Aldershot asked. "Most young actors starting out would give their eyeteeth for such an opportunity." There was an acerbic underlay to her tone. "I don't know any of your work, so I assume you *are* just starting out."

Fenella considered, a little discomfited by the rather hostile undertone. But she couldn't fault the statement. "It's precisely because I am untried, Miss Aldershot, that I'm hesitant. The character's very complex. Have you read the play?"

"Some of it," the woman replied, watching Fenella narrowly.

"Then you'll know what I mean." She took a deep draught of ale just as a serving girl put a heavy platter of oysters nestling in ice on the table in front of her.

Fenella wondered why Edward was saying nothing. It was as if he was deaf to the exchange. She glanced questioningly at him as he calmly reached for an oyster, tipping the open shell to his mouth and swallowing with a distinct slurp.

"Have one," he said, taking another from the platter and holding it to her lips.

Fenella swallowed the succulent morsel, aware of the conversational buzz resuming around her. It seemed that the subject of Edward's play was closed for the time being. But not for long.

"So what about a theatre, Ned? Any closer to coming up with a venue?" This from the bewhiskered elderly gentleman on Fenella's other side.

Edward drank ale before saying with a careless gesture, "I'll have to see what I can afford first. It won't be one of the big West End theatres, that's for certain. Unless, of course, I can find a wealthy backer," he added. "Eat some more oysters, Fenella. Marcus," he addressed a man across the table, "are you touring again this summer?"

Fenella absently took another oyster, savoring this very different Edward, this *Ned*. He was with his own people, that was obvious from his clear relaxation, the total absence of that sardonic twitch that underscored so much of his manner and conversation. He didn't despise these people, his mother's people, as he despised his father's familiars, the people who inhabited Society's upper circles. Here, in a pub in Covent Garden, eating oysters, drinking Guinness, talking theatre, he was at home, he was Ned, the playwright, son of an actress.

She let herself relax again, content to listen to the animated theatrical gossip around her. It fascinated her, so different from the colorless and somewhat malicious conversations she was used to . . . and now found so tedious.

Finally, Edward drained his tankard and swung his leg back over the bench. "Come, Fenella, we'll miss curtain up if we don't hurry. I hadn't realized the time."

Fenella scrambled hastily and somewhat inelegantly over the bench amid a chorus of goodbyes. She responded as best she could over her shoulder as Edward propelled her quickly to the door and out into the street.

"Here, you'll need this." He draped her cloak over her shoulders, took her hand and they hurried to the theatre. The sounds of Covent Garden and the Piazza were loud: music, laughter, raised voices not always in merriment accompanied them into the foyer of the Theatre Royal. Fenella looked around, hoping she wouldn't see anyone she knew. She couldn't avoid an accidental meeting and it would be awkward, but she'd taken the risk with open eyes. However, to her relief, they reached their seats in the center orchestra without running into any familiar faces.

The hushed talk, the sounds of the orchestra tuning up, the rich scents of the theatre—plush seats, perfume—the rustle of silk gowns, all filled her with the same deep pleasure she had experienced as a small child when, one Christmas, she had been taken to see *Robinson Crusoe* at this very theatre.

Edward could feel her pleasure as she sat close beside him, her arm on the shared rest between their seats. It was the same pleasure he had always felt himself. He had faint memories of afternoons spent sitting in a corner of the stage while his mother rehearsed, and later in the front stalls watching dress rehearsals. He was such a familiar figure to his mother's fellow actors that no one paid him much attention. He ran errands eagerly when asked, brushed the stage, moved props, struggling underneath the cumbersome weight on many occasions but delighting in every task. That had all come to an end on his seventh birthday when, without warning, his mother had told him that he was to go live with his father and brother and sister in Cornwall.

He could feel even now the stab of fear, the confused sense of abandonment during the long journey with a stern gentleman wearing a dog collar, who spoke little except to say lengthy prayers during the tedious hours of the interminable rail journey into

Cornwall. He preferred not to remember his arrival at Tremayne Court, his introduction to his half siblings and the misery of that long, lonely summer, followed by all the other summers until he finally escaped under the sheltering roofs of academia. His time at Oxford had been pure delight, largely because he had quickly found his own social circle among the academically inclined students, and had managed to steer clear of his half brother. Carlton had inhabited a very different social world. He was a member of the exclusive Bullingdon Club, a select group of wealthy, aristocratic undergraduates with no interest in scholarship, only the drunken delights of privilege, their clubs, their horses, their gambling and preying on those less fortunate.

The siblings barely exchanged two words during the months they were up at Oxford together, and when Carlton was sent down in his second year for some particularly vicious prank in Town, Edward remained sequestered, spending even the long vacation in college, with frequent trips to London to visit his mother, when he would eagerly participate in her world, one that gave him a different kind of pleasure and excitement from that of academia.

"I always get a thrill at this moment," Fenella whispered, unconsciously grasping his hand tightly as the lights dimmed.

Edward was more than happy to relinquish his memories and settle into the rhythms of the play, aware always of Fenella, rapt beside him. At intermission, he suggested they go to the bar, but she shook her head. "No, if you don't mind, I'd rather just stay here. I don't like to break my concentration." She didn't say that she would also prefer to keep away from the crowded bar and foyer. Meeting someone she knew would really destroy the mood the play had created for her.

Edward merely shrugged. "As you wish. Would you like an ice cream?" A young woman with a tray of ices around her neck was walking down the aisle.

"Perfect," Fenella said happily.

Edward left his seat and walked down the aisle to where the young woman stood. He debated over the offerings, trying to guess what Fenella's favorite would be. Not chocolate, he decided; she was not a chocolate type of person. But neither was she in the least vanilla. Strawberry? No. "Coffee," he decided.

The girl scooped coffee ice into a small glass bowl, added a little wooden spoon and handed it to him. "One shilling, sir."

He took the bowl back to his seat, handing it to Fenella. "Did I guess right?"

She took a tiny taste on the tip of her spoon. "I adore coffee, so yes, you did. Was it hard to guess?"

He shook his head, smiling. "Not very. I'm getting to know you, sweetheart."

The endearment caused her to swallow the icy spoonful in one gulp, making her eyes water. She took a moment to recover, then said, "I liked your pub friends. Are they all professional actors?"

"Actors, directors, writers, scenery painters, dressmakers . . ." He shrugged easily. "They all live and breathe for the stage."

Fenella took another spoon of coffee ice. "You're the same, aren't you, Ned?"

He turned his head sharply and she offered him a questioning smile. "Am I allowed to use your *stage* name?"

"When we're alone or with my friends," he responded.

She nodded. "I understand. Edward doesn't inhabit the same world as Ned. It must be fun to have two personas. Or is it confusing?"

"Until I met you, Miss Grantley, I didn't find it in the least confusing," he replied drily. "But somehow, my generally well-ordered worlds have become chaotically entangled since you first burst upon me."

"Is that a good thing, d'you think?" She moved her knees aside to let returning patrons back to their seats.

"To be completely honest, my dear girl, I have absolutely no idea." He turned his attention to the stage as the curtain came up.

Fenella did the same, smiling slightly. He didn't sound particularly concerned about his lack of knowledge.

Chapter Thirteen

"Well, I don't know whether I'm supposed to be disappointed or uplifted by Candida's sacrifice," Fenella declared as the curtain came down and the audience applauded with typically English restraint. "It was a wonderful production, though, and the cast was very good."

"You have problems with Shaw's premise itself, then?" Edward escorted her through the departing crowd and across the foyer.

"Didn't you?" she asked, looking sideways at him as she adjusted the high fur collar of her cloak against the wind.

"Let's get into the warm and discuss it over supper and a bottle of claret." Edward tucked her hand into his arm and hurried her into the brightly lit, rowdy Piazza, filling with people spilling out of the nearby theatres and the Royal Opera House. "I booked a table at Marco's for supper."

"Lovely," Fenella said. "I'm famished." Marco's was one of the most expensive restaurants in Covent Garden. Edward's mother must have left him a substantial sum to supplement whatever meager salary he received as a university researcher. She had no right to be curious about something so personal—it was none of her business, as he'd so forcefully pointed out—but she couldn't help still feeling a little concerned that he not overspend on her. His sister had made it clear he had no financial support from his father.

She remembered the question he'd been asked about finding a theatre for his play. He'd been quite unequivocal about the expense there, and that he couldn't afford any of the playhouses in central London unless he found a financial backer. So he *did* have financial constraints, however little they affected his day-to-day life. But she would sooner cut out her tongue than trespass again into that territory.

"Here we are." He held the door for her and she went ahead of him into the restaurant foyer.

"Mr. Tremayne, a pleasure, sir. It's been a long time since you were last here." The maître d'hôtel came forward, smiling and bowing. "Miss Grantley . . . madam, how nice to see you again." He bowed to Fenella, who returned the courtesy with a smile.

"Nice to see you too, Mr. Simpson."

Edward slipped off her cloak and handed it to a hovering footman together with his own outer garments, including his hat, which, Fenella had noticed, had not once graced his head. "I must just freshen up, Edward. If you'll excuse me a moment," she said, moving toward the ladies' cloakroom. "I'll see you at the table."

She knew she was taking a coward's way out by ensuring that they didn't walk together through the dining room. People were less likely to notice them once they were seated and buried behind menus. But she did need the cloakroom, she told herself, and besides, there was no point precipitating any social awkwardness if it could be avoided. She just hoped that Edward wouldn't notice her devious maneuverings because he himself seemed quite untroubled about the public aspect of this outing. But then, of course, given his outspoken contempt for Society's opinion, he would be.

Edward followed Mr. Simpson into the dining room to a secluded corner table. "You requested a quiet table, sir. I trust this is to your satisfaction?" Simpson said, gesturing.

"Perfectly, thank you." He took his seat. "Bring a bottle of Bollinger, will you?" He leaned back in the gilt chair, taking in the scene as he waited for Fenella. The tables were well spaced and their corner table was discreetly shielded by a potted plant of some species. Edward was not a horticulturist, but he appreciated the privacy of the large spreading plant and guessed that Fenella would appreciate it even more. He didn't give a damn about being seen together in public, but the subsequent need for social chitchat exasperated him, and he had a feeling that Fenella, for all her professed nonconformity, was, at this point anyway, less cavalier about public appearances than he.

"Oh, this is good. We're quite invisible to our

fellow diners," Fenella said cheerfully, proving the wisdom of his caution. She appeared from behind the plant with Mr. Simpson, who pulled out a chair for her before signaling to the accompanying waiter to open the champagne. "Not that I can see too many familiar faces; can you?" she asked, wondering if he had bothered to look for any.

"Not that I noticed," he returned, leaning back in his chair as the waiter poured the champagne. "But I tend to be fairly unobservant in situations like this. The fewer people I recognize, the happier I am."

Fenella picked up her menu, hiding a relieved smile. "What do you think about the consommé? It's a perfect night for soup."

"I think that if that's what appeals to you, then that's what you should have," he responded, examining his own menu.

"How nice not to be told what I'm to eat," Fenella mused aloud.

"What do you mean?" Edward looked up from his menu. "Who tells you what to eat?"

Fenella hadn't meant to express her thought aloud and searched for a seemingly careless explanation. But really only the truth would work, she decided. "I'm always infuriated by men I'm dining with who assume it's their responsibility to order for me. It drives me crazy that they think they know better than I do what I should have."

"Ah." He nodded. "I can certainly understand how annoying that could be. Is there any gentleman in particular who's guilty of such appalling condescension?"

She shook her head and prevaricated. "No . . . no one in particular. They all do it."

"I see. And do you dine alone with these gentlemen often?" His eyes flicked from the menu to her face and stayed there, watching her expression closely.

She shrugged. "As you would expect, I have numerous friends; escorts, you might call them." She sipped her champagne. "Despite my advanced years, I've not yet joined the quilting circle of those left on the shelf."

At that he laughed with rich enjoyment. "Oh, Fenella, what an abominable image. I applaud your discrimination and strength to resist the pressures that must be brought to bear . . . by your mother, perhaps?"

"There's nothing she would like better than to be able to announce my engagement in the *Times* and the *Gazette*," she responded with a chuckle. "But she's never been one to bring pressure, and my father wouldn't countenance it anyway. If I want to end up an old maid, I'm free to do so."

"And do you think you will?"

She shrugged. "Who knows? Maybe . . . or maybe I'll be swept off my feet by some Prince Charming when I least expect it." She turned her attention back to the menu. "We should order."

Edward accepted the abrupt change of subject and waited until the waiter had left with their order before saying, "Don't you ever tire of the endless social round and its rituals?"

"Frequently. But I have Diana and Petra, and we

manage quite successfully to fly above the tedium whenever we wish."

"Nevertheless, how will they react to you on the public stage? How will Lord and Lady Grantley take it?"

Fenella's expression grew somber. "Diana and Petra are very supportive; they find it exciting, if anything. But my parents . . . well, that's another matter. I try very hard not to think about it."

"But you must," he said flatly. "If you agree to play Rose, you'll be committed. You must be certain nothing will get in your way. Too many other people's lives and commitments will be depending on you. This isn't a dilettante proposition, Fenella."

"You think I don't know that?" she demanded in a fierce undertone. "How insulting can you be?" She glared at him across the table. "If I make a promise, I keep it." She turned her head away abruptly, resisting the urge to get up from the table to leave.

"I merely wished to be sure you understood," he said, apparently not in the least dismayed by her anger, and certainly not apologetic.

There was silence for a few moments as waiters brought their first courses, and when they'd gone, Fenella picked up her spoon and dipped it into the clear broth in front of her. She was still too angry and hurt to continue conversation of any kind, and Edward, after watching her for a moment, seemed to accept her silence and turned his attention to his mussels.

"So, would you have made the same decision as Candida?" he asked after a while, his tone neutral.

"To sacrifice the chance of happiness with the man I love in order to stay and look after the man who needs me?" She frowned, considering, before saying ruefully, "I'm not certain I'm *that* good a person . . . that unselfish."

"That's honest, at least," Edward said with a small smile. "But it's hard to absolve her would-be lover from his own selfishness. Just believing that the woman he adores is far too good for the life she has chosen, a mere wife, whose only object in life is to care for and love her husband, doesn't to my mind give him the right to unilaterally break the chains of trust and affection Candida shares with her husband."

Fenella sliced into the veal scaloppine that replaced her consommé. "Shaw's view of marriage as a sort of female imprisonment in a life of service and drudgery is certainly interesting. Perhaps I'll suggest that to my mother and see what she thinks . . . although I know perfectly well what she'll say."

He laughed. "I doubt Lady Grantley leads a life of service and drudgery."

"No, but she is in service to my father. His opinions are hers, his orders final. And she believes that in return she is entitled to his care and protection. He will ensure that nothing changes, nothing disturbs her sense of order . . . hence her inability to imagine a woman voting or even having a political opinion."

"She's far from alone in that," Edward observed.

"No," Fenella agreed with a sigh. "And that's why the WSPU has such a hard row to hoe. The Union needs more men in its ranks, which is ironic when you think about it."

Edward nodded, about to say something when a hearty voice declared, "It *is* you, Fenella," and a figure sporting a curly mustache and a head of ginger hair appeared from behind the potted plant. "See chaps, I'm right. It is Fenella. I'd recognize that voice anywhere." Two other male figures appeared beside him, crowding the small space.

"Charles, Peter, David, where did you spring from?" Fenella asked. "Are you acquainted with Edward Tremayne?" She gestured to her companion, whose expression was not that of a happy man.

"Oh, yes, of course. Tremayne . . . haven't seen you around at all in . . . Lord, it must be at least a year. Thought you'd gone abroad or something," Peter Mayhew said.

"No," Edward said without embellishment and continued with his dinner.

"So, what have you been up to this evening, then, Fenella?" the ginger-haired gentleman asked.

"The Theatre Royal . . . Bernard Shaw," Fenella responded, wondering how to get rid of them. Edward was seething with annoyance, not that they'd notice. Their slightly glazed eyes indicated they were all somewhat the worse for wear and probably oblivious to any gentle hints.

"Oh, that damn socialist," one of them declared. "His plays should be banned. Certainly not fit for the ladies."

"And there, David, we must disagree," Fenella said firmly. "I think you should all go back to your table and leave us to our dinner." She sounded rather like a schoolmistress, she thought, but she had had sufficient experience of handling inebriated young gentlemen to know that the tone usually worked.

"Yes, of course. Forgive the intrusion, couldn't help recognizing your voice, m'dear girl. Didn't expect to find you dining à deux with Tremayne, here." He stared pointedly at Edward.

Fenella heard the note of disdain in his voice. "I can't imagine why not, Charles," she said with a touch of ice. "However, whom I dine with is no business of yours."

There was a moment of awkward silence; then Edward said quietly, "Gentlemen, I believe the lady gave you your congé a few minutes ago. I suggest you take your leave."

The trio left at once, looking rather discomfited. "Damned drunken idiots," Edward declared.

"They were too drunk to remember any of this," Fenella said. "I'm sorry I brought them down upon us."

He shook his head. "No matter. It's going to be inevitable if we continue to be out in public together."

"Yes."

"Does it embarrass you to be seen with me?" He raised his wineglass to his lips, watching her over the lip.

"No, of course not," she exclaimed. "Whatever made you say that? It's just that I don't like drawing attention to myself in any circumstances."

He set down his glass. "Why do I have the impression there's something you're not telling me, Fenella?"

"I can't imagine," she said shortly. "Except that I'd like treacle tart for pudding."

He inclined his head in acknowledgment and signaled the hovering waiter.

Fenella tried to recover her equilibrium. Of course she wasn't telling him about George. There was no reason to. Her friends and acquaintances were no business of Edward Tremayne's. But if that was so, why was she so anxious to hide behind a potted plant? And why had the encounter with the three young men unnerved her? But most of all, why was she shying away from mentioning George Headington at all? If she had nothing to hide, why was she acting as if she had?

Edward made no attempt to break her brooding silence. He was certain she was keeping something from him, but he couldn't imagine what or why. Her business was her business, except where it concerned *Sapphire*. Then it was most certainly his business. But he didn't think his play had anything to do with Fenella's present discomfort.

"So, are you prepared for Wednesday's reading with Cedric?" he asked, as if none of the previous conversation had happened.

"A little nervous actually," she confessed. "I wish I had a copy of the play so I could get really familiar with it before then."

"I'll send Harvey to Albemarle Street with a copy," Edward said. "Unless, of course, you'd care to come back with me now and collect it." He raised a questioning brow, his lips quirked in a half-smile of invitation.

Fenella shook her head. "No, not tonight. I think I want to go straight home."

"Any particular reason?" His voice was quiet. "Any way I can change your mind?"

Again she shook her head. "It's nothing to do with you, Edward. I just don't feel right tonight. I'm sorry."

"Don't apologize," he responded easily. "There's no obligation, sweetheart. If you want to go home to your own bed, that's your right. I'll settle up here and we'll take a cab."

Fenella wasn't sure what she'd expected, but this calm, relaxed acceptance of her rejection probably wasn't it, she thought. A small attempt at persuading her to change her mind wouldn't have come amiss, but then she scolded herself for such hypocrisy. She should be grateful he made things so easy, not a word of recrimination, a hint of disappointment to make her feel guilty, just a simple shrug of acceptance.

She thought of how George had behaved that morning, his sullen anger at her suggestion they become less exclusive. Did it mean George's feelings for her were stronger than Edward's? But what did it matter if they were? Feelings, apart from lustful passion, hadn't so far had a place in her brief relationship with Edward Tremayne. Words of love didn't come into anything they did together. Love involved possession; she had learned that much in her twenty-four years. She only had to look at Rupert and Diana to see that. But it had to be willing possession on both sides.

Edward watched her face in the flickering light of the hackney on the way to Albemarle Street. She hadn't spoken beyond the occasional monosyllabic response to a mundane question he'd asked as they'd left the restaurant. He wished he knew what she was thinking. Whatever her thoughts were, they troubled her, flying across her mobile features like greyhounds on a racetrack. He wondered if she'd tell him if he asked her. But they weren't close enough yet for confidences, he decided. He wasn't even sure he wanted to develop that closeness. Not, at least, until the uncertainties of *Sapphire* were resolved. He needed her clearheaded to play her part.

Fenella, suddenly aware of his close scrutiny, turned her head aside to look out of the carriage window. They were making slow progress through the thronged streets as the evening drew to a close, rowdy people in various stages of inebriation pouring onto the pavements from pubs and restaurants. And the closer they came to Albemarle Street, the more uncertain she became. Her head was telling her to bid Edward good night at her doorstep, but the prospect brought her only a sense of deep disappointment. Dinner had been unsettled and the evening felt unfinished. And she had the feeling that if they parted with this unfinished business between them, it would become permanent.

It wasn't so much the absence of lust, of passionate lovemaking, that made the evening feel unfinished. It went much deeper than that, but Fenella couldn't put her finger on the problem.

"You may not have noticed, my dear, but we've been sitting outside your house for nearly five minutes." Edward's voice broke her reverie and she shook her head as if to dispel cobwebs.

"Oh, I'm sorry. I was miles away."

"Yes," he agreed in the same coolly amused tone. "You certainly were. Are you back?"

She looked helplessly at him. Was she? For some reason, she seemed stuck to the seat. Her house was a few steps away, the privacy of her own bedroom a staircase away. All she had to do was get up and step out of the carriage. Collins would open the door for her. That was all she had to do . . . and yet she couldn't make her body obey the commands of her brain.

Edward stroked his mouth with a fingertip, regarding her thoughtfully in the dim light; then, abruptly, he made up his mind. "For God's sake, woman, if you can't decide, then, much as it goes against the grain, I'll decide for you." He reached for her hands and pulled her across the small space between them, drawing her onto his lap in a tight embrace. He kissed her hard and long, and with a little sigh, Fenella yielded her will to one that for this moment was much stronger than her own.

Her eyes closed, her arms went around his neck and she lost herself in the familiar earthy yet lemony scent of his skin, the heat of his body, the pliable warmth of his lips on hers. His mouth tasted of champagne and cream and she was barely aware when he reached up and knocked on the roof of the cab, which instantly started forward.

After a few moments, Edward disentangled himself from the ermine folds of her cloak and placed her once more onto the opposite seat.

"Does he know where to go?" Fenella asked, dazed, her mouth tingling from the pressure of his kiss.

"I told him when we got in the cab where to take me after I'd left you at your house," Edward replied, smiling slightly. "Is coming with me what you want?"

"Apparently," Fenella said, hugging her cloak tightly around her.

Chapter Fourteen

Fenella noticed only slowly that they seemed to be going back into the late-evening chaos of Covent Garden. Praed Street was in the opposite direction. She looked out of the window. "I thought we were going back to your lodging."

"I wasn't ready to call it a night alone after you said you wanted to go home," he responded, leaning back, his arms folded, watching her with an amused glint in his eye. "The fire will be out at home and it'll be generally unwelcoming, so I had somewhere else in mind."

"Oh. May I ask where?"

"Wait and see." He smiled in the shadowy dimness of the carriage.

Despite her mixed feelings, her sense of confusion over her abrupt change of mind and the way it had been changed, Fenella felt a surge of excitement. It had been such a long time since she'd felt this simple excitement, this pleasurable anticipation, and she savored it like the marzipan on a childhood birthday cake . . . How she'd delighted in peeling off the icing to reveal the rich, golden, almond paste. She could almost taste the sweetness now, lingering on her tongue.

She couldn't imagine where they were going, but it had to be somewhere that fierce kiss could have its natural conclusion. It had aroused too great a need in her to be ignored.

The carriage drew up on a quiet street away from the Piazza, although the raucous noise of late-night revelry could be heard on the crisp air. Edward jumped down and held up a hand for Fenella, who took it and stepped to the cobbled street in front of a handsome, double-fronted house, its windows discreetly curtained, a lamp over the front door lit in welcome.

"Who lives here?" she asked as Edward paid the cabbie and turned to the front door.

"Madam Elizabeth runs the establishment," he said, pulling the bell chain. "And she runs it with the utmost discretion, I can promise you." The door opened, and a liveried servant stood in the entry, examining the new arrivals before bowing.

"Mr. Tremayne, sir. A pleasure indeed. It's been a while since you visited us." His eyes flicked to Fenella, and she had the impression that however quick the glance, she had been assessed, from the pearls in her hair, to the ermine cloak and the bronze slippers on her feet.

"Please, come in. I'll tell Madam you're here." He held the door wide for them to enter the large, square hall, softly lit with gas lamps, the air faintly perfumed, a few brocade armchairs scattered around. Laughter and the sound of a piano came from behind a pair of double doors to the right.

"What is this place?" Fenella demanded in an undertone. "Who is Madam Elizabeth?"

Edward gave her a wicked grin. "Guess." He set his hat and gloves on a small table, then shrugged out of his evening cloak.

Fenella's eyes widened as she stared at him, the impossible truth taking shape. He was looking far too pleased with himself. "It's not . . . it couldn't be . . . a *brothel*," she managed finally, and was rewarded with a chuckle.

"A house of ill-repute," Edward said, still chuckling. "A very select establishment, my dear. And totally discreet. Just leave everything to me, and don't say anything, if you can manage not to."

She should of course walk out in justified indignation, horror, outraged modesty, Fenella thought, but she had not the slightest inclination to do any such thing. She was fascinated, and her earlier excitement increased a hundredfold by the forbidden nature of their surroundings.

"Edward, my dear man, how lovely of you to visit us this evening. I understand you have brought a companion." The lady who spoke seemed to sail into the hall from a passageway behind the stairs. She was dressed in a deeply flounced gown of crimson and black silk, pale, slightly plump shoulders rising from a dramatic décolletage that revealed full white breasts almost to the nipples. Her hair was dressed in a high pompadour, which, together with a pair of impossibly high-heeled scarlet shoes, accentuated her tall figure.

"Elizabeth, forgive my neglect. I've been busy with

my play," Edward said, sounding as natural as if they were conversing in a conventional drawing room. "Allow me to introduce Miss Phoebe Adams." He drew Fenella forward. "Phoebe, my dear, this an old friend of mine, Madam Elizabeth."

Madam Elizabeth took Fenella's hand in both of hers as she looked her up and down with the air of one accustomed to scrutinizing and assessing young women. "Well, my dear, you're not the usual gentleman's companion we see around here, but if Edward vouches for you, you're most welcome."

How often did Edward avail himself of the services available in Madam Elizabeth's establishment? Fenella wondered. And then she wondered if she really cared about the answer. She responded to Elizabeth's comment with a blandly neutral smile and gently removed her hand from the clasp.

"The gold suite is available at present, Edward," Madam said, turning away from Fenella. "Will that suit your needs?"

"Perfectly, and would you send up a jug of negus with some of those wonderful lobster patties?"

"Right away, sir. Let me escort you to the suite." She turned to the stairs, mounting with a stately tread.

Fenella followed, wondering how on earth the woman managed to walk on those impossibly high heels. She glanced over her shoulder at Edward, a step behind her. He raised an eyebrow in question, and when she nodded, a deeply sensuous glow illuminated his eyes, his lips quirked in a wicked smile she hadn't seen before. She was suddenly breathless; her heart seemed to race, her blood to run swiftly in her veins.

"Here we are. The gold suite." Madam Elizabeth opened a pair of doors onto a large chamber. A fire burned brightly in the grate, long yellow velvet curtains were closed over the windows and the big four-poster bed was enclosed with similar hangings. A sofa, a chaise and two armchairs upholstered in gold brocade stood on the yellow, ochre carpet.

"Gold" was definitely not a misnomer, Fenella thought, her eyes momentarily dazzled by the richness of the furnishings. "Gaudy" was her final judgment. But what else would one expect from a brothel, even a high-class one such as Madam Elizabeth's?

The door closed behind the departing mistress of the establishment and Edward turned to Fenella, still with that wicked little smile. "Are you shocked?"

The ordinary question gave her a moment to compose herself despite that come-hither smile. "Surprised," she responded as blandly as she could. "This seems to be a home away from home for you?" It was her turn to raise her eyebrows in question.

He shrugged. "I expect that gaggle of young fools in Marco's are as at home here as I am."

"I doubt that." Fenella sat on the high bed, idly swinging her legs, trying to ignore the tingling of her skin, her fast-beating heart. "I'm sure they've all visited a brothel in their time, but I doubt they'd do so with your ease and familiarity."

"Does my ease and familiarity trouble you?"

Did it? Should it?

Fenella looked around, taking in the unreal surroundings once again. She had entered a different world, one where anything could happen, a secret world where she could indulge her wildest fantasies.

It was so far removed from the pedestrian day-to-day she was used to, ordinary considerations didn't apply. She touched her tongue to her lips, giving him an up from under look, her long lashes concealing the glint in her gray eyes. "No, not in the least. I don't know how the game is played, but I'm ready and willing to take instruction."

"In that case, I'd like you to take off your clothes." His own eyes narrowed as he stood with his back to the fire, an arm stretched along the mantel, one foot on the copper fender.

"Shouldn't that wait until they bring up the negus?" she asked, goose bumps of anticipation prickling her skin.

"Ordinary standards of behavior have no place in houses like this," he responded, watching her expression closely.

That might be so, Fenella thought, but despite the excitement of these novel surroundings, she couldn't bring herself to stand naked in front of whatever servant brought up the refreshment. To her relief, before her hesitation became too obvious, a brief knock at the door heralded the entrance of a maid with a laden tray. "A jug of negus, sir." She set a tray with two pewter cups and a silver salver of lobster patties on a small table, then set the jug on a raised trivet in the hearth, close to the fire's heat. "Will that be all, sir?"

Edward nodded. "Yes, thank you. I'll ring if we need anything else."

The girl bobbed a curtsy and disappeared, the door closing softly in her wake. Fenella realized that the maid had not once looked toward her; it was as if she was not in the room at all. That must have been what Edward meant by conventions having no place here. Had she been naked, the girl still would not have looked at her. As far as the maid was concerned, she was merely a woman of the night.

Edward was watching her, guessing at her thoughts. He hadn't known how she would react to finding herself in what was to all intents and purposes a bawdy house, however distinguished its clientele. He knew that as soon as she had changed her mind about going home, he should have redirected the cabbie to Praed Street, but some devil, a not unfamiliar one, had taken over his better nature. He wanted to know how far outside the familiar and comfortable she would go. Part of him offered the excuse that it was a necessary test, to see if she had the adaptability to play Rose at her most manipulative, but in truth, he knew he had wanted to see if she really was as daring and careless of convention as she appeared to be.

To his delight, not only had she taken the situation in her stride, she had immediately recast it as a game throbbing with sensual excitement. Now she stood by the bed, her hands at her sides, her head slightly tilted as if in question.

He turned away to pick up the jug of negus, pouring a cup for himself before turning back to her and repeating quietly, "I'd like you to take off your clothes."

Fenella swallowed, aware of the hot surge of anticipation flooding her body, lifting her nipples, moistening her sex. Slowly, she began to undress, reaching awkwardly behind her to unbutton her gown. Edward didn't offer to help her, just watched steadily, and that watchful gaze, sharp with lust, made her fingers quiver at their task. Slowly, she slid the gown to her feet and stepped out of the puddle of emerald taffeta. She untied the ribbons of her stiffly starched petticoat and stepped out of that, then very slowly unfastened the tiny pearl buttons of her chemise.

Edward didn't move, except once to take a sip from his cup, but his eyes never left her. When she stood naked except for her gartered silk stockings and her bronze slippers, he held up an arresting hand and she remained as she was, standing quite still as he looked at her, her nakedness accentuated by her stockings and slippers.

"Come to me," he instructed softly, and she stepped away from her discarded clothes, crossing the small space between them until she stood in front of him.

"You are so beautiful," he murmured, holding his cup of negus to her lips. "Drink some. It'll keep you warm."

She sipped the hot spiced port as he tilted the glass for her, lost now in this strange, dreamlike world where only desire mattered, where every inch of her skin was sensitized, her blood racing through her veins. She wanted his hands on her and took a step closer until her skin touched the soft silky wool of his coat, until her bared breasts were pressed close to the starched white linen of his waistcoat. She could detect a hint of lavender from his shirt, as she inhaled the familiar scent of his skin.

At last he gave her what she craved, his hands moving over her body, cupping her breasts, sliding over her belly, fingering the hard knobs of her hip bones, slipping between her stockinged thighs.

"Tell me what you want, sweetheart," he said against her ear as his fingers moved within her.

"This, *you*," she returned in a fierce whisper. "I'm on fire, Edward. I need you now."

For answer, he lifted her against him, moving to the bed, letting her fall onto the coverlet as she kicked off her slippers. He bent to untie her garters and with agonizing slowness inched her silk stockings down her legs, over her feet, tossing them to the carpet. She gazed hungrily up at him as he hovered over her for a moment, then straightened, shrugging out of his coat, unbuttoning his trousers. He came down on the bed, still wearing his shirt and white silk waistcoat. He knelt astride her, and she reached for his erect penis, stroking it with long, sweeping caresses of her fingers, delicately teasing the moist tip.

He took her hands in a firm clasp, putting them firmly on the bed on either side of her body. "Don't touch me. Lie as perfectly still as you can," he murmured, his eyes heavy with arousal, his mouth set in a firm line of intent.

Fenella lay still, aching to touch him but more than willing to play the game according to his rules.

He slid his hands under her bottom, lifting her on the shelf of his palms as his penis slid inside her open, welcoming body. She gasped with glorious sensation as he seemed to fill her, possess her, become one with her. He moved inside her, leaning backward so that only their loins touched, until he moved a hand to touch her where their bodies met. The touch electrified her, her body jumping involuntarily on the bed, and the climactic flood of sensation overwhelmed her.

Edward let himself go then, watching her face, as his own climax ripped through him. Her eyes were wide open, fixed upon his as her body convulsed a second time with the pulsing of his sex deep within her.

The fire was burning low when Fenella at last came back to some semblance of her senses and realized she was alone on the bed. She rolled onto one side, resting her head on an elbow-propped hand, watching Edward, who was fully dressed, kneeling in front of the fire, stirring the jug of negus with a hot poker. Sensing her gaze, he turned toward her, sitting back on his heels.

"Awake?"

"I'm not sure I was actually asleep. More like knocked unconscious." She smiled a little. "What time is it?"

"Almost three o'clock." He stood up, bringing a steaming cup to the bed. "Drink this, and then I'll take you home."

"I wish we could stay here all night." She hitched herself up against the pillows and took the cup from him, inhaling the rich scents of nutmeg and cloves.

"Well, you haven't written any letters establishing an alibi, so I think that's probably impractical," he responded, taking a lobster patty from the plate. "Want one?" He gestured to the salver.

Fenella shook her head and drank deeply from the glass. "I'm still full from dinner." Reluctantly, she swung her legs off the bed. "Where are my clothes?"

"I put them all together on the chaise. There's water and towels and other necessities behind the screen."

For the first time, Fenella noticed the tall screen that closed off a corner of the room. She went over and peered behind it, eager to see what amenities were provided in a brothel suite. A washstand, towels, soap and a commode. "All very convenient," she declared, ducking behind the screen to make use of the offerings.

When she emerged, she was dressed again, this time with Edward's help with the fastenings of her gown, then she said directly, "We didn't use anything, and you didn't come out."

"No," he said. "I was carried away in the moment. When did you last bleed?"

"I'm due to start any time now," she said, wondering why she didn't find it in the least uncomfortable to talk with him about such an intimate subject, one that was generally considered to be faintly shameful and therefore taboo. She doubted her mother and father had ever mentioned this monthly inconvenience to each other during the years of their marriage. "It should be all right."

"Let's hope so. I'm very sorry, my dear. It was my fault."

"I think we were both swept away in the moment," Fenella said, sitting on the bed to tie her garters.

Edward held her fur cloak for her and then went to the door. "The major domo will send a page to get us a hackney."

Feeling rather as if she had just woken from a dream, Fenella followed him downstairs and, a few minutes later, into a hackney. The night doorman opened the door for her at Albemarle Street and she stood for a moment on the threshold, watching the cab drive away in the direction of Praed Street before entering the house and hurrying up to her own room.

Alice knew not to wait up for her, and the fire was down to glowing embers, but Fenella was too exhausted to care. She threw off her clothes, leaving them in a heap on the floor, pulled on her nightdress and climbed into bed, pulling the covers tight around her. Within a minute, she was asleep.

Chapter Fifteen

"He took you to a brothel?" Petra asked incredulously. "In Covent Garden?"

"Wardour Street," Fenella responded from her position curled up in the corner of the chaise in front of her bedroom fire. She was still in her dressing gown, sipping coffee. Her visitors, on the other hand, were bright-eyed, pink-cheeked from their brisk walk through the cold and showed no inclination to allow her to escape their questions.

It was late morning after her return from Madam Elizabeth's establishment and she was finding it difficult to clear her head. Her body bore all the signs of vigorous lovemaking, her limbs aching pleasantly, and she could hardly stop yawning. Late nights didn't normally reduce her to this floppy state of happy immobility, but then, she had never had a late night like the last.

"What did it feel like? Did you see any of the women?" Diana asked, helping herself to an almond biscuit and dipping it in her coffee.

Fenella shook her head. "I saw a butler, a maid, a page and Madam Elizabeth."

"Was she scary?"

Fenella laughed. "Not in the least, although I think she probably could be if she was annoyed about something. But she seemed very fond of Edward. I gather he's a regular visitor."

Her friends absorbed the implications of this. "I suppose it's not shocking or surprising. He is a bachelor, after all," Petra ventured. "But to take *you* there." She shook her head. "Whatever would people say if it got out?"

"That I was no better than a whore myself," Fenella responded with a little chuckle. "And, just between us and the gatepost, I very much enjoyed pretending to be one."

"Anyway, it won't get out," Diana stated. "No one saw you there, and we're not about to spread gossip. I really would like to meet Edward Tremayne properly. I have only the vaguest memories of him from a few years ago. And he didn't make a favorable impression, standing their glowering with contempt for everything and everyone in the room."

"Yes, he does do that," Fenella admitted with a grimace. "I don't think it's an act either. I think he really does despise the life that people like us lead."

"But he doesn't feel that way about you, of course." Petra regarded her friend closely, a hint of question in her voice.

Fenella frowned. "I don't think so. Not all the time anyway," she added, wrinkling her nose a little.

"You're certain you know what you're doing, darling?" Petra leaned over to pat her arm.

Fenella shook her head. "No, I'm not certain at

all, but I *am* certain that for as long as I go on enjoying it, I have no intention of stopping."

"So what happens next?" Diana, ever practical, asked.

"Well, a read-through of the play on Wednesday with Cedric and the rest of the cast. I'm hoping Edward will send me a copy of the play today, so I can familiarize myself with it before then."

"And when are you going to mention this to Lord and Lady Grantley?" Diana asked, drinking down her coffee.

"After Wednesday," Fenella said firmly. "The shaky way things have gone with the play thus far, plans may all fall apart on Wednesday when it's supposed to become reality."

"And if it does, what will that mean for you and Edward?" Petra nibbled a biscuit.

"I have no idea," Fenella said honestly. "Nothing good, I suspect. Edward identifies with *Sapphire*. It seems, for the moment at least, to be the most important, defining factor of his life. If his plans fall apart, I don't know how he'll react . . . if he'll blame me."

"For what?" demanded Diana.

Fenella grimaced. "For not being good enough, for not giving enough of myself, for not realizing what a masterpiece of creativity it is . . . for not seeing it with his eyes."

"But that's so self-centered, so *unfair*," exclaimed Petra.

"It's the artistic temperament for you," Fenella said. "Of course, it might be quite different. He might take it all in his stride. We shall see."

"Well, I hope he makes himself visible to the naked eye soon. I can't wait to meet him properly." Diana stood up. "I have a fitting for my new riding habit in half an hour. I must be on my way. Are you coming, Petra? Or staying here?"

Petra glanced at Fenella. "You're looking peaky, dearest. I think I'll leave you to recover from the exertions of last night. Tell us how things go on Wednesday . . . promise."

"Promise," Fenella agreed. "You don't mind if I don't get up, do you? I'm so comfortable here and my limbs don't seem to want to move."

"Stay right where you are, my dear." Diana bent to kiss her. "But I'll be expecting you in Grosvenor Square after your play reading on Wednesday. Don't fail us."

"As if I would." Fenella embraced her friend and reached for Petra to kiss her goodbye. "I'll come for tea."

"See you then." Petra straightened from her embrace. "I should get home. Mama is in a tizzy because Jonathan is supposed to arrive from Paris this afternoon and she wants a family dinner to welcome him, but he keeps promising to come on a particular date and then cancels at the last minute. He's so insensitive to poor Mama's feelings, but then she spoils him rotten. He can't do anything wrong in her eyes. Sometimes it makes me quite cross with him."

Diana bit her lip. Memories of her brother, killed two years before at the siege of Mafeking, were still vivid, and she thought she would have given anything to be able to grumble about him as Petra was doing about her own brother.

"Oh, I am sorry, darling." Petra gave her a convulsive hug. "Now I'm being insensitive. I didn't mean to remind you of Jem's death."

"It wasn't your fault," Diana said, returning the hug. "Rupert and I often talk about him. It hurts, but it keeps him real. Goodbye, Fenella, love. See you on Wednesday."

"If you get your energy back by then." Petra blew her a kiss on her way to the door.

Fenella smiled as the door closed on them. In the last ten minutes, she had begun to feel faintly nauseated, her belly cramping fiercely. It explained her unusual lassitude, but instead of moaning about it, she welcomed the discomfort this month, uncurling herself from the chaise to get what she needed from the dresser on her way to the bathroom. They had escaped the consequences of their carelessness last night and she must send a note to Edward to put his mind at rest.

She had just returned to her position on the chaise when Alice entered with a brown paper parcel. "This just came for you, Miss Fenella. How are you feeling now? Is there anything I can get you?"

"Something for cramps, Alice," she said, taking the parcel and swiftly untying the string. "Negus," she said, suddenly reminded of the spiced, soothing warmth of the drink. "D'you think the kitchen could manage to make me a mug? I think it will be just the thing."

"I'll make it myself, Miss Fenella. And I'll bring you one of Lady Grantley's new tablets for her headaches."

"Aspirin, you mean? No, just the negus, Alice. I don't need anything stronger."

"Well, if you're sure. Does wonders for her ladyship's headaches, so Elsie tells me." Alice bustled from the room.

It was true, as her mother's maid reported to Alice, that aspirin, the new, so-called miracle tablet, relieved her mother's frequent headaches, but Fenella decided her own discomfort could be managed well enough with a day of indolent self-indulgence and the relaxing effects of negus.

She opened the parcel to reveal a neat pile of typewritten pages. There was a handwritten note on top, just a few lines in Edward's distinctive hand. There was no soft greeting, no salutation, even, and not a mention of the previous night's activities.

> *I only have 2 typewritten copies, so please protect this with your life. I thought the impersonal typescript might make it easier for you to develop some detachment, to avoid any personal issues that might get in the way of an impartial reading. E.*

Fenella frowned, thinking that the short note, despite its brusqueness, revealed Edward's anxiety all too clearly, although he'd hate to think so. And it put even more pressure on her. What if, after reading it through again, slowly and without distraction, she really hated it? Or simply decided that the part was too much for her?

Well, that was a bridge to be crossed if and when she got there.

"Here's your negus, Miss Fenella. And Lady Grantley said you should take one of her aspirin tablets. You'll feel better quickly." Alice set a steaming mug on a low table by the chaise and laid a small white tablet beside it. "There now. And Lord George was here a few minutes ago. I told Collins to tell him you were indisposed and he said he was very sorry to hear that and hoped you'd feel better soon. He went into the library and wrote you a note." Alice handed her a folded sheet of paper, glancing curiously at the pile of papers in Fenella's lap.

"Thank you, Alice." Fenella took the note and then picked up her mug, cradling it between both hands and inhaling the spicy comfort. "I'll ring if I need anything else."

"Right you are. Now you just rest there and I'll bring you some hot broth and a lightly boiled egg for your lunch a bit later on."

The prospect didn't sound very appetizing to Fenella, but she smiled her thanks, waiting until Alice had left her before taking a sip of the negus and then opening George's note.

Dear girl, I am devastated to hear that you're under the weather. I do hope you didn't eat something at Marco's last night that upset you. I know you don't particularly like dining à deux. I am wondering what changed your mind. I do hope you'll be well enough for the Warehams' ball. Your mother has invited me to dinner first, so I look forward to seeing you then, if not before. Your devoted George.

Fenella drank some more negus, feeling its warmth curling in her belly, soothing the cramping. She reread George's note. As she had feared, one of the drunken oafs who'd accosted her at the table had reported back to him. As George would see it, she had refused to go to the opera with him and had instead gone to the theatre with Edward Tremayne. Which was only the truth. George would see it as a direct slap in the face and she could hardly blame him. The tone of his note resonated with entirely justified resentment.

She leaned back, closing her eyes on a deep sigh. It was all going to be as miserably messy as she'd feared and she had only herself to blame. She was committed to attending the Warehams' ball with George, but was it possible she could smooth George's ruffled feathers beforehand while sticking to her guns? It had to be done whether Edward Tremayne was in the picture or not. She owed it to George. There were women aplenty who would give their eyeteeth for a smile from him and he deserved to find someone who was truly fond of him as more than a convenient escort.

Resolutely, she put George's note aside. She would write him a charming note a little later. For the moment, she had work to do. She picked up the first typewritten sheet.

Two hours later, she put down the last sheet. There was no question in her mind that Edward's play was brilliant. The dialogue ran smoothly, the characters were all clearly defined—all except Rose.

She was a conundrum, an enigma, but for the first time, Fenella had an inkling of how to play her, how to get *inside* her character. The evil Rose was difficult, and portraying her meant suppressing much of her own nature, but that, after all, was the essence of acting, Fenella told herself. She just needed to create her own character history because Edward had supplied very few details, except for the murder of Rose's baby sister. Part of the play's fascination was the question, did she or didn't she? The audience would have to decide that for themselves.

But Fenella had made up her own mind. She didn't know Rose well enough as yet, but well enough to start deepening her understanding. She would be ready on Wednesday for the full cast read-through.

She looked with distaste at the luncheon tray Alice had brought up to her. She'd had no interest in eating its sad contents an hour ago and even less now. She was still feeling a rather pleasant inertia from the negus, but otherwise much better than before, and her mother's aspirin still lay on the table. And she was hungry. An image of lobster patties drifted into her mind.

She had two letters to write, one to George and one to Edward. She reached behind her for the bellpull on the wall.

Alice appeared within a few minutes. "Oh, Miss Fenella, you haven't eaten any of your lunch," she exclaimed.

"I'm sorry, Alice, but I need something rather

more robust," Fenella said, offering what she hoped was a winning smile. "Toasted cheese, perhaps?" It wasn't lobster patties, but it had been one of her nursery pleasures.

"I'll see to it right away." Alice picked up the untouched tray. "Glad to see you're feeling better."

"Thank you, Alice. I have two letters to write. Could you ask Collins to arrange for them to be hand-delivered? I think it's too late for the regular mail."

"Certainly, Miss Fenella." Alice departed.

Fenella cast off her quilted coverlet and uncurled herself from the chaise with some reluctance. She sat down at the pretty writing desk, pulled a sheet of vellum toward her, dipped pen in the inkwell and wrote, *Dear George.*

She stopped. Dear George *what*? She was in no mood to apologize and she couldn't make promises she had no intention of keeping. It wasn't possible for things to be the same between them. Finally, she dipped her pen again and wrote: *I'm sorry I couldn't receive you today, but I look forward to seeing you here for dinner before the Warehams' ball. With affection, Fenella.*

She read the note twice, frowning. She did feel affection for him, so that wasn't a lie or even an exaggeration. There was nothing she wanted to say to him about his reference to Marco's. He could read what he liked into her silence on that subject. It would have to do. It was polite, not unfriendly and very much to the point. Satisfied, she reached for an envelope, addressed it and turned her attention to

Edward, nibbling the tip of her pen before writing swiftly.

Night was drawing in when Edward returned to his lodging after a day working in college to find Fenella's letter awaiting him. He had put all thoughts of the play, of Fenella and her reaction, out of his mind, losing himself in the intricacies of *The Decameron* as compared with Chaucer's *Canterbury Tales*. It was a challenging task, as his grasp of Medieval Italian was shaky, but the research project had worked its usual magic and he had escaped the urgencies of his own world into the cerebral world of academia.

Now the sight of Fenella's delicate handwriting, each cursive letter perfectly formed as one would expect from a graduate of an elite girls' boarding school, brought his own world rushing back. He threw a log on the fire, poured himself a glass of wine and sat down in the leather armchair, slitting open the envelope.

Edward, my dear, I've read the play slowly and with reflection. I think it's wonderful. I believe I now understand Rose in a way that shows me how to portray her. As you know, I was afraid I wouldn't be able to do her justice, particularly the evil side of her character. But I see a way in and look forward to Wednesday, when I can show you what I mean.
I have missed you today; the memories of last night are still so vivid. On that subject, I should tell you

that there will be no unwanted consequences. Think of me tonight as I shall think of you. F.

Edward sat with the letter in his lap, looking into the fire, a slight smile on his lips. Wednesday couldn't come soon enough.

Chapter Sixteen

Fenella pushed open the door to Cedric Hardcastle's studio on Wednesday morning, feeling unusually nervous. She had read *Sapphire* so many times in the last two days that she felt she could almost recite it by heart, but what happened in the next hour or so would determine so much, not just the future of Edward's play, but any future she and Edward might have.

"Good morning, everyone." She greeted the group gathered around the table with a warm smile. "I'm sorry to have left you all in the lurch last time."

"We're honored you could join us this morning," Cedric stated on an abrasive note, glowering at her from beneath beetling brows.

"So am I," Fenella returned pleasantly, ignoring the tone. Cedric was not going to intimidate her. She glanced around the room. "We seem to be missing Mr. Tremayne, however."

"Not so, Miss Grantley. Here I am." Edward walked into the room behind her. "Ah, good, I see you have the script with you." He took the folder from Fenella's hand with an eagerness akin to anxiety. He was, she thought with a degree of sympathetic amusement, overly anxious to have his baby back in his own hands. "Has everyone else had a chance to read it through?"

A murmur of agreement answered him. "And you're all quite familiar with your parts?"

"I have already established that everyone around the table is ready for the read-through, Edward," Cedric said brusquely. He was not about to let the author assume the role of director, a not unfamiliar happening, he knew from experience, with writers who were reluctant to relinquish their creations to someone else's authority.

Edward looked put out and Fenella could see that he was about to respond with one of his acerbic snaps. She broke in swiftly. "I'm sure everyone's as excited as I am to be part of this project." Pulling out a chair, she sat down at the table. "I can't wait to begin." She held out her hand for the folder Edward still held. "May I have the script back? I almost know it by heart, but I'd feel more comfortable with it in front of me."

Edward seemed almost visibly to steel himself before handing back the folder. "Of course, Miss Grantley."

"Oh, surely we can dispense with the formalities, Edward," Fenella murmured, fluttering her eyelashes with the wicked intention of breaking through his grim tension. Experience told her the tension was taking him far too close to the edge of ill temper, which didn't augur for a peaceable morning. "We have a lot of work to do together; I'm sure it will go more smoothly if we all relax in one another's company."

His eyes narrowed, and for a moment she thought she had pushed him too far, taken the initiative too quickly, but then she saw the taut muscles around his mouth relax and a little glint of understanding sparked in his blue gaze. "I'm sure you're right as usual, Fenella. Let us by all means drop the formalities . . . Cedric, ready when you are."

"Act one, scene one," Cedric responded, tapping his hand on the table. "Cora enters the drawing room . . ."

For almost an hour the reading continued with no interruptions, and Fenella began to enjoy herself. Perhaps they would get through this morning without any caustic comments. Edward was making notes, scribbling fiercely on his high stool in the corner of the room, but so far quietly.

She had relaxed too soon. She had spent a long time puzzling over how to portray Rose in a particularly complex scene and had finally found an interpretation that seemed true to the character. She plunged into the scene, confident in her reading, and was thrown off course when Edward suddenly jumped from his stool.

"No, no, that's not what she's feeling," he exclaimed, crossing to the table in three long strides.

"Fenella, you haven't understood what's happening here. Rose is planning—"

"Could we talk outside, please?" Fenella interrupted him, her eyes shooting sparks. She was determined that any further arguments between them would not be public spectacles. "There are some things I don't believe *you* understand, Edward."

She stood up as she spoke, pushing back her chair. "Would you excuse us, please, Cedric?" She stalked to the door.

Edward hesitated for a second, thrown by the abruptness of her departure. Then his ready anger rose to the fore. He strode after her, closing the door with a bang behind him. "What the hell's this all about, Fenella? You make a mistake—"

Fenella was standing on the landing, her arms folded. "I did not make a mistake," she broke in, keeping her voice low, but nonetheless vehement. "Maybe I see the scene differently from the way you do, but my view is just as legitimate as yours." Her need to stand up for herself, for *her* interpretation, infused her with a passionate intensity, a renewed sense of being truly alive that had nothing to do with exciting nights in a brothel.

Edward looked astounded. "How could you possibly believe that? Rose is my creation. I know her inside out."

"No, you're wrong," she stated flatly. "Yes, you conceived her, you put her on paper, but until someone embodies her that's all she is . . . words on paper. Admittedly, *your* words on paper, but they're flat and without substance until they're spoken."

She could see from his startled and infuriated expression that he had never really acknowledged that his creation needed something else . . . *someone* else . . . to be complete, a three-dimensional character. "It's my job to put the flesh on the skeleton, Edward."

"You're tampering with my vision," he responded. "If you don't adhere to *my* vision of the character, none of the play will make sense."

"No, I believe you're wrong." She remained standing, arms folded, unmoving, her eyes fixed upon his countenance. "There's room within the play for interpretation; it wouldn't be much of a play if there wasn't. After all, there's a central question, which is never really answered. Did she or didn't she kill the baby? You want the audience to make up their own minds; I've made up mine. But I think I know how to preserve the ambiguity for an audience."

She paused, expecting him to say something, but Edward remained silent, those bright blue eyes seeming to penetrate her innermost thoughts. His face was expressionless and she couldn't tell whether she was getting through to him or not. But at least he was no longer explosive.

Finally, she asked, "Do you want me to do this or not, Edward?"

The question seemed to shake him out of his reverie. "Yes, of course I do. How could you think otherwise?"

"Very easily, as it happens," Fenella responded. "Just one look at your face is all it takes. But listen to me now, Edward. You have to let me do this the way it feels right to me. Rose is me. She has to be, otherwise none of this will work. If I can't inhabit the character in the only way that fits me, you'll have to find someone else to play her."

Edward rubbed his eyes with finger and thumb. Finally, he'd met his Rubicon. If he insisted on his vision, Fenella would refuse the part. And he was absolutely convinced she was the right person to play Rose. If he wanted her, he had to let her play the character her way. But relinquishing control of this precious thing he had worked on for so long, that was almost dearer to him than anything he could think of, was like tearing off a piece of his flesh.

"Will you trust me?" Fenella asked, reaching out a hand to touch his arm. "I promise I will listen to everything you have to say, we'll talk over differing opinions, but in return, you have to promise to listen to me and not lose your temper, or become acidulous and unpleasant, as you do."

He was silent for a moment but didn't move his arm away from her hand. Finally, he said, "You drive a hard bargain, Miss Grantley."

"Is it a bargain?" She looked at him, head tilted to one side in a way that reminded him of an inquisitive sparrow.

"I suppose it must be." He took her hand. "I will hear you through today without another word. But I will continue to make notes, and when the reading is over, we will go through them together and try for a consensus. Agreed?"

"Agreed. Now, let's get back in there before they all decide to go home."

Edward followed her back into the room, where she took her seat again with a half-apologetic smile to her fellow actors. Edward said nothing, ignoring Cedric's questioning glance, as he returned to his stool and his notepad.

An hour later, the reading was over and the group around the table sat for a long moment in silence. "I'm exhausted," one of the players said at last with a deep sigh. "I felt at times as if I was drowning in emotions. How do you feel, Fenella? It has to be really hard for you."

Edward looked as if he was about to say something, but Fenella jumped in before he could open his mouth. "It is exhausting, Meg, I agree. But I felt that as a whole, we were reaching some kind of shared understanding. Did anyone else feel that?"

"I certainly did," Cedric announced. "We've a long way to go, but plenty of time to be at ease with the script before we go into full rehearsals. We still haven't found theatre space as yet. That's so, isn't it, Edward?"

Edward nodded. "I'm going to look at a community space in Fulham this afternoon."

"Fulham," Robert exclaimed. "But that's so far off the beaten track. Who's going to trek to Fulham to see an obscure bunch of actors performing an obscure play?"

"It depends on advertising," Fenella said swiftly. "I have contacts, friends, I'm sure we all do, who could spread the word, get up parties to cheer us on. Besides," she added, "it's early days yet."

"Thank you for your optimism, Fenella." Edward didn't sound in the least thankful. He stood up, tucking his notepad into the inside pocket of his jacket. "But until we have a play that's fit for public consumption, I think talk of staging is somewhat premature. We have a very long way to go, my friends, judging by this morning's efforts." He wrapped his muffler around his neck. "I bid you all good morning." The door closed sharply behind him.

Fenella was the only member of the group who was not surprised at Edward's irritable and decidedly discourteous departure, but she deeply resented for herself and her companions his implied criticism of their morning's work.

"The artistic temperament," she said lightly. "One must make allowance, I suppose. I thought we all did splendidly. What's your opinion, Cedric?"

"For a first run-through, it wasn't too bad," he said. "Still rough around the edges, but only to be expected at this stage. We'll meet again Saturday morning, if that suits everyone." He looked interrogatively around the table.

There was a murmur of agreement and Robert remarked acidly, "I hope we won't be honored with the playwright's artistic temperament on Saturday. I for one could do without that glower. He makes me nervous."

Fenella held her tongue, although her instinct was to jump to Edward's defense. But then she reflected that it would be a very good thing if he did modify his arrogance with the folk who were going to fulfill his dearest ambition, to see his play performed. And she had every intention of telling him so.

She said her goodbyes and hurried down the stairs and out onto Gower Street. Edward stood waiting for her, tapping his foot impatiently. "You took your time."

Fenella put up her chin. "It would have been courteous if you had done the same," she retorted, starting to walk toward Bloomsbury Square.

"Now what's that supposed to mean?" he demanded, falling in beside her.

"You know perfectly well. For all that so-called chip you carry, you were taught decent manners and elementary courtesy, I assume." She increased her speed. "If you'll excuse me, I have somewhere else I need to be." It wasn't strictly true; she was engaged to have tea in Cavendish Square later, but the church clock was only now striking noon. Edward's unpleasant behavior had annoyed her more than she'd realized.

"Oh, damn, now what am I supposed to do?" he said, stepping in front of her. "I would cast myself at your feet and beg forgiveness, but it doesn't seem practical here." He gestured with a comical expression of dismay to their surroundings, the busy street, the vehicles crowding the square.

Fenella held herself aloof for as long as she could, but in the end she couldn't control a bubble of laughter at the absurd image. This habit he had of suddenly switching moods was hard to keep up with. "Now you've made me laugh," she complained. "And I don't want to. You are impossibly rude, Edward Tremayne."

"I know," he agreed with an unconvincing attempt at a penitent smile. "Forgive me?"

"I'm not the one you should apologize to; it's everyone else. They were all trying to do justice to your play, and all you could do was scornfully dismiss their efforts." She moved to go past him, but he laid a restraining hand on her arm.

"No, you can't just walk away like that, Fenella. I won't part with you on bad terms; everything will just fester and never get resolved. I've said I'm sorry for my ill temper, and I accept that I should apologize to the others, only that's not going to happen right now. I'll say something on Saturday, but now come and have lunch with me and we'll discuss my notes."

Fenella frowned. Edward's habit of sweeping aside her objections or her wishes if they didn't coincide with his own was one of his most annoying traits, which was saying something. But at the same time, she could see his point about not letting a grievance fester. It would be all too easy to simply give in, but a streak of obstinacy, of refusal to have her legitimate complaints swept aside wouldn't let her.

"I'm not really hungry, Edward, and I'm too drained by this morning's reading to summon the energy to go over your notes. Let's just part friends now, and we'll see each other tomorrow, perhaps."

"Don't sulk, Fenella, it doesn't suit you." His tone was sharp and her anger finally got the better of her.

"Oh, how *dare* you accuse me of sulking?" she demanded furiously, ignoring the crowds around them. "I'm not a child. If either one of us is behaving childishly, it's you. Everything has to be the way you want it, and you ride roughshod over anyone else's opinions or feelings. I have nothing more to say now and I don't want to spend any more time with you. Let go of my arm."

She twitched her arm free of his hold. "When you've recovered your temper, send me a note and I might consider discussing your reactions to the reading with you." Seething, she stalked off down the street without a backward glance.

Edward took a step after her and then stopped. No one had ever challenged him the way Fenella did, and even as his anger blossomed at her abrupt dismissal, he couldn't deny the nagging feeling that she might have a point. He had been fighting for himself from childhood, fighting to be acknowledged, simply to be noticed as a living presence a lot of the time, so that it had become an entrenched way of conducting himself with others. But Fenella was forcing him to see himself as others saw him, when he was at his most morose and demanding. And he wasn't sure he liked himself that much.

And now what was he to do? He watched her straight-backed stride down the crowded pavement, restraining himself with difficulty from following her. He saw her hail a cab and disappear inside.

What did a man do in these circumstances? Send flowers, an apologetic note, linger on Albemarle Street gazing up at the windows, hoping to catch a glimpse of her?

Or storm the citadel?

With a sigh, Edward turned his steps toward Praed Street. The long walk in the cold would do him good. Citadel storming could wait until he had recovered his equilibrium, and with any luck, Fenella would have recovered hers.

Chapter Seventeen

"You're looking very disgruntled, darling. What's happened to cause the black brow?" Diana asked, jumping up from the tea tray when Fenella walked into her parlor later that afternoon. "What's making you glower?"

"Oh, am I glowering?" Fenella unpinned her hat, a particularly unlovely felt concoction that she disliked intensely, though somehow wearing it had suited her dark mood. "Well, it's hardly surprising in the circumstances." She cast aside her hat and coat. "Where's Petra?"

"She'll be along in a minute. She sent a message to say she was running late, something to do with her brother." Diana resumed her seat. "Shall we wait for her before you tell me what's happened to put you in such a mood?" She poured tea and handed the delicate cup to her friend. "Have a piece of shortbread. Fortnum's finest." She held out a plate.

"Thank you." Fenella took a piece and bit into it. "Maybe it'll sweeten my temper," she said, brushing crumbs from the front of her striped silk blouse.

"Well, I'm on tenterhooks," Diana declared. "I'm guessing it has something to do with your Mr. Tremayne?" She raised eloquent brows.

"Not too difficult to guess," Fenella responded, sipping her tea. "I can't remember when I was last this angry. Oh, and he's not *my* Mr. Tremayne."

"Wait for me." Petra's voice came from the doorway as she entered the parlor. "You can't tell secrets without me here."

"It's not exactly a secret, Petra, but don't worry, we were waiting for you," Fenella reassured her, exchanging a kiss of greeting with her friend. "You've become very flamboyant these days." She looked admiringly at Petra's hat, which sported a wide, floppy brim and a scarlet ostrich plume in the band. "I wish I could wear a hat like that. And I love that feather boa."

"Oh, the weather was making me dreary; I thought it would cheer me up," Petra said lightly, discarding hat, scarlet boa and coat. "Tea, please; I'm parched." She sank onto the sofa next to Fenella and took a large gulp of tea from the cup Diana passed her. "Oh, that's better. So, what's made you angry, dearest?" She turned to Fenella with an inviting smile.

Fenella hesitated. "For some reason, being with you two has banished my annoyance. I was rather enjoying it, actually. Righteous indignation, I think it could be called."

"But what caused it?" Diana prompted.

She and Petra listened intently to Fenella's account of the morning's events. Fenella didn't spare

Edward in her narration; she saw no need. The story would go no further than Diana's parlor, any more than would the facts of the Honorable Fenella Grantley's outrageous foray into the world of the public stage. At least until she was ready for a public disclosure.

"Is he ever polite?" Petra asked in her customary, straightforward fashion. "Forgive me, Fenella, but I'm beginning to wonder what you see in the man."

"I don't blame you," Fenella said with a sigh. "I find myself wondering the same rather too often. But . . ." The rest of the sentence faded into another sigh.

"Lust?" inquired Diana shrewdly.

"Yes, of course," her friend agreed with a wry smile. "I can't seem to get enough of him in that respect. And he's also funny, frighteningly intelligent, holds all the right opinions when it comes to politics and such, and he's really, really good company, and . . ." She stopped in midsentence and sipped her tea.

"And?" inquired Diana.

Fenella pursed her lips. "It's hard to describe, but just recently, I don't know . . . I've been feeling a bit, what's the word? Drear," she said. "You know, when the sky always seems gray and life has no color. D'you know what I mean?"

"I think so," Petra responded. "To be honest, dearest, Diana and I had both noticed you seemed down, not like yourself at all. But since you met Tremayne, you seem much livelier, like you used to be."

Fenella nodded. "Exactly, that's how he makes me feel. He drives me mad some of the time. I'd like to hit him over the head with a coal shovel, but then he makes me laugh, and he excites me, and makes me *think* again. I want to know things and things interest me again. And Rose fascinates me; I can't stop thinking about her, about who and what she really is, and how to make her real for an audience." She looked helplessly at her friends. "Am I making any sense?"

"In a Fenella kind of way," Diana said, smiling. "You always were a bit complicated."

"So, of course you have to persevere with the play," Petra stated. "And persevere with Edward, however much you want to hit him with a shovel."

Fenella laughed, suddenly feeling absurdly light-hearted. "Yes, I'm afraid so. It's almost got to the point where Edward and *Sapphire* are inseparable." She shook her head with an air of resignation. "I know that's why he gets so tense when the play's exposed to other people, and when he's tense, he's impossible. He knows perfectly well he has no choice if he wants it performed, but he can't bear the idea of anyone else having a look-in."

"So the question really is, how much of the *impossible* Edward you're prepared to put up with," Diana said, reaching for another biscuit.

"Well, I don't seem to have reached my limit yet," Fenella told her. "And I don't know if that makes me a pathetic victim."

Petra laughed. "*You* a victim, Fenella? Of course you're not. It seems to me that our friend Edward is struggling with some pretty fierce demons of his own and you understand that. It's only reasonable to give him some rope."

"Enough to hang himself?" Fenella questioned with an ironic smile. She glanced at her watch. "I must go, my dears. I have a heap of correspondence to tackle and Mama wants some help with the menu for the dinner before the Warehams' ball, although I don't know why she asks me; she knows perfectly well what she's going to serve. I think she's trying to make me feel useful. Or at least," she added, shaking her head, "she's attempting to educate me in the duties of the Society hostess she hopes I will one day become."

"Is she still hoping for Lady Headington?" Diana asked.

"Probably," Fenella returned with a sigh. "And I have to disabuse her, although she's never openly said that's what she's hoping for. Oh, how did life become so tangled up all of a sudden? No, don't tell me. It's all the fault of Edward Tremayne." She pulled on her gloves. "Farewell, my loves. Anon . . ." She kissed them both and made her way downstairs. A footman opened the door for her and she stepped out into the square.

The gray, overcast afternoon was just sliding into evening when she arrived home, looking forward to a little solitude and the warmth of her bedroom fire. Even the correspondence awaiting her no longer felt like a chore. Collins greeted her as she came into the house.

"Could you tell Alice I won't be needing her before

the dressing bell?" Fenella said as she headed for the stairs, knowing that her maid would appreciate an hour to herself when she knew it wouldn't be interrupted by a summons from her mistress.

Edward stood on the pavement outside the Grantley's house on Albemarle Street, looking up at the now-lighted windows, wondering which if any at the front was Fenella's bedroom. Finding it impossible to concentrate on a word of *The Decameron*, he'd spent the better part of the afternoon considering how best to storm the citadel, and now it was time. He resolutely pressed the doorbell, then he stood back a little.

Collins opened the door and surveyed the gentleman standing outside. "Good evening, sir."

"Is Miss Grantley at home?" Edward held out his card.

Collins took the card. He recognized the gentleman from his previous visit, when he'd escorted Miss Grantley to the theatre. "Allow me to ascertain, sir." He held the door wide in invitation.

Edward stepped into the warmth of the hall. His own lodgings seemed mean and shabby in comparison, something that had never struck him before. He had always been indifferent to the elegance of the Tremayne family's town house, to the lavish expenditures on the little luxuries that made life so pleasant, much preferring the rough and tumble of the theatre world and his mother's simple but comfortable apartments on Long Acre, which were always filled with her theatre friends. Now, he felt a faint unease. How did Fenella manage to fit so easily into his sparse rooms on Praed Street? Or was she just a very good actress?

"Oh, good evening." He turned at the sound of a woman's soft voice.

Lady Grantley had come into the hall from the library. She smiled with a hint of a question.

"Good evening, Lady Grantley." He bowed. "Edward Tremayne, ma'am. I am hoping to see your daughter."

"Oh, I see." Lady Grantley looked pointedly at the long case clock and Edward winced. Conventional visiting hours were long over. "Has Collins gone to tell Fenella?"

"Yes, ma'am. I apologize for the late hour, but there was something urgent I needed to discuss with her."

"Indeed," Lady Grantley said with a vague, slightly puzzled smile. "Well, if you'll excuse me . . ." She fluttered past him to the stairs.

Edward paced the hall, wondering what was keeping Fenella. He told himself that if she had refused to see him, the butler would have brought the message by now and he wouldn't be kicking his heels uncomfortably in the Grantleys' hall.

The library door opened again and Lord Grantley appeared. He regarded the visitor through his pince-nez. "Good evening?"

The question was clear in the raised eyebrows, the unsmiling lips.

"Edward Tremayne, sir. I was hoping to have a word with Miss Grantley."

"I'm so sorry to have kept you waiting, Edward." Relief came with Fenella's lightly melodious voice and her quick descent of the stairs. She had been unsure how to greet him when she'd told Collins that she would receive her unexpected and untimely visitor, but seeing him facing her father made only one approach possible. She gave him a warm smile, extending her hand as she reached him. "Papa, are you acquainted with Mr. Tremayne?"

"I wasn't," Lord Grantley said. "But I am now. Good evening again, Mr. Tremayne."

Edward bowed again. "I realize it's an unconscionable hour for visiting, sir, but I have something very urgent that I most particularly wished to discuss with Fenella."

"None of my business, I'm sure," Lord Grantley declared. "I am going to dress for dinner, if you'll excuse me." He nodded a farewell and mounted the stairs, disappearing into the shadows at the top.

"Oh, dear," Edward said with a rueful headshake. "Somehow I forgot about correct visiting hours in my anxiety to see you."

"Oh, don't mind about that. My father's not a particular stickler when it comes to convention, unless it suits his purposes. Mama will be curious, but she would never pry. Come into the library."

Fenella led the way into the book-lined room. "Sherry, or would you prefer whisky?" She moved to the sideboard, where several decanters were displayed. "Or anything else. Most things seem to be here," she added, examining the decanters in turn. "Gin, brandy, claret . . . I think this is claret?" She lifted a decanter, holding it to the light.

"Whisky, please. It's a cold evening."

Fenella poured whisky into a cut-glass tumbler and brought it over to him where he stood with his back to the fire. She turned back to pour sherry for herself, then perched on the arm of a chair, regarding him quizzically. "To what do I owe the honor, Mr. Tremayne?"

He shook his head. "Please don't play games, Fenella. You know I'm here to put things right between us." He put his glass on the mantel and held out his hands, palms up, to her. "Sweetheart, I can't bear to be out of sorts with you. I don't know why it should be so; I've never minded being at odds with anyone before, but there's something about you . . ."

He took a step forward, seizing her hands in a firm clasp, his thumbs stroking her palms. "About being with you, your voice, those lovely gray eyes, that pale beauty and that challenging spirit . . . oh, it's everything about you, the very essence of you." He brought her hands to his lips, pressing a kiss into each palm. "I need you, Fenella. I need you to play Rose, I need to make love to you, to talk with you, to feel you. I need you in my life, to give it color and texture."

At first his words brought Fenella a rush of pleasure, of warmth, a responding sense of her own need for him, but then, as his words took concrete shape, she felt a prickle of doubt. His first stated need was for her to play his Rose. Everything else seemed to stem from that. And how genuine were they? These feelings described with such elegance and passion? For all his self-centered irritability, his undiluted rudeness when the mood took him, Edward could be utterly charming, irresistible even. But was he just turning that charm on her because he had a use for her?

"Fenella, say something, for God's sake," he said, breaking into her thoughts, tightening his grip on her hands. "I've just opened my heart to you and you're just standing there looking confused."

"I am confused," she said. "Being with you is like being on one of those switchback railways. One minute we're going one way and the next, the complete reverse."

"I suppose I deserve that," he said, releasing her hands slowly. "Come out with me this evening and I promise I will keep us both on an even keel. What d'you think?"

"I'm not dressed for dinner," she demurred.

"You don't need to dress for dinner with Ned." He watched her expression, a slight smile on his lips as he read her mobile countenance, the instant understanding of what he was offering, an evening in theatre company, well away from the provocations and irritations of Edward Tremayne's intense company and ambitions. He saw the quick flash of anticipation in her eyes, the spark of excitement, and knew he'd made the right move.

"I'll fetch my coat," Fenella said. "Wait here; I won't be a moment. Help yourself to the decanter."

She whisked herself out of the room and upstairs just as the dressing gong chimed.

Alice was in her bedroom waiting for her as she hurried in. "Alice, I'm going to be out for the evening," she said. "I'm going out with a friend. I'm not going to dress as it's going to be a very informal affair. I'll just write a quick note to Lady Grantley." She sat down at the writing desk and scribbled a few lines before handing the folded sheet to Alice. "Could you give this to my mother? And then have the rest of the evening to yourself. There's no need to wait up for me."

Alice took the letter. "Of course, Miss Fenella. Are you certain you won't be needing me anymore this evening?"

"Positive." Fenella slipped her arms into her sable coat. Informal dress might be the order of the evening, but there was no reason to freeze in her less-dressy wool coat. She turned the collar up to cover her ears, thrust her gloved hands into the sable muff and ran downstairs.

Alice shook her head on her mistress's hasty departure, reflecting that Miss Grantley was not behaving like herself these days. She went to take the note to Lady Grantley's bedroom, where she would be dressing for dinner.

Lady Grantley read Fenella's hasty scribble with a puzzled frown. She too had noticed something different about her daughter in the last several weeks. For a while she had seemed rather sad, lacking her usual sparkle. Her mother had put it down to the weather, the short days and gray skies, and had assumed her daughter would return to her usual cheerful self when the Season picked up and the social whirl was in full swing. But very recently, she had felt something a little unpredictable about Fenella. She was never one for rigid convention; she and her friends had a rebellious streak when it came to protocol, but it had never overstepped the bounds, and as long as it didn't do so, Society's grumbles would be muted at most. But Lady Grantley had recently detected an extra edge to that rebellious streak. Receiving an unknown male visitor at a most unsuitable time of day was bad enough, but to go out for the evening with that man on what was clearly the spur of the moment was quite worrying. And where did that leave Lord George Headington?

She turned on the dresser stool as the adjoining door to her husband's bedroom opened behind her. "My dear, did you meet Fenella's visitor in the hall? Edward Tremayne, I believe Fenella said."

Lord Grantley, immaculate in evening dress, held a large, cut-glass tumbler of whisky in one hand. He bent to kiss his wife's powdery cheek. "Yes. Seemed an innocuous enough fellow," he declared, standing behind her so that she could see him in her mirror.

"Well, it was a very strange time to visit, and now she's gone out for the evening with him." Lady Grantley waved Fenella's note. "She wouldn't even have had time to dress for dinner."

"Well, Fenella can be impulsive on occasion,

my dear," her husband said, taking the note from her fingers.

"But who is the man? I don't know anything about him. Is he related to Julia and Carlton Tremayne . . . to their father, Lord Pendleton?"

"He's their half brother, I believe. I seem to remember he was around briefly several years ago, did the Season, elected to White's but was never seen there. As I recall, he preferred the Garrick, one of those artist types . . . then he just disappeared."

"Half brother?" Lady Grantley questioned. "I didn't realize the earl had been married before."

"No, my dear, he wasn't. According to fairly reliable gossip in the clubs, Edward's the son of his mistress, an actress. The circumstances of his birth are not the boy's fault, and Pendleton, to do him justice, did make an effort to give him all the advantages. Eton, Oxford, London Season. Don't know what happened, but suddenly, he seemed to be persona non grata among the Tremaynes. As I said, he disappeared from the social scene completely."

"Well, he seems to have reappeared now," his wife said. "I know it's not his fault that his birth was irregular, but I can't quite like Fenella's being so free and easy with him."

"Oh, Fenella's sensible enough," Lord Grantley declared with a dismissive wave. "She's got her head screwed on straight."

"Well, I can't help feeling a little anxious," Lady Grantley said, rising from her stool, the delicate ruffles on her dark blue, silk skirt settling around her with a gentle swish. "I do so wish the darling girl would settle for Lord George. It would be such a suitable match for her, but if she's seen around with someone unsuitable, the gossips will have a field day and she'll lose all chance of an advantageous marriage."

"Grace, my dear, Fenella and George Headington would be a disaster. She would make his life a complete misery and be utterly wretched herself," her husband stated. "And I think you know that. The girl's intelligent enough and old enough to make up her own mind and steer her own course. Let us go down for dinner. I'm famished."

"I suppose you're right," Lady Grantley said, accepting defeat with a sigh. "You always are. But sometimes I wish dear Fenella were just a little more ordinary." She slipped her arm through her husband's.

"And I thank my lucky stars every day that she is not," her husband returned with a little smile as they descended the wide staircase to the dining room.

Chapter Eighteen

Fenella stretched lazily under the thick quilt covering Edward's bed. Her body felt used and satisfied, their lovemaking after a wonderfully rowdy, companionable evening in the King's Head had carried no burden of ulterior motive or unspoken need, no meaning beyond the sheer physical joy of their bodies joined in exquisite pleasure.

"What time is it?" she murmured.

"Almost two in the morning," Edward replied, straightening from the fireplace where he had been poking the logs into renewed flame. "Must you go home?" He stood naked, a smile quirking his lips.

"You look very smug, Mr. Tremayne," she said, smiling her own complacent smile over the bedclothes pulled up to her chin.

"I feel very smug," he responded. "You haven't answered my question."

Fenella debated with herself. "I should go home," she said eventually. "But I don't wish to. Not just yet. It's so cold out there and wonderfully warm in here. Besides, I'd never get a hackney at this time of night."

"No, I'm sure you're right. So that's settled. How about a nightcap?"

"What did you have in mind?" Her gray eyes gleamed.

"Hot milk and brandy, I thought," he answered.

"Is that all?" She made a comical moue of dismay.

"Have mercy, sweetheart; after that marathon, I need a little recovery time," he said, shaking his head in mock reproof.

"I could help there," she suggested, twitching a corner of the bedcovers aside in invitation.

"Insatiable creature . . . not that I don't appreciate the offer, but I'm going to heat some milk. We both need our strength."

With a sigh of resignation, Fenella propped herself against pillows, keeping the covers tight under her chin, watching as he set a pan of milk on the trivet over the fire. "I meant to ask, how did the visit to Fulham go this afternoon?"

Edward watched the first bubbles appear on the surface of the milk before answering. "Robert was right. It's a dreary space and I can't imagine anyone voluntarily trekking to an insalubrious part of Town to see a play by an unknown playwright with no known players."

Fenella grimaced. "That's harsh."

He poured the milk into a tall glass, his back to the bed. "I wish it were. But it's the unvarnished truth, I'm afraid. We'll have to find a space more inviting for the right kind of audience." He turned to the bed. "D'you want brandy in this?"

"Just a splash." Somehow, the languid warmth of afterglow had dissipated, and rather too soon for Fenella's liking.

He poured a generous slurp from the brandy bottle and brought the glass to her. "Be careful, it's hot."

She took it with a nod of thanks, inhaling the rich steam. "Aren't you having milk?"

"No, my sweet. I gave up milk in the nursery. Just brandy for me."

"Pity; you should try the adult version. It's very relaxing and soporific." She took a careful sip of the concoction. "So what now? If Fulham won't work?"

"It has to be the West End," Edward said decisively, sitting heavily on the side of the bed with his glass. He reached out a hand and lightly stroked the shape of Fenella's thighs under the covers.

She stirred lazily beneath his hand. "To attract Society, I suppose. I thought you didn't have any time for *our* kind of people."

"As a rule, I don't." He shrugged. "But I can compromise my principles for the greater good."

"How very pragmatic of you," Fenella said, only half-joking. "But you said in the pub that you don't have the finances for a West End theatre."

"Not entirely true." He stood up with a small gesture of his hand, which seemed to Fenella almost unconscious, but she read it as a signal that the subject was closed. "Have you finished that?" He took the empty glass from her.

Reluctantly, Fenella pushed aside the covers reaching for the crimson velvet dressing gown.

"Where are you going?"

"Lavatory." Holding up the voluminous, trailing skirt of the robe, she shuffled in the direction of the closet that was the nearest thing to a bathroom Edward could lay claim to. She was back in a few minutes; it was too cold for lingering. She cast aside the robe and jumped swiftly into bed. "Have you got your strength back?" She fluttered her eyelashes at him, lifting the covers.

He turned down the gas lamps and slid into bed beside her. "Oh, you're so cold," Fenella protested. "Let me warm you up." She wriggled on top of him, molding her body to his. "Is that better?"

"Much," he said, twining his hands into the golden spill of her hair, pulling her face down to his.

It was close to dawn when Fenella slipped her key into the lock and entered the house on Albemarle Street. The night doorman was no longer on duty, and already the household staff were up and about, maids clearing ash and relaying fires in the down-stairs salons, the kitchen alive with preparations for both staff and family breakfast. There was no one in the hall and Fenella hoped she could make it unseen and unnoticed to her bedroom. A maid was on her hands and knees sweeping the grand stair-case and she dodged past her with a smile of greeting and apology before finally reaching the safety of her own quarters.

Another maid was relighting the fire in the grate and looked up, startled, as Fenella came in. "Oh,

Miss Fenella, ma'am . . . I'm sorry, I thought you was still asleep."

Fenella glanced at the bed. It was conspicuously empty, but the room was dimly lit and the young girl had such a load of work to get through, she probably hadn't so much as glanced at the bed. "Don't mind me, Lizzie . . . it is Lizzie, isn't it?"

"Yes, 'm." The girl sat back on her knees and wiped a smudge of coal dust from her cheek with the bottom of her apron. The fire crackled into life and sent a warm glow through the room. "Should I draw back the curtains, Miss Grantley?"

"No, don't worry. I'll do it myself in a few minutes." Fenella smiled reassuringly and discarded her sable coat over an otttoman at the foot of the bed. The maid scurried off with her pan of ashes and Fenella undressed. It was barely six o'clock and she decided to go to bed until Alice came to wake her at her usual time. Surprisingly, she fell into a deep and dreamless sleep almost immediately, and when Alice came in and drew back the curtains, letting in a watery sunlight, it was an effort to force herself awake.

"What time did you get in, then?" Alice asked, picking up Fenella's discarded clothes. "Well, after midnight it must have been. You weren't here when I took myself to bed."

"I don't know what time it was," Fenella prevaricated, "but it was certainly sometime in the early hours."

"Well, here's your tea, nice and hot. That'll set you

up proper." Alice poured tea and handed her the cup. "Will you dress before breakfast?"

"No, I'll wait to have my bath afterward," her mistress responded, sipping her tea, her eyes half-closed. It was considered acceptable in the Grantley household for any ladies in residence to breakfast in dishabille.

In the country, at Grantley Court, Lady Grantley hosted a continuous house party, guests coming and going throughout the shooting season and well into the New Year. Fenella's mother was in her element with a house full of guests, planning meals, entertainments, placidly handling any of the complicated domestic issues that always arose at some point.

Fenella smiled to herself. Her mother was admirable in her way, the perfect product of her aristocratic, Victorian upbringing; it was no wonder she found her only daughter an unknown quantity. She was remarkably forbearing, Fenella reflected, swinging herself out of bed. It was going to be interesting to see how she reacted to the idea of her daughter on the public stage. The time had come to find that out.

She draped herself in a very fetching peignoir, put her feet in satin slippers and paused at the dresser to brush her hair and confine it at her nape with a blue ribbon. Bending close to the mirror, she examined her complexion. By rights, she should look exhausted after such an energetic night and so little sleep, but she looked the opposite: positively glowing. Her mother would see nothing amiss.

"Put this around your shoulders, Miss Fenella."

Alice bustled over with a cashmere wrap. "Silk is all very well, but it doesn't do much to keep you warm." She draped the wrap over Fenella's shoulders. "You go down and have a good breakfast. I'll have your bath drawn when you come up."

Fenella smiled her thanks and hurried downstairs to the breakfast room. Away from the cozy warmth of her own fireside, the house seemed very draughty and chill, and it was with relief that she entered the fire-warmed breakfast room, where the smell of kippers and kedgeree dominated.

Lord Grantley, reading his freshly ironed copy of the *Times*, peered over the top to greet his daughter. "Nice of you to join us, m'dear," he said. "It's not a pleasure we have very often."

"No, because I'm usually a lazy slugabed," Fenella teased, bending to kiss him.

"No wonder, with all this gadding about through the small hours," her father said, folding over his paper. "Pour me some more coffee, would you?"

Fenella did so before helping herself to a poached egg. "Mama isn't up yet?"

"Oh, she'll be down in a minute. Some crisis in the kitchen, apparently. God-awful hour for a kitchen crisis, if you ask me." He stirred sugar into his coffee.

"Oh, I'm sorry to have kept you waiting, dear . . . why, Fenella, I wasn't expecting to see you at breakfast. I'm sure you had a late night with Mr. Tremayne."

"I did, Mama, but there is something I most particularly wish to discuss with you both."

"Oh, how exciting," Lady Grantley said, her eyes shining with anticipation. "Is it about George, dear?"

Fenella sighed. "No, Mama, it's not about George. George and I are good friends, but that's all it will ever be. I'm sorry."

Lady Grantley's face fell. "Such a pity, so suitable . . . but you must know your own mind best, I suppose."

"I do, Mama."

"So, what do you need to discuss with us?" Lord Grantley prompted, spreading Gentleman's Relish liberally on a piece of toast.

"A part in a play," she said, deciding to start rather vaguely and become more concrete as the idea settled.

"Oh, that's nice, dear," her mother said, stirring sugar into her tea. "You've loved the theatricals we put on at Grantley Court during the Christmas festivities since you were a very little girl."

"Yes, that's true, I do love to act," Fenella agreed. "But this is not a play for Christmas festivities. It's a play that I hope will be put on in London in the next couple of months."

"Oh, that's unusual." Her mother looked askance. "Are your friends in it?"

"Just what is this play, Fenella?" Lord Grantley interrupted before Fenella could answer her mother.

"It's called *Sapphire*, and Edward Tremayne wrote it."

"Mr. Tremayne? Was that why he was here last evening?"

"We did have some matters about the play to discuss," she prevaricated.

"And it's to be performed in Town?" Her mother

looked even more puzzled. "It's a country house entertainment usually. Where will it take place? Whose house?"

"Not a house exactly," her daughter explained. "We thought of finding a small private theatre, where we could put on the play for friends and family." It was no good, she realized. There was no way she could even suggest the possibility of a commercial production. But if she could get them to accept a nonprivate venue, maybe the rest would be less of a shock.

"Well, I don't know, dear. It's most irregular. What do you think, my love"

"I think there's more to this than meets the eye," Lord Grantley stated, regarding his daughter closely. "You seem very well acquainted with Mr. Tremayne."

If you only knew. Fenella swallowed the inconvenient and involuntary reflection together with the bubble of laughter that came to her lips. It was far too serious a matter for misplaced humor. "I met him at a drama class I've been going to for a while," she said calmly. "Just a hobby."

"You never said anything about drama classes." Lady Grantley looked rather put out. "Who else attends them, any of your friends?"

"Actually no," Fenella admitted. "But it's all perfectly respectable, Mama. Surely you've heard of the classical actor Cedric Hardcastle . . . he has a small drama studio on Gower Street in Bloomsbury."

"Bloomsbury? That's a hotbed of socialists," declared Lord Grantley. "Full of painters and writers and so-called poets. Idle, mischief-making drifters, the lot of 'em."

"Oh, dear, it doesn't sound in the least respectable, Fenella, dearest. Is Mr. Tremayne a socialist too?"

"Probably," Fenella responded, struggling to keep a straight face. "He's a great admirer of George Bernard Shaw anyway. But then, so am I."

"Well, I want none of that socialist nonsense under *my* roof," Lord Grantley stated, pushing back his chair. "I'm going to my club." He tucked the newspaper under his arm and left the dining room.

"Oh, dear, I think you've upset your father." Lady Grantley sighed. "I do wish you'd try not to upset him with your strange notions, Fenella."

"I don't do it deliberately, Mama." Fenella drained her coffee cup. "I'm very sorry to have ruined your breakfast. I shan't say another word to upset anyone." She pushed back her chair and bent to kiss her mother's brow. "Try not to fret."

"Sometimes you make that difficult," her mother responded with a most unusual touch of acerbity.

Fenella beat a hasty retreat. At least she'd broached the subject, and even if she hadn't told the worst, she'd made a start. She felt guilty nevertheless, and for the first time was aware of a niggle of self-doubt. Was she perhaps being more than a little selfish following her dream with such single-minded passion?

But it wasn't just her dream of performing on the stage that she was following, it was also the dream of a future with Edward Tremayne, which in and of itself would be far from Grace Grantley's heart's desire for her only daughter. The two dreams were inseparable, and the biggest hurdle she could see at this point was how far she could trust Edward's stated feelings for her. If he was using her feelings for him to ensure her cooperation in fulfilling his ambition, she was being played for a fool.

A lovesick fool?

Lady Grantley, alone in the breakfast room, absently spread marmalade on a piece of toast. She felt out of sorts, and that was not the way she liked to start her day. She turned as the door opened behind her and her husband came in again.

"Did you forget something, dear?" she asked with a vague smile.

"No, Grace, but I've been thinking about this play business with Fenella."

"Oh, yes, it troubles me too," his wife said. "It's not like her to be secretive. Why has she not mentioned these drama classes before?"

"I don't know, but I don't care for it either. I've been thinking we should make an effort to get to know this Edward Tremayne. I had very little impression last evening."

"He behaved with perfect propriety," Grace pointed out.

"Well, so you'd expect. He grew up in a gentleman's household, went to all the right schools, mingled with all the right people," Lord Grantley said, a touch impatiently. "But now he's something of an unknown quantity, a renegade from Society.

If Fenella is going to continue to have dealings with him, we need to know him better."

"Yes, if you say so, dear. Of course you're right. What would you wish me to do?"

"Invite him to your dinner before the Warehams' ball."

"Oh, but George will be there," his wife protested.

"Let Fenella sort that one out. If she has dueling suitors, it'll give her a chance to sort them both out."

"Oh, dear, I do so hate it when people are at odds at my dinner table. And particularly on this night. The Warehams' masked ball marks the opening of the Season. Everyone will be there, and the gossips' tongues will be working overtime."

"You are the best, most accomplished hostess in all London, my dear. I know you'll ensure smooth sailing." His lordship bent to kiss his wife. "I'll lunch at my club."

Lady Grantley sighed as the door closed behind him. She reached for the handbell and rang it vigorously. "Ah, Collins," she said as the butler appeared in answer. "Do we have an address for Mr. Edward Tremayne?"

"Yes, my lady. He's left his card twice."

"Good. I must send him a dinner invitation . . . although it's such short notice, it's almost impolite. But Lord Grantley wishes it done." She rose from the breakfast table. "Have one of the pages deliver it as soon as I've written it, please."

"Of course, my lady." Collins held the door as Lady Grantley swept through it on the way to her parlor, where she wrote an invitation to Edward Tremayne, begging the pleasure of his company at eight of the clock on Saturday, March 1, for dinner before the Warehams' masked ball.

She read the invitation again, tapping her pen against her lips as she frowned at her perfect hand-writing. Maybe she should invite the other two Tremaynes. If Fenella was making a friend or some-thing else of Edward, it would be politic to include Julia and Viscount Grayling. Their presence would lessen any dramatic impact of Fenella's involvement with the illegitimate branch of the family and would lend family respectability to their half brother's some-what parlous position in Society.

She drew two more engraved invitations toward her.

Chapter Nineteen

Fenella took her morning bath in leisurely fashion. "Could you put out my riding habit, please, Alice?" she called through the bathroom door on a sudden whim. "And send someone to the stables for Firefly. The sun's shining and I've a mind to blow away the cobwebs."

"Certainly. It's a fine morning for a ride, Miss Fenella." Alice went off to do her errand and Fenella got out of the bath, wrapping herself in a thick toweling robe. She wrote two notes, and when Alice returned asked her to have them delivered at once to Mrs. Lacey and Miss Rutherford. If they weren't able to join her in Hyde Park on the spur of the moment, she'd ride alone.

Half an hour later, dressed in a very fetching gray tweed riding habit with a dark gray silk waistcoat, a neat bowler hat pinned to her tightly braided coronet, Fenella left the house. Her mare was standing patiently with a groom, who held the reins of his own horse as well as Fenella's at the front step. Fenella could tell from the gleam in the mare's soulful brown eyes that the horse was ready for a gallop. Galloping was frowned upon in Hyde Park, but it was one of Society's protocols that Fenella and her friends ignored at will. Firefly would get her gallop. She mounted gracefully, the maneuver made easier by the unseen, soft, chamois trousers she wore strapped beneath her boots, and nudged the mare into a walk, the groom falling in behind them.

Edward had just turned the corner onto Albemarle Street as Fenella and the groom moved off. It was a fairly safe bet they were heading for Hyde Park, and without further thought, he hailed a passing cab, giving the address of a hacking stable just outside Stanhope Gate. He wasn't dressed for riding, but then, neither was anything he was wearing practically unsuitable for the activity.

Fenella had suggested to her friends that they meet her at Speakers' Corner at Marble Arch inside Cumberland Gate, and as she trotted decorously to the meeting place they both rode into the park side by side. "What a good idea, darling," Diana declared, drawing rein. "It's such a beautiful day for once, not even that cold." She leaned sideways to brush cheeks in a fleeting kiss of greeting.

"I wish I shared your passion for horsemanship," Petra grumbled but smiling nevertheless. "It's all right in the country on a summer's day, but a sedate trot around the tan in midwinter is no fun for horse or rider."

"Then let's gallop the circuit." Without waiting for a response, Fenella nudged Firefly into a canter and then a full gallop. Her friends needed no encouragement, and the groom, perfectly accustomed to his mistress's habits, followed at a more subdued canter.

Edward was just entering the Park on his jobbing horse, a raw-boned, hard-mouthed hack, with a way-ward temperament, when he first caught sight of his quarry flying past the gate, followed closely by her friends. He watched them for a moment, chuckling at their blatant disregard for the unspoken rules. Then he kicked his horse firmly into motion and, after a startled second, the animal broke into a canter and then a gallop, throwing up his head with a snort of pleasure.

Petra heard the pounding hooves behind them first and turned her head briefly. The rider's long scarf flew behind him, his hair whipped away by the wind. He was not dressed for riding, not even wear-ing a hat, was her first impression; then she turned her attention back to her own mount, who was slow-ing gradually. She let the animal slow to a genteel trot and her companions followed suit.

"Magnificent, ladies," Edward said, drawing level with them, offering a mock bow even as he kept a firm hand on the reins of his unruly horse, whose ca-vorting seemed to indicate resentment at the end of the gallop. "I couldn't resist joining you; you seemed to be having such a good time."

"Diana, Petra, are you acquainted with Edward Tremayne?" Fenella asked, catching her breath after the energetic ride. "Mrs. Lacey, Miss Rutherford, Edward." She waved a hand between them. Edward's tweed jacket with leather-patched elbows and his faded corduroy trousers were definitely not Hyde Park wear, but she couldn't ignore how well he sat his horse. His tall, powerful figure looked very much at

home even on the jobbing hack and his easy hold on
the reins was exerting sufficient authority to control the restless animal.

"I believe we may have met a few years ago, Mr.
Tremayne," Diana said pleasantly.

"Yes, before you disappeared from Society altogether," Petra put in with her customary bluntness.
"Not that anyone would blame you, with such an unpleasant family. Julia is pure poison and Carlton is
dumber than a dodo."

"Were dodo's dumb?" Edward inquired with a
quizzical smile. "How are we to know?"

"Well, they allowed themselves to die out," Petra
said, laughing. "Bad analogy, I accept, but you know
what I mean."

"I do indeed. Should we continue? We don't want
the horses to get chilled after a sweaty gallop."

They fell into an easy group, continuing on the
sandy path devoted to horse and carriage traffic that
ringed the park, a pedestrian path running alongside.

Edward seemed to be turning his full charm on
her friends, Fenella thought with amusement, even
as she wondered why, instead of his usual disdainful
distance, he had chosen to be so charming. He could
be the most entertaining companion when it suited
him and, apparently, for some reason, it suited him
right now. Diana and Fenella responded to his wit
and light banter, and they were all laughing when
they reached Stanhope Gate once again.

"I wish I could continue this ride, but I have people
coming for lunch," Diana said. "They're fellow officers

and Rupert is not happy about entertaining them, so I need to be there to smooth troubled waters."

"Why's he not happy?" Petra inquired with customary curiosity.

"Too complicated to go in to now, dearest. I'll tell you when I see you next time. Goodbye, Mr. Tremayne. I'm delighted to have become properly acquainted." She reached over with gloved hand outstretched.

Edward shook it warmly. "The pleasure is all mine, ma'am." He turned his attention to Petra. "Are you leaving us too, Miss Rutherford?"

"Unfortunately I must," Petra said, shaking his hand. "Besides," she added with a mischievous wink, "I have no desire to overstay my welcome. I'll see you anon, Fenella."

"Yes . . . before the Warehams' ball anyway. I want another opinion on my dress."

"At your service as always, darling." Petra blew her a kiss and turned her horse toward the gate.

"I'll see Miss Grantley home," Edward said to the groom. "There's no need for you to wait around." He swung off his horse. "Take Miss Grantley's mount back to the mews with you. I'm leaving mine at the jobbing stable. We can take a cab from here." He came to Fenella's stirrup and offered her a hand to dismount.

"I suppose it doesn't occur to you that I might have another pressing engagement?" Fenella asked as she slid to the ground, speaking softly enough that the groom couldn't hear as he secured the stirrups on the mare and looped her reins over his free hand before leading her off.

Edward frowned. "Do you?"

"Well, no, as it happens."

"Then why say you do?"

"I said I *might.*" She bit her lip, wondering whether to continue. But there was no point not saying things because she was afraid of putting him in a bad mood. That was no basis for a friendship, let alone for anything more intimate. She took a breath. "It's just that sometimes I feel you take me for granted, Edward."

He stared at her, the frown darkening the intense blue of his eyes. "Do I? Is that what it seems to you?"

"Sometimes, yes." She met his gaze steadily.

He pulled at his chin, considering what appeared to be a novel idea. After a minute, he said slowly, "I suppose that's true. I'm not accustomed to considering the views and wishes of other people. I live alone."

"Is that cause or effect?" she asked. His answer seemed to matter a great deal and she was barely breathing as she waited.

"I don't really know," he said finally. "There are people whose company I love and others whose company I would do anything to avoid. You come into the first category. Is that good enough, Fenella?"

It would have to be, she thought. One thing was clear: In general, the people whose company he enjoyed came from his mother's world, the world of his early childhood years. He had no time for his father's world, and given how that world had treated him, it was not surprising. But where did she come in? Her interest in drama perhaps enabled her to straddle both worlds in his view.

"Fenella?" he prompted as her thoughtful silence continued.

She looked up, focusing her attention once more. "Why did you join us this morning? As you just said, in general you avoid contact with Society, and my friends are well entrenched in that world, as am I, but you were all charm. You even seemed to enjoy them."

"Is it beyond the realm of possibility that I might want to get to know people who matter to you?" he inquired, his eyebrows raised. "Am I really such an irredeemably graceless wretch?"

Fenella wondered if she had gone too far. She said hastily, "No, that wasn't what I said. But you are a man of contradiction. You must admit that."

"That rather depends on your viewpoint. Now, do we have to continue this dissection of my admittedly deeply flawed character in the middle of the street, or can we go somewhere more private?"

She *had* gone too far. She said with a contrite smile, "Oh, dear, I'm sorry, Edward. The conversation seemed to take charge of itself. Forgive me."

He nodded curtly, then led his horse toward the entrance to the stables. Fenella followed, wondering what was to come next, unsure whether he had accepted her apology or not.

The horse safely returned, they left the stables and stood for a moment on the street. "Lunch?" Edward said as if it was a suggestion. Fenella felt a surge of relief. He was obviously prepared to let the uncomfortable conversation lapse.

"Where did you have in mind?" she asked. "Have you reserved a table somewhere?"

"No, I didn't start this morning expecting it to end like this," he stated. "But if you won't consider it too presumptuous, I have a suggestion. There's a decent pub in Shepherd Market. Just around the corner. I'm not really dressed for anywhere special."

"You haven't accepted my apology, have you?" She faced him, meeting his gaze.

Edward looked at her for a moment, then suddenly laughed. "I have many flaws, but I don't hold grudges, and I actually accept some of your points." He spread his hands wide in a gesture of concession. "Now, will you allow me to take you to lunch at the Shepherd's Crook? They do an excellent Lancashire hotpot, as well as shepherd's pie, as you might expect. But they do have rather more refined offerings . . ."

"Both sound delicious and I'm famished. Come on, let's go." She took his hand and pulled him urgently after her, determined now that there would be no more bickering over lunch. Unless, of course, he insisted on discussing his notes from yesterday's rehearsal. Fenella suppressed a sigh.

"Why the sigh?" He slowed his step, regarding her with a raised brow.

"No real reason," she replied. "I assume we're going to discuss your notes from the run-through?"

"And you don't wish to," he stated, eyebrow still quirked.

"It's not that exactly. But I would like to enjoy lunch without quarreling."

"I swear, there will be no arguing on my part," he

declared, laying a hand on his heart. "But can you answer for yourself, Miss Grantley?"

"That rather depends on what you have to say."

"How about we declare a *Sapphire*-free zone over lunch?" he suggested. "I know I am bound to put your back up with some of the things I have to say about yesterday's rehearsal."

Fenella grimaced but acknowledged the suggestion with a nod of acceptance and took Edward's proffered arm for the short walk down Curzon Street to bustling Shepherd Market. The pub was full, but Edward pushed through the crowd, a protective arm around Fenella, toward the back of the saloon bar, where a narrow door opened onto a small snug. It was mercifully empty after the noisy crowd in the saloon bar.

"Sit down by the fire and I'll order a drink from the bar." Edward guided Fenella into a deep armchair by the inglenook fireplace. She sat down and was instantly engulfed in its tobacco- and beer-smelling depths.

"I'm lost in here," she complained with a laugh, waving her booted feet, which barely touched the floor.

"Too insalubrious for you?" he inquired with the touch of sarcasm she hated.

"Not in the least," she returned smartly, "so don't look so supercilious. It doesn't suit you."

Edward threw back his head and laughed. "You are a wondrous companion, Miss Grantley. I can always be certain you will pull me up if I show the slightest indication of getting above myself."

Fenella bit her tongue on the retort that came to mind. They had agreed not to bicker, and while sometimes it was fun to cross verbal swords, it was probably better it didn't become their preferred method of communication.

"What does one drink in a pub?" she asked. "I'm not in the mood for beer."

"Well, most of the women here are probably drinking shandy or port and lemon," he said. "But I know you drink sherry, so let me get you a glass."

Fenella sat back in her chair, growing accustomed to its various smells and feeling oddly comfortable in its cushioned depths. The rise and fall of the voices from the bar beyond the snug became a pleasant background noise and she felt her eyes drooping.

"Wake up, sweetheart. All that cold, fresh air and exercise seem to have knocked you out." Edward set a schooner of sherry on the table beside her and stood smiling down at her as she came back to full awareness. He held a pewter tankard of Guinness in one hand, one foot negligently resting on the brass fender before the fire.

"That and a sleepless night," she reminded him with a small smile, lifting the large glass of pale, straw-colored sherry. "This is huge, Edward. A schooner of dry sherry will knock me flat. An ordinary-size glass would have done."

"You don't have to drink it all. Now, what would you like for lunch? As I said, I can recommend the shepherd's pie and the hotpot. But if you'd prefer smoked salmon and brown bread, or vegetable soup, or veal and ham pie . . . ? Your choice."

"Hotpot," she replied promptly.

"Two hotpots it is. I'll be right back." He went to the door and called above the voices, "Two pots, Nick, if you please." Then he stepped back into the snug and half-closed the door. "Warmer now?"

"Very cozy," she replied, taking a sip of sherry. It seemed to go straight to her toes. "By the way, I told my parents over breakfast about this theatrical project."

Edward's expression seemed to tighten, his mouth to straighten. "Well?"

"Well, nothing really. My mother seemed convinced it was merely a theatrical game we were planning to play, as we always play them around Christmas at home in Grantley Court, and other country houses. She was puzzled as to why we would want to interrupt the fun of the Season with such an activity, but I gave up trying to get her to understand the reality." She shrugged, stretching her booted feet to the fire.

"And Lord Grantley?" His eyes narrowed as he watched her expression. He had the conviction that her father would be a lot more likely to be on the ball than his lady wife.

"Hard to say. He's often quite difficult to read, but I don't believe he was satisfied with my description of a small production in a small theatre. But fortunately, he got onto the subject of the heresy of socialism and Shaw and that drove other considerations out of his mind."

"He doesn't approve of either, then?"

Fenella laughed. "Oh, dear me, no. He'd drive 'em all out of Town with a horsewhip given the chance."

"Well, we cannot choose the families we're born in to," Edward said lightly.

To Fenella's relief, he let the statement stand without further elaboration and she turned with relief to the door as a server came into the snug with a laden tray giving off the most toothsome smells.

They ate in a voracious silence until Edward pushed aside his empty plate and leaned back in his chair, watching Fenella finish her own lunch, a reflective smile hovering on his lips. He loved the way she never hid her appetites for whatever gave her pleasure, never exhibiting any of the social pretenses of ladylike reticence. He'd observed his sister often enough waving away some treat on the grounds that she couldn't possibly eat another morsel, while her eyes told quite the opposite story, just as she sat through musical recitals that bored her stiff and afterward poured fulsome praise on the musicians. He'd watched her droop in the sun, waving a bottle of sal volatile under her nose until she'd gathered sufficient audience to ensure she was the center of attention. To his knowledge, Julia had never fainted in her life and was as strong as an ox.

"That was delicious." Fenella finally set down her fork and took a last sip of sherry. "I didn't realize how famished I was."

"What would you like to do now?"

"Have a long nap," she responded promptly. "I'd happily stay here all afternoon."

"I can promise a warm fire and a comfortable sofa if you can force yourself outside and into a hackney," he offered.

Fenella considered the offer, her eyes narrowing. "But does that come with a helping of critical commentary on my performance at yesterday's read-through?"

"We have to go through it sometime," Edward said. "But I promise you a long fireside nap first, followed by tea and madeira cake. Then, and only then, will we have a civilized discussion, and I stress *discussion*. You are free to respond in any way you wish to anything I may say."

"In other words, we have carte blanche to fight to the death," she said, only half in jest.

"It doesn't have to be that way, sweetheart." He took her hand and gently pressed his lips into her palm. "Indeed, I have mostly praise for your reading; there are just one or two small points."

Fenella closed her eyes for a moment. It was too hard to think with that penetrating blue gaze fixed upon her and the warmth of his fingers enclosing hers. Eventually, she opened her eyes and looked directly into Edward's steady but slightly questioning gaze. "Why can't we go through your notes, the whole cast, at the next rehearsal? Why do you need to do this with just me now? You're not the director. Cedric should be part of this critique."

"But I thought you'd like my direct input, I thought you'd benefit from it," Edward said, sounding both confused and disconcerted.

But Fenella had made up her mind. She wanted to love . . . to make love . . . with Edward Tremayne. She could think of little else, and when she wasn't with him, she felt a void, an all-encompassing sense that some piece of herself, of her life was missing. Somehow, she had to separate Rose and *Sapphire* from any other aspects of her growing feelings for their creator.

"No, Edward, I don't want any direct conversations with only you about my performance in rehearsals. Our personal relationship has nothing to do with the project. I'll hear what you have to say when everyone else does."

His face closed and he let her hand drop. "And if I consider that unacceptable . . . ?"

"Then we've reached an insurmountable problem." Her voice was soft but determined as she fought to hide her internal struggle from him. So much was at stake, even, she now acknowledged, her future happiness. This was no casual liaison fueled simply by lustful delight in each other's body. She was in love and couldn't imagine a future without him. But some part of that future had to be on her terms.

She wanted to get up and walk away, feeling her definitive statement required some physical punctuation, but she was so deeply ensconced in the chair, she couldn't see how to get out of it with the determined grace the gesture required.

"Your mind is made up?" Edward asked into the silence.

Fenella nodded. "I don't see any other way except to keep the two things separate. I seem to have feelings for you, Edward, and for that to work for me, we have to have an equal playing field. *Sapphire* is a part of you, but it isn't a part of me. I'm learning to be an actor, and that's vitally important to me. Your play is one way I have of learning, and that's what it means for me. I know and respect the fact that it goes much deeper for you, and I will continue to respect that and give you everything I can onstage, but offstage, we're different, *real* people. Can you understand what I mean?"

He stared into the fire for a few moments as Fenella waited, holding her breath. Then Edward shrugged and turned back to her. "So be it. Come, let's go home." He leaned over to grasp both her hands, hauling her up and out of the chair, giving her a final pull so she landed against his chest, his arms tight around her so that she could feel the steady beat of his heart.

Fenella couldn't quite believe in his swift concession. She'd been braced for a major storm and the possible end of everything; instead she was enclosed in a powerful hug, inhaling the familiar, faintly spicy scents of his body, his breath rustling through her hair.

Chapter Twenty

Edward's apartment was warm, the fire bright and the gas lamps lit, their wicks turned low. "Good," he pronounced, escorting Fenella into the sitting room. "Harvey did what he was supposed to. Shall I take your jacket?"

"In a minute. I'll just warm up a little first." She went to the fire, stripping off her kid riding gloves to hold up her bare hands to the fire's warmth. Her eye fell on an engraved card on the mantel. She stared at the familiar, elegant cursive lettering. She would know her mother's writing anywhere. She also recognized the card without having to read it. It was an invitation to the dinner Lady Grantley was giving before the Warehams' ball.

"Ah," Edward said, following her astounded gaze. "Yes, I received a most kind invitation from your mother to dinner before that masked ball that's supposed to kick off the Season."

"But . . . but you're surely not going to the ball," she stammered, turning slowly to face him.

He shrugged. "I received an invitation. I always do

for such events. I may be a by-blow, but I still bear the Tremayne name." His tone was lightly cynical. "I declined it, as I always do, very comme il faut."

"So you declined the dinner invitation as well," Fenella said, wondering why she felt so relieved.

"No, of course I didn't. I accepted Lady Grantley's kind invitation with all due protestations of thanks."

So much for relief. Fenella shook her head, bemused. "But you're not going to the ball, you just said so."

"Yes, I know I did," he agreed calmly. "But no one will remember that if I did decide to put in an appearance. The world and his wife will be there; no one would even notice me."

All of which was probably true, Fenella acknowledged. There would be several hundred masked guests at the ball, and even though the masks were not truly intended to disguise anyone's identity, they could certainly make it easier to blend in with the crowd.

"You don't look happy," he observed, with a slight twist of his lips. "Would you prefer that I declined your mother's invitation?"

"Yes, of course I would," she said with more than a touch of impatience. "She's curious about you after your unorthodox visits and the fact that I went out for the evening alone with you . . . and there's George . . ." Her voice faded.

"George?" he questioned with raised brows. "What George is this?"

"Lord George Headington," she replied, telling

herself there was no reason to prevaricate. "He's the second son of the Duke of Wellborough."

"And he's been lavishing attention upon you?"

"We've been friends since my first Season," she said vaguely. "He acts as my escort on various occasions."

Edward frowned. He had the feeling Fenella was holding something back, but he had no right to pry. "I see," he said. "And Lady Grantley would obviously like to see her daughter married to the son of a duke, even if he's not the heir." His tone was dryly matter-of-fact.

"You've got it in one," Fenella agreed. "And George will be at the dinner party. My mother knows I have no intention of marrying him, but she still has hopes, although she tries to hide them, poor soul. My father doesn't mind one way or the other," she added.

Edward tried to imagine what it must be like to be a conventional Victorian mother to a daughter as unusual and freethinking as Fenella. He was still struggling with his decision to reenter the world he so despised, but as his interest in Fenella grew, the more necessary it became. And it would be essential that he make a good impression on Lady Grantley. He would also like to see this Lord George for himself.

"Tea?" he suggested, picking up the kettle.

Fenella unbuttoned her riding jacket, tossing it untidily over the back of the sofa, from which it slipped to the floor. "Yes, thank you."

Edward set the kettle on the trivet over the fire

and went to pick up her jacket, shaking it out and then hanging it on a hook on the back of the door. "There's no lady's maid here, my dear girl."

"How very prissy of you," Fenella accused. "It's not in the least like you."

Edward merely laughed. "You look so neat and trim in that waistcoat and silk shirt. I've always approved of female riding habits." His eyes narrowed, enlivened by a sudden, unmistakable gleam of pure lust. "Take off the skirt?"

And that was the end of any clear thinking as far as Fenella was concerned. She unhooked the flowing riding skirt at her waist and stepped out of it, bending to pick it up, shake it out and very deliberately hang it on the hook with her jacket. Then she turned to face him, hands on her hips, an unmistakable challenge in her eyes.

The chamois leather britches molded her hips, thighs and calves and were strapped under her boots. The gray silk waistcoat was nipped in at her waist over the black-and-gray-striped silk shirt. A wide cravat formed the neckline of the shirt. "Satisfied, sir?" she queried.

"God, but you're so provocative," he murmured, running his gaze over her. "I want you *now*." The kettle whistled from the trivet and he swore softly, turning to lift it off the heat, setting it down on the brick hearth.

When he turned back, Fenella was naked, except for her boots. She smiled mischievously. "I'll pick up my clothes once I've taken off my boots."

For answer, he pushed her back onto the sofa, lifted her feet one by one and yanked off her boots and stockings. He reached for her hands and pulled her to her feet. "Now, you can pick them up."

Fenella was aware of his eyes on her as she bent to pick up her clothes, making every movement slow and seductive, turning from side to side so that his view was constantly changing. She arranged her garments carefully over the back of a chair at the table, standing back for a moment to assess the arrangement. "Will that satisfy you, sir?"

For answer, he caught her up in his arms, holding her naked body easily as he looked down at her, his eyes smoky with desire. "Just be quiet and still," he directed. "I'm in the mood for a plaything."

Somewhere in the recesses of her mind, Fenella registered that he had said play*thing* and not play-*mate*. It sounded as if he wanted total control of this lovemaking, and for the moment she was content to give it to him. She relaxed her limbs, lying heavily in his arms as he leaned over and half-dropped, half-laid her on the sofa. She lay watching him as he stripped off his clothes, letting them lie where they fell. She was about to point this out to him when she remembered his demand for silence. If he wanted to play, Fenella was very happy to be played with.

And played with she was; he moved her body as he wished, raised her legs over his shoulders and put his mouth to her core, his tongue teasing the nub of her sex until she heard herself groan with pleasure and need. He raised his head long enough to tell her to make no sound before returning to his goal, his hands slipping beneath her, lifting her hips off the cushions as his tongue dipped deeper within her, and she bit her lip hard to keep from crying out as her body convulsed around his tongue. And when he was done there, he flipped her onto her belly and nibbled his way down her spine from the nape of her neck to the cleft of her buttocks, his tongue licking and tickling until her skin was so sensitized, it would take the merest flick of a touch to send her over the edge again.

She felt him move away from her, leaving her for a second to feel lonely and abandoned, and then he was back, turning her over again onto her back.

"Close your eyes."

Fenella was so lost to herself now that she obeyed automatically and then felt something on her nipples. They were already hard and erect, and the light touch of whatever he manipulated so skillfully was more than she could bear in silence. As pleasure flooded her body, invading every hidden corner, every private, sensual spot, every inch of her sensitized skin, she heard herself scream with uncontrollable delight. His mouth came down on hers, silencing her as her body jerked beneath his, dominated now only by the all-consuming consummation of passion.

When it was over, she lay still, exhausted by sensations that had overwhelmed her, made her merely a sensate being with no will, no mind of her own, and now, as her senses slowly returned, Fenella felt a tiny tremor of dismay that someone could have the power to do that to her. What if she had fought him, refused to let him have his way? Could she have retained control of her responses, kept her clarity of mind? It was a disconcerting question.

Edward looked down at her, a soft smile on his lips. "I didn't know what to expect, but you exceeded every possible expectation, my sweet. I have never experienced such a sensitive and responsive lover. And I know I have no right to say this, but I do hope no one else has experienced that with you."

Fenella managed a faint smile and shook her head. "I have never experienced anything like that before this moment. But now I should reciprocate, only I don't have the energy. I'm so sorry."

"There'll be another time," Edward said. "Besides, I took enormous pleasure from yours. I am satisfied, my love. Would you like tea now?"

"No, I'm going to sleep," she replied. "I don't seem able to help it."

He went into the bedroom and came back with a quilt, tossing it over her. "I have to go to the college library for a while. No more than an hour or so. The fire should stay on, but if you should happen to wake and think to put more wood on, that would be helpful."

"Yes," she murmured dopily.

He bent and kissed her forehead. "Sleep well, now."

The door closed behind him and Fenella turned her head idly on the cushion, settling more comfortably. Her eye fell on something white on the floor beside the sofa. It was a feather. So that was what he had used to stimulate her breasts. She fell asleep thinking of how she could return the favor, and what part of Edward's body would be most sensitive to the feathery torment.

She awoke an hour or so later, stretching languidly beneath the coverlet before slowly hitching herself up onto her elbows to look around the room. There was no sign of Edward yet. Throwing off the coverlet, she got to her feet still a little groggy.

Fire, that was what she was supposed to do. She knelt to throw another log on the diminishing glow and poked it into life, then sat back on her heels gazing into the renewed blaze. It still felt as if she was inhabiting a dreamworld, the edges blurred and her mind foggy. Her eye fell on a scrap of paper that must have fallen from the piles of them on the table, and she leaned sideways, stretching her arm to pick it up, thinking to return it to the table.

Her gaze sharpened. There was a name: *William Garrett. Manager.* And an address*: Music Box Theatre, Wellington Street.*

Fenella smoothed out the crumpled sheet, frowning. Was Edward considering this venue for *Sapphire*? It was in the heart of Covent Garden, but he'd said he needed a less expensive location than the West End. Maybe he had more money than his lifestyle indicated, but that didn't mean he could afford a West End theatre to put on his play. It would be a hugely expensive project.

She stood up to put the paper back on the table, memorizing the name and address, a vague idea forming in her still somewhat foggy brain, her mind and body still reverberating with the vivid physical memories of the afternoon's play. *Tea*, she thought; that would clear her head.

She had just set the teapot on a trivet in the hearth when Edward came in. "Nice sleep?" he asked, unwrapping his scarf.

"Delicious," she replied. "I've just made tea. Shall I pour?"

"Lovely, yes. And then we'll go out."

"Oh, must we?" she groaned, pouring tea into two cups. "It's so warm and cozy in here and I feel too languid to go out in the cold."

"A breath of fresh air will do you good," he responded without a hint of sympathy, taking the cup from her. "We'll have supper in Covent Garden if you care to."

That put a different complexion on the matter. "Ah, an evening with Ned?" Fenella queried, looking up at him over her teacup.

"Most certainly," he replied with a chuckle.

"Then how can I refuse?" She set aside her empty cup and unwound herself from the quilt. Edward went into the bedroom and reemerged carrying an opera cloak of the finest gray wool, lined with black silk.

"You need something warmer than just that riding habit," he said. "It's colder than this morning." He held up the cloak. "You can carry this off. It was the one I had when I was about thirteen. I can't think why I still have it."

Fenella wrapped herself with a flourish in the soft wool and silk. "It's lovely. Warm, but so stylish."

"The design of opera cloaks doesn't change much over the years . . . come now, let's go and find a cab." He swept her ahead of him down the stairs and back out onto the lamplit street. A cab appeared just as he pulled the door shut and he waved it down. "Tavistock Square," he instructed the driver before opening the door for Fenella.

"Oh," she said, stopping dead, one foot poised on the footstep. "I forgot my gloves."

"I'll fetch them. Get in the cab." He turned back into the house.

Fenella stepped back into the street and called up to the driver on the box, "Could we go down Wellington Street?"

He shrugged, saying amenably, "Good a way as any."

"Thank you." She climbed hastily into the interior just as Edward came out of the house, holding her gloves in one hand.

"Here." He dropped them on her lap as he climbed in opposite her.

Fenella pulled them on with a smile of thanks. "I can't think why I forgot them." She leaned sideways to look out of the window as the cab started forward. When they turned down Wellington Street, she stared out into the shadowy, narrow, cobbled street. There were only two gas lamps quite far apart, so it was hard to distinguish the buildings, but as luck would have it, the light from one of the streetlamps spilled onto a neglected-looking building bearing a faint sign seriously in need of a coat of paint: *Music Box Theatre.*

She sat back, satisfied. "So, where are we going on Tavistock Square?"

Chapter Twenty-One

Fenella had not expected an evening of charades in an upper room of the Rose and Crown on Tavistock Square. At first, she'd been a bit intimidated by the game played with people who made their living on the stage but had quickly overcome her anxiety. In Ned's company and the company of his friends, she became a different person, or at least it felt like it. She could lose her sense of self, forget the rules that circumscribed her daily life, forget the idly malicious gossip that passed for conversation. She laughed until she cried, drank far more wine than was good for her and reveled in seeing the real Edward, a man who laughed, created ingenious clues that he acted out with vigorous enthusiasm, who thought nothing of kissing her with sheer exuberance regardless of an audience.

"That was the most wonderful evening I've ever spent," she declared, stumbling out into the cold night just before midnight, her arm firmly tucked into Edward's. "I don't think I've ever had so much fun."

"I'm glad," he said, holding her up as her foot

caught in a space between the cobbles. "Careful, now. You've had at least one glass more than is wise."

"Oh, I couldn't care less," she said, flinging her free arm wide. "I wish I could stay in this world forever."

"Is your world that bad?" he asked, pausing as he continued to hold her tight against his side.

"No, it's not bad, it's just dull . . . very, very dull," she pronounced. "There's no color to it anymore, and this world . . ." Again she flung out an expansive arm, "this world is bright and full of color."

"Not always," Edward said quietly. "There's unhappiness and tedium here too, my dear girl."

"Well, there wasn't any tonight," Fenella returned stoutly.

"I'll give you that," he said, smiling and bundling her into a hackney that had stopped beside them. "Albemarle Street," he called up and leaned in to kiss her. "I feel like walking home, so good night, sweetheart." He stepped back before she could demur and closed the door firmly.

Fenella leaned out of the window as he walked away, feeling a sudden sense of loss. She didn't want to go back to her own drab world, to worrying about George's feelings, her mother's aspirations, a daily routine that wasn't worth anticipating. And even as she acknowledged that, she knew how ungrateful she was, how very fortunate she was to live as she did. The recognition didn't help, just made the feeling of anticlimax worse.

The cab drew to a halt outside the house on Albemarle Street, and Fenella stepped out, aware that her eyes were suddenly misted with unbidden tears. Anticlimax after too much wine and excitement, she told herself severely. She fumbled in her coin purse to pay the driver, unsure what coins she gave him, though he seemed happy enough, and the hackney pulled away as she hurried to the front door, which opened as she reached it.

"Good evening, Miss Grantley." Collins greeted her with a bow. "Lady Grantley's last guests have just left and I was about to lock up."

Fenella managed only a murmur and a brief nod of acknowledgment before hurrying, head down, to the stairs.

"Good heavens, darling, why are you in such a hurry . . . and what on earth are you wearing?" Lady Grantley's voice from the galleried landing at the head of the stairs stopped Fenella in her tracks.

"Mama, forgive me, but I'm so very tired, I can hardly take another step." Fenella climbed the last few steps and brushed past her mother, praying only to reach the sanctuary of her bedroom without extending the encounter.

Lady Grantley looked astonished. "Did you see Fenella, my dear?" she asked her husband, who was walking toward her along the gallery. "Whatever was she wearing?"

"Looked like an opera cloak to me," Lord Grantley responded.

"But it was a *man's* cloak," Lady Grantley said. "And why was she running as if a pack of fox hounds were on her heels?"

"I suggest you ask her, my dear," her husband said patiently. "But not at this hour. It's gone midnight.

I'm looking forward to a single malt in front of the library fire before bed. Will you join me in a glass of madeira?" He offered his arm.

Lady Grantley hesitated, as if unsure what to do, but then, as usual, accepted her husband's wisdom and took his arm to descend the stairs. "I confess I am getting ever more worried about Fenella."

"The girl's quite capable of looking after herself," her husband declared in bracing tones.

"But what if she's . . . if she's in some kind of trouble?" his wife finished with a deep sigh.

"What kind of trouble?" Lord Grantley asked sharply as he ushered his wife into the library.

Lady Grantley shook her head. "Oh, I don't know, I really don't know. But she's not herself, hasn't been for several weeks. Could it have anything to do with that Mr. Tremayne?"

"Your guess is as good as mine, my dear." Her husband handed her a glass of madeira before pouring himself a generous measure of single malt from the cut-glass decanter on the sideboard. "But I trust Fenella not to do anything stupid, and I suggest you do the same. She's just a bit emotional at the moment . . . probably some kind of female thing," he added with a cough.

"Perhaps you're right." Grace sipped her madeira, trying to take comfort from her husband's sanguine attitude.

Fenella, unaware of the turmoil she had caused her mother, was standing in front of the fire trying to stop the ludicrous flow of tears for which she could

find no cause when the knock on the door brought
Alice, alerted to Fenella's return by Collins. She
turned and waved her away. "I don't need you this
evening, Alice, thank you."

Alice frowned at her usually calm and composed
mistress, noticing the tear stains on her cheeks, her
slightly puffy, reddened eyes, and her strange costume. "I don't recall seeing that opera cloak before.
May I hang it up for you?" She moved to divest
Fenella of the unknown garment.

"Don't worry, Alice, it doesn't belong to me. I'll
send it back in the morning." Fenella tried not to
sound ungracious. "And I'll put myself to bed,
thank you."

"Very well, Miss Fenella." Alice added coal to the
fire and adjusted the velvet curtains tightly against
the cold darkness outside. "Would you like me to
draw you a bath?"

The idea was instantly appealing. "Yes, please,
Alice, it's just what I need." She threw off Edward's
cloak and began to undress for the second time since
lunch. Soon she lay in the soothing, rose-scented
water and stayed for a long time, her eyes closing as
her body relaxed into its warmth. Slowly, she allowed her mind to examine the idea that had come
to her earlier. She pictured the deserted theatre on
Wellington Street. It had looked in need of some renovations; obviously it was not in present use. But how
difficult would it be to put it back into service?

Her spirits lifted with a surge of anticipation at the
prospect of such a project and what it would mean for
Edward. Her inexplicable low mood vanished as if it

had never been, and she wriggled her toes beneath the water as she made plans.

Sitting before the fire in her dressing gown later, she wrote notes to Diana and Petra, asking them to come around as soon after breakfast as they could. She set the letters aside to give to Alice first thing in the morning and took herself to bed, where she fell instantly into a deep and dreamless sleep.

She awoke just before dawn and lay listening to the sounds of daybreak on Albemarle Street. The heavy wheels of a dray on the cobbles, the clatter of horses' hooves, the clang of milk churns and the growing chorus of birdsong. It was growing louder these days, the first real harbinger of spring. A girl tiptoed in with a dustpan and brush and a coal scuttle, closing the door with exaggerated quiet behind her. She knelt before the cold grate and riddled the ashes, cleaning the grate before restarting the fire.

Fenella wanted to say good morning but was afraid the girl would assume she had been guilty of waking the sleeping Miss Grantley. It wouldn't give her day a good start at all, so she lay still, waiting until the maid had tiptoed out with her ashpan and now-empty coal scuttle. Then she pushed aside the covers and stood up, curling her toes into the lush softness of the Axminster carpet. The fire was already warming the air as she padded to the window to pull back the curtains. The sun was making a weak and watery appearance, but it was definitely going to be a bright day.

Diana and Petra would arrive after breakfast, unless curiosity brought them earlier. She had deliberately given them no reason for the urgent summons, partly because her thoughts were still fuzzy, her plan unformed. The evening's wine hadn't encouraged clarity, of course, but her mind was like crystal this morning. She reached for the bell to summon Alice.

"Why d'you think Fenella needs to see us so urgently?" Diana asked Petra as they stepped out of a hackney on Albemarle Street. "She's usually so imperturbable, but her note sounded almost . . . almost . . ."

"Excited," Petra supplied. "And I'll lay odds it has everything to do with Edward Tremayne."

"She's certainly less composed since she met him," Diana said thoughtfully, reaching for the lion's head door knocker. "And more like her old self. She'd seemed a bit gloomy until just recently." She lifted the knocker and let it fall with a clang against the metal plate beneath it. "Did you like him, Petra?"

"He was certainly charming, but—" she broke off as the door swung open.

"Good morning, ladies." Collins greeted them with a bow. "Miss Fenella is waiting for you in the yellow salon."

"Thank you, Collins." Diana stepped past him and hurried for the stairs. "We'll show ourselves up." She knocked once perfunctorily on the salon door and opened it. "What's going on, dearest? Petra and I are agog."

"Yes, agog," Petra repeated, coming in behind Diana. "We're all ears."

"I want you to come with me to look at a run-down theatre," Fenella said without preamble. "I've just sent a message to the manager to expect us at ten o'clock."

Petra glanced up at the clock on the mantel. "It's only half past eight and I haven't had any breakfast."

"I'm sorry to drag you out so early, but I am on tenterhooks and can barely contain myself." Fenella pulled the bellpull beside the fire.

"Well, so far you've only given us a fraction of the story," Diana pointed out. "Why are we going to look at a dilapidated theatre?"

Fenella opened her mouth to explain just as Alice opened the door. "Good morning, Mrs. Lacey, Miss Rutherford. Is there something I can get for you, Miss Fenella?"

"Coffee, please, Alice, and . . . ?" She glanced interrogatively toward her friends.

"Muffins," Petra declared. "We passed a muffin man on the way and the smell was heavenly."

"Do you think you could find muffins, Alice?" Fenella asked with a smile.

"Oh, I think we can manage that, Miss Fenella." Alice bobbed a curtsy and left.

"So . . ." Diana prompted once they were alone.

"Edward needs a theatre for *Sapphire*," Fenella began. "And I am going to surprise him with one.

I suspect he can't afford a West End venue; in fact, he basically said as much. But he must have been looking, because I found an address and the name of the manager of a theatre on Wellington Street, which is just off the Piazza, in his rooms. We went past it in a hackney last night. It looked rather run-down, but I thought I'd take a proper look and just see . . . oh, thank you, Alice." She turned to smile as Alice and a footman came in with laden trays.

"Hot muffins, butter, jam and honey, coffee, cream, sugar," Alice said, unloading the trays as the footman stood patiently. "Anything else, ladies?"

"No, that's perfect," Petra declared, sniffing hungrily. "They smell delicious."

Alice nodded, then gestured to the footman and they left the room.

Petra wasted no time in splitting a muffin and buttering it liberally. "What d'you intend to do?"

Fenella took a sip of coffee and waved away the platter of muffins Diana offered. "No, I'm too excited to be hungry . . . I don't really know what I intend to do. It depends how much work it will take to make it a serviceable venue, and, of course, the rent. And, once we have a theatre, we can rehearse in the space. It would be so much better than Cedric's freezing studio and so much more *real*."

She gave an expressive shrug, extending her hands palms up. "Covent Garden: What could possibly be better?"

"It certainly sounds ideal," Petra said, beginning to get into the spirit of this adventure. "Let's go take a look."

Chapter Twenty-Two

A stout man with a set of magnificent curled whiskers was standing outside the Music Box when Fenella and her friends stepped down from the hackney. He took off his top hat, sweeping them a flourishing bow. "Ladies, at your service."

"Mr. Garrett? Fenella Grantley." Fenella held out her hand. "Mrs. Lacey and Miss Rutherford." She gestured to her friends.

The stout man bowed to each in turn. "Delighted, ma'am." He turned back to Fenella. "You wish to see the premises, I understand?"

"Yes, I do," she replied. "I have a question first, though. Is anyone else interested in the venue, Mr. Garrett?"

He shook his head. "Not at present, ma'am. There was a gentleman a week or so ago who showed some interest, but he has not returned." He turned to the double doors and pushed them open. A gas lamp was already lit, showing them a dim foyer. "Please, ladies, come in. It's rather chilly, I'm afraid. The heating is not on when the building's not in use."

Fenella looked around her. It felt rather spooky in the shadowy light of the gas lamp, despite the bright sunshine without. She could smell the dust in the chill air and turned up the collar of her fur coat with a tiny shiver.

"Let me light some more lamps." Mr. Garrett struck a match to light two more gas lamps. He handed one to Petra, the other to Diana. "D'you care to take this one, Miss Grantley?" He offered her the other lamp.

Fenella held it up high to illuminate the small foyer. "I feel like Florence Nightingale," she observed. "You know, the lady with the lamp?"

"Well, it's certainly as cold as the Crimea in here," Diana declared, drawing her furs closer about her.

The manager opened a set of double doors at the rear of the foyer, flinging them wide onto a theatre. A theatre with a stage, an orchestra pit and rows of plush seating. There was only the one floor, no mezzanine or balcony and the space was small, but Fenella instantly saw its possibilities.

"How could this not be perfect?" she asked, awestruck by its potential. Just off Covent Garden with all the ambience of a real theatre.

"I don't know." Petra sounded doubtful as she looked around the gloomy space. "It's hard to imagine what it will look like."

"Imagine it filled with people, the chandeliers lit . . ." Fenella gestured to the ceiling. "Red velvet curtains across the stage, strains of music from the orchestra."

"It will take a lot of work," Diana said hesitantly. Like Petra's, her imagination was not as vivid as Fenella's.

"Yes, it will," Fenella replied cheerfully. "Let's see what it's like backstage." She plunged into the gloom in front of the stage, holding her lamp high as she headed for the steps that would take her onto the stage. Mr. Garrett followed rather more slowly, Petra and Diana bringing up the rear.

Fenella climbed up onto the stage, where she stood looking out over the gloom of the auditorium and for a heady moment imagined it packed with an attentive audience. Then she turned and made her way more tentatively into the wings, the lamp lighting her path. It was chaos backstage, but nothing that couldn't be tidied and put right. "Oh, there's a prop room. It's full of all sorts of great stuff. Come and see."

The manager peered over her shoulder at the jumble of props gathering dust in the shadows. "Of course, everything here can be rented with the theatre."

"It needs to be included in the rental," Fenella told him firmly. It occurred to her that her overt enthusiasm might encourage Mr. Garrett to inflate the price. "The place is dirty and needs fresh paint, even the sign outside. The stage curtain's dusty and will have to be cleaned, so that everyone's not sneezing throughout the performance. And while it's Covent Garden, it's not the best part."

Diana and Petra exchanged looks. This was the Fenella they knew, levelheaded and quick-witted.

Mr. Garrett looked somewhat taken aback by this sudden change in his potential tenant. He coughed. "Well, I'm sure we could come to some agreement, ma'am."

"How much a month?" Fenella demanded. "For the theatre and the props."

"Two hundred guineas."

Fenella shook her head. "One hundred and fifty guineas a month paid in advance with a three-month lease. And you'll have the curtain cleaned and the auditorium and foyer repainted, including the sign outside."

He shook his head, saying sadly, "It'll cost a lot for the cleaning and repainting. That's usually undertaken by the tenant."

"Not by this tenant," Fenella stated. "Take it or leave it." She turned and picked her way back to the stage followed by her friends, who wisely kept silent.

The manager huffed and puffed, then said, "Three months in advance?"

"Yes," she agreed. "I'll send you a banker's draft once you've drawn up the lease." She looked around the theatre again, holding her lamp high. "It's not as if you have potential renters beating down your doors."

"You drive a hard bargain, ma'am." He extended his hand.

Fenella shook it and nodded. "Let me give you the address to send the lease." She took a visiting card from her wallet and handed it to him.

A few minutes later, they were back on Wellington Street as Mr. Garrett locked the doors from the outside and, with a short bow, strode off toward the Strand.

"Well, that was some bargaining, Fenella," Diana said. "Congratulations."

"Let's go to the Piazza and get some coffee to celebrate," Fenella suggested. Covent Garden in the day was very different from its nighttime hustle and bustle; even the market was quiet, but it was usually at its busiest in the early hours before dawn, when traders brought in their produce and various establishments around Town sent their buyers for the fruit, flowers and vegetables available.

Petra stepped around a street sweeper and into the colonnade. "There's a coffee shop over there." She pointed to the far side of the square. "I went there with Joth once. I remember it because they had the most delicious éclairs. I can't think why my brother thought he needed to treat me. It's not like him at all. Maybe it was my birthday," she added cheerfully.

Her friends followed her across the cobbles to the small shop. Petra's relationship with her older brother was a subject of much amusement, blowing hot and cold as it did, but secretly, both Diana and Fenella knew that she actually adored Jonathan and he returned the affection in full measure.

"Café crème and an éclair, please." She gave her order to the waitress. "I'm so pleased with this theatre. It's an intimate space, perfect for the play itself, which is very intense and with a small cast, and the location is perfect. A lot better than Fulham."

"Fulham . . . why Fulham?" Diana inquired. "And yes, I'll have the same, please," she said to the waitress.

"I will too," Petra put in. "Fulham's a bit out of the way, isn't it?"

"Yes, that's exactly why it wouldn't do," Fenella told

her. "Edward looked at a space there and dismissed it out of hand."

"And how's George these days?" Diana bit into her éclair, catching a dollop of cream with the tip of her tongue.

Fenella frowned into her coffee, slowly stirring the thick, golden cream into the dark brew. "I don't know. He wrote me a rather snippy letter because one of his cohorts had seen me at Marco's with Edward when I'd told George I wouldn't go out with him à deux." She took a sip of her coffee. "I can't really blame him for being snippy when he heard that I was dining alone with someone else."

"No, I suppose not," Petra agreed, taking a large bite of her éclair. "He's still escorting you to the Warehams' ball, though, isn't he?"

"Oh, that's another pretty pickle." Fenella sighed. "I discovered yesterday that for some reason my mother has invited Edward to the dinner she's giving before the ball. And he accepted, although I can't imagine why. He makes no secret of his contempt for such social diversions. And George will be at the dinner expecting to be my escort for the evening." She shook her head. "I don't know how I'll get through the evening, but at least Edward declined the invitation to the ball, so it'll only be dinner to survive."

"Ritual will get you through that." Diana scooped up a smear of chocolate with her finger. "Just follow the usual rules for a formal dinner and you can't go wrong."

"You, my dear Diana, are an impossible optimist,"

Fenella said with a slight laugh. "And you don't know Edward. He has no time for Society's rituals and rules."

"He wouldn't do anything to make you uncomfortable, would he?"

"No, not deliberately," she said definitely. "He can be morose and ill-tempered, but he's not malicious or spiteful. And he can play the gentleman with the best, if he chooses to."

"Well, it'll make for an interesting evening," Petra declared. "Don't worry, Fenella. Diana and I will be beside you to fend off any uncomfortable encounters between dear George and your Edward . . . Now, I need another éclair." She raised a hand toward the hovering waitress.

Fenella was well aware that for all her lightheartedness Petra spoke only the truth. She and Diana would be beside her every step of the way. It was reassuring but didn't lessen her apprehension about the evening.

Fenella was at home in the yellow salon later that afternoon when a messenger brought the lease from Mr. Garrett. She read it through carefully. Then she went to the writing desk, picked up her pen, dipped it into the inkstand and signed her name. She wrote out a bank draft for the full three months' rent and attached a note saying that she expected the renovations to begin immediately. With a smile, she folded the papers into a neat package and sealed them closed before writing the address.

She rang for a footman and gave him the package. "Boris, would you see that this gets to Wellington Street right away, please?" Then she sat back and took a deep breath, visions of the spruced-up Music Box Theatre on opening night dancing in her head. How proud Edward would be to present his play to the world, and how proud she would be of him.

A tap at the door brought her out of her reverie. "Ah, darling, there you are." Lady Grantley came in with a somewhat strained smile. "I was hoping you'd be in this afternoon."

"Is something the matter, Mama?" Fenella got to her feet. "You don't look happy."

"Your father and I are worried about you," Lady Grantley stated, sitting down on an armless chair beside the fire, smoothing the pleats of her pale green afternoon dress. "You seem distracted, dear, and you've missed going to several soirees in the last weeks. Oh, I know you spend a lot of time with Diana and Petra, but you can't drop out of Society altogether."

Fenella resumed her seat on the sofa. "Oh, Mama, I haven't done that," she protested. "But the weather's been so inclement and it's so early in the Season, there really isn't much going on. All's well, I promise you. There's nothing at all for you to worry about."

"You don't seem to see as much of George as you used to."

Fenella sighed. "No, that *is* true. I felt that George had got the impression that we were all but engaged, and I realized that I had let him think that and it wasn't fair to him because there's no way that could happen. I couldn't possibly marry him."

"Oh, dear," Lady Grantley said. "That's what your father said. I had hoped . . ."

"I know you had, and I'm sorry to disappoint you." Fenella came over and knelt beside her mother's chair, taking her hand. "But it really wouldn't do, Mama."

Lady Grantley sighed. "Well, I suppose you know your own mind, dear." She hesitated before saying, "As to that, Fenella, what of this Mr. Tremayne? You appear to be seeing quite a lot him at the moment. I don't know much about him at all, except what your father told me about his . . . his personal circumstances," she added awkwardly.

"Ah." Fenella considered her answer. "I do enjoy Edward's company, I'll admit. If you remember, I told you I was involved in a play. Well, Edward wrote the play, which is why I'm seeing quite a lot of him at the moment." Half-truths were better than outright lies, Fenella told herself. And the less her mother knew, the better for her peace of mind.

Grace absorbed this in silence for a moment, before saying, "I do remember, yes, and I'm glad I decided to invite Mr. Tremayne to dinner before the Warehams' ball. I must ask him all about that."

"You didn't tell me you had invited him to dinner," Fenella said, slowly getting to her feet. "It was rather short notice, wasn't it? All the other invitations went out weeks ago."

"I didn't know Mr. Tremayne weeks ago," her mother said, standing up. "And I certainly didn't know that he would be taking up so much of your time. I felt that it was time your father and I made his acquaintance properly."

"Of course, I understand," Fenella responded swiftly. This was about as sharp as her mother ever got. She was clearly very put out. "I'm sorry, Mama, I should have told you before, but I've been so wrapped up in the play and my part in it that social proprieties were the last thing on my mind."

"Well, once we've been properly introduced to the gentleman and he knows he's welcome to visit you here, I trust matters will regularize themselves." Lady Grantley moved to the door. "Will we see you for dinner?"

"Yes, I'm in this evening." Fenella waited until the door closed behind her mother before sinking onto the sofa again. She couldn't stop her mother from being a mother, but it was irksome nevertheless.

Chapter Twenty-Three

"Well, it's coming together slowly," Cedric announced. "This room's not ideal, but it'll have to do until we get a proper space." He turned to where Edward was perched on the windowsill of the large empty room in the drama studio that they were using as a makeshift stage. "Any news on that front, Edward?"

Fenella held her breath. It was three days since she'd signed the lease for the Music Box and she hadn't yet told Edward, hoping to delay until repairs were further along.

"There's a community hall I'm looking at in Marylebone," Edward responded. "It's not perfect, but it might do. I'm taking another look tomorrow morning."

"Mmm. Well, sooner rather than later would be better. Actors need to become accustomed to the performance space. We can't start to block out scenes until we have a proper stage."

Edward made no answer. Cedric was preaching to the choir and knew it. Fenella bit her lip, suddenly nervous. It was time to show Edward his surprise, even if the renovations weren't yet complete.

She shrugged into her coat and went over to him. He was scribbling notes on his script and for a moment didn't look up even though he was aware of her standing beside him. This would have annoyed her a few weeks ago, but Fenella knew him better now. She guessed that he was annoyed with Cedric and was trying to master his irritation before he turned it on any unsuspecting person in his vicinity. Which in this case would be herself.

He looked up finally. "Fenella?"

"Edward?" she responded, gently mocking. To her relief, she saw his eyes warm and his lips twitch into the semblance of a smile. "I have something I want to show you. When you're ready . . ."

"Sounds intriguing." He bundled his papers into a worn leather satchel and hitched off his coat from the back of his chair. "Where are we going?"

"Wait and see." She turned to the door of the rapidly emptying room, calling goodbye to those who were left. If her fellow cast members guessed that there was something between herself and the playwright, they kept their assumptions to themselves.

Edward followed her down to the street. "We'll have a better chance of getting a hackney if we go to the corner of Bloomsbury Square," she said, turning in that direction. Edward nodded agreeably and walked beside her.

"I hope this outing includes lunch." He stepped

sideways into the street to wave down an approaching cab. "I'm ravenous."

"So am I." Fenella climbed into the hackney, deciding swiftly that after a good lunch and a bottle of wine, Edward might well find her surprise less of a shock. "Where should we go?"

"The Shakespeare Head," he said. "So what have you got to show me?"

"After lunch all will be revealed." She smiled, hoping she didn't look as nervous as she felt.

Edward said nothing, but his blue gaze intensified as he leaned his head back against the squabs, watching her. She was up to something, and as a rule, he didn't like secrets and was deeply suspicious of surprises. Despite that, he would do his best to respond as Fenella wanted him to. It wasn't her fault he was such an ill-tempered bastard so much of the time. At least he knew himself for what he was, he reflected, with a twisted smile.

Fenella's nerves settled somewhat over lunch. Edward was his most entertaining self, refrained from any adverse comment on the morning's rehearsals, and the steak and kidney pie was rich and comforting, accompanied by a robust claret.

"So, where to now?" Edward asked, pulling on his gloves as they stepped out onto the colonnade.

"This way." Fenella set off down Russell Street. At the junction with Wellington Street, she paused, looking up at him. His expression was now wary. She quashed the little prickle of alarm and turned right onto Wellington Street. She walked halfway down the street to the Music Box. The sign was freshly painted, the doors stood open to the pavement and the smell of fresh paint and turpentine wafted on the air, the sound of men's voices coming from the depths within.

"Here we are," she said, struggling to sound strong and confident. "What do you think?"

Edward stood very still, staring at the theatre. "What have you done, Fenella." But it wasn't a question.

She swallowed. This was not the reaction she'd been expecting, and she suddenly felt horribly awkward. "I . . . I found the address in your sitting room . . . and I thought you'd been considering it as a venue. It seemed so perfect," she stammered. "I've taken it for three months. I wanted to surprise you. We should be able to start rehearsing here next week."

He turned his gaze on her, a white shade around his mouth, his eyes glacial. "You've taken it for three months. Without discussing it with me first. What on earth were you thinking? What could possibly have made you think I would want this?" He gestured with supreme contempt to the building.

"Dear God, Fenella, I had thought you different. But I see now . . ." he said scornfully. "This is what *you* want—to act in a Covent Garden theatre, to impress your Society friends. You, a rank amateur indulging her playacting *hobby* just because she can afford to. The last thing I want is fanfare and fuss. I don't want my play, my *first* play, exposed to an audience I despise. I'm not interested in fame and fortune, however much you might hanker after such things yourself. I want critical appreciation from people I respect and I won't get that by prancing around Covent Garden like some self-aggrandizing idiot."

"But you *did* look at the theatre yourself," she said, bewildered by the ferocity of his attack. "I wouldn't even have known about it otherwise."

"Why didn't you *ask* me about it? How hard would that have been? Why would you jump to conclusions? I looked at it purely for comparison's sake."

"You don't have to use it," she said, her voice muffled by tears. "It doesn't matter. Just forget about it." She turned away and left, half-running toward the Strand.

Edward swore under his breath but made no move to go after her. He was too angry to trust himself. After a moment, he walked through the open double doors and went into the theatre.

Fenella slowed as she reached the safety of the crowds along the Strand. Her tears dried on her cheeks and slowly, she regained her composure as anger at his cruelty overcame her sense of shame. She had tried to do a good thing, to give a present she had been sure, obviously mistakenly, would be appreciated, at least once he'd recovered from the first shock. It wasn't true that she only wanted to exhibit her dramatic skills in public. And Edward had never implied that he didn't want to expose his play to Society's opinions. He'd talked about the West End as a financial impossibility, nothing else.

But she should have asked him first—she saw that now. She had been so sure she was giving him what he wanted. It was something she had the means to do, and she'd wanted him to have it.

She walked the streets for an hour until a dull numbness replaced her anger and disappointment. Then she flagged down a hackney and told him to take her to Cavendish Square. If Diana wasn't at home, she'd leave a note asking her to call in Albemarle Street.

As luck would have it, Diana was just returning from the park with the dogs as Fenella stepped down from the cab.

"This is a surprise, Fenella . . . oh, something's wrong . . . what is it, dearest?" Her eyes filled with concern as she embraced her friend. "You look wretched."

Fenella smiled weakly. "I *am* wretched. And angry and cross with myself . . . oh, it's a mess, Diana." She bent to stroke the dogs, who were pressing against her legs, radiating welcome. "Hello, you two."

"Come inside." Diana ushered her up the steps and into the house.

"Good afternoon, ma'am . . . good afternoon, Miss Grantley."

"Good afternoon, Barlow." Fenella returned the butler's greeting with as much equanimity as she could muster.

"Come upstairs to my parlor. Could you send up

tea, Barlow?" Diana unhooked the dogs' leads and flung an arm around her friend's waist, urging her toward the stairs, the dogs racing ahead of them. She opened the door onto her square parlor at the back of the house. "Here we are; sit by the fire and tell me what's happened."

Fenella sat down before saying, "Petra's going to want to hear this; should we send her a note?"

"Of course. I'll send a footman straightaway. Just sit by the fire and relax." She hurried away, and Fenella closed her eyes. The dogs flopped in front of the fire with breathy sighs and looked up at her, heads resting on their forepaws.

Their silent but attentive presence was oddly soothing. She felt drained of all emotion, physically tired from her long walk, and sleep nudged at her.

When Diana came back from her errand with a tray of tea, Fenella forced her eyes open, but then it seemed too much trouble to keep them that way and she closed them again. "Sorry, I'm feeling feeble."

"Have a doze while we wait for Petra," Diana said. "You really look as if you've been through hell, darling."

Fenella raised a limp hand in acknowledgment. Diana poured tea, placed a cup on the side table beside her friend and then sipped her own, wondering what on earth had happened. It wasn't hard to guess that Edward Tremayne had something to do with it, or that the Music Box Theatre was probably involved.

Petra burst in upon them within half an hour.

"Whatever's happened? Has there been an accident? Your message sounded so urgent, Diana."

Fenella sat up, drained the last of her tea and said, "It's not urgent, Petra. I just needed a shoulder or two to cry on."

Petra discarded her coat and hat. "Is there any tea left?"

Diana poured her a cup and they both regarded Fenella. "Tell us."

Fenella took a breath and told the whole, trying to be as objective as possible. "I should have asked him first, of course, but, oh . . . I meant well. I thought this would make him happy. How stupid I was." Her fingers quivered and she closed her fists tightly. "But now I'm just angry at both of us. Me for being stupid and him for being so nasty and hurtful. And I'm just so disappointed."

"I'm so sorry, Fenella." Petra came over and hugged her. "I'd like to stick a knife in his ribs."

"Me too," Diana said.

"Me three," Fenella said, and they all laughed. It was a subdued laugh but it served to lighten the mood a little.

"But seriously, what are you going to do?" Diana asked.

"Nothing. I've paid for the theatre and it can stand empty for three months. It's no one's business but mine." Reluctantly, she got to her feet. "I should go home. My mother's taking a sudden and inconvenient interest in my doings. I couldn't face her questions just now."

"Why don't we visit you in the morning? We can do something fun to take your mind off all this."

"I'd like that." Fenella drew on her gloves. "Are you coming too, Petra? We could share a cab."

"Absolutely," Petra said cheerfully. "Bye, Diana. See you in the morning."

Fenella slept fitfully that night; her mind wouldn't let go of the hideous scene with Edward . She was a rank amateur, was she? Playacting in front of her friends? Was that what he thought of her? How ridiculous she'd been to think he respected her as an actress. Had there ever really been a future with Edward? The present was so seductive and exciting that she had defined the future only in terms of the continuation of it. But now she realized that despite the odds, deep down she had nurtured a seedling of hope that there might be something more.

She got up and dressed, trying to respond to Alice's cheerful morning conversation, but after a while she gave up and restricted her conversation to questions about Fenella's plans for the day and evening as they related to her wardrobe needs.

"Will you be going down for breakfast, Miss Fenella?" Alice fastened the last tiny button at the back of Fenella's broderie anglaise blouse.

"No, I'll just have toast and coffee up here." The idea of eggs and bacon was repellent, and the effort of making conversation with her parents was too much.

She was dressed and in the yellow salon flicking

through the pages of the *Gazette* when Diana and Petra were announced.

"So, we are come to distract you with something amusing," Petra announced, looking her over with an air of concern. "You still look a bit peaky, dearest."

"I didn't sleep very well," Fenella admitted. "But I'm all the better for seeing you both. What shall we do to take our minds off this dismal business?"

"We thought—" Diana broke off as Collins came in with a silver salver.

"A messenger brought this for you, Miss Fenella."

"Thank you." She took the letter from the salver and her stomach jolted. Edward's writing on the envelope was unmistakable. Her fingers quivered slightly and she felt a little queasy as she broke the seal with a fingernail and extracted the single sheet.

Petra glanced knowingly at Diana, who nodded and sat quietly as her friend read the letter.

Fenella, we must talk. If I was unduly harsh, I apologize, but you should have known better. Nevertheless, the deed is done and there are things we now need to discuss. I'll come by this afternoon, around three o'clock. E.

"Sweet heaven," Fenella whispered in a fury too deep to express. "After the terrible things he said . . . of all the arrogant . . ."

"May we see?" Diana held out her hand. Fenella gave her the sheet of paper. "Oh, yes, indeed, of all the arrogance," she said when she'd read it, before passing it on to Petra. "He sounds like some exasperated schoolmaster."

"It's a habit he has," Fenella said caustically. "I have no wish to see him in this mood; it'll do no good for either of us. I won't be here this afternoon. Should I leave him a message or just ignore him? How *dare* he just announce in that supercilious way that he's coming to see me? After everything he said yesterday . . . he's sorry for being harsh, but it was all *my* fault. Oh, no, that's more than I can bear." Her voice shook with a muddle of emotion.

"I suggest you ignore him," Diana said. "Just be out of the house, as if you didn't receive his message."

Petra shook her head. "No, I think you should ask Collins to tell him that you wished him to know that you're not at home. He'll get the message more clearly that way."

Fenella considered her options. "Yes, I think delivering a message through Collins is the answer. I won't dignify this piece of patronizing rubbish with a proper response. But, oh, Lord, it's the Warehams' ball tomorrow. And the dinner party here."

"Well, he wouldn't come now, would he?" Petra declared. "It wouldn't be . . ." She sought for the right words. "It wouldn't be *gentlemanly* to put you in such a position."

"Edward's a gentleman only when it suits him," Fenella said bitterly.

"Well, if you make it clear this afternoon that you want nothing more to do with him, he's bound to send his regrets to Lady Grantley," Diana stated. "No one, not even the ungentlemanly Edward Tremayne, would be so barefaced as to present himself in those circumstances."

"I wouldn't be so sure of that," Fenella muttered. Then she shook her head vigorously. "I'm not going to think about it anymore; it only makes me even more upset." She jumped to her feet. "Come to my room and tell me what you think of my gown for tomorrow."

Her friends followed her without demur to her bedroom. Fenella went straight to the wardrobe. "It's rather unusual, and Mama is not at all convinced it's appropriate." She lifted out a hanger and turned dramatically to face her friends, holding against her a gown of stunning black velvet, so deep and dark it seemed almost luminous. The sleeves were tight to the elbows, then flared in silver lace ruffles to her wrists.

"It's *gorgeous*, Fenella," Petra declared in awe. "I love those tight sleeves. Everyone else will be wearing leg-of-mutton or melon sleeves, if they're wearing them at all."

"Who made it?" Diana asked, fingering the luscious material.

"Madame Lecourt. She had this vision and I fell in love with it." Swiftly, Fenella returned the gown to the wardrobe, averting her face from her friends. She had been secretly treasuring the thought of Edward's reaction, anticipating his response when he saw her in the gown set off by her mother's sapphires. Anticipation was the very devil; it only led to heartbreak, she thought.

"So," she said, forcing a cheerful note to her voice as she turned away from the wardrobe. "What shall we do for the day? Something that will keep me out of the house until at least five o'clock."

"There's an Egyptian exhibition at the British Museum," Petra suggested. "I'd quite like to see that."

"Good, then lunch first at the Trocadero and the exhibition after, then we can have tea at Fortnum's, by which time Mr. Tremayne will have been and gone," Diana declared.

And hopefully her mother would have received his regrets for tomorrow's dinner, Fenella thought. It was inconceivable that he would force his presence upon her.

Edward knocked on the Grantleys' door at precisely three o'clock. For once, he was dressed impeccably for an afternoon visit in a gray tweed frock coat and matching trousers, carrying his top hat. He had decided that if, as was likely, he were to meet Lady Grantley at an impeccable hour for visiting, he should do what he could to erase any previous unfortunate impressions.

Collins answered his knock and said with a bow, "I'm sorry, Mr. Tremayne, but Miss Grantley asked me to tell you that she is not at home this afternoon." He stood foursquare in the doorway.

Edward regarded the obstacle in front of him with a slight frown. "Is Miss Grantley in the house, Collins, or has she gone out?"

"She is out for the afternoon, sir."

"I see." Edward's lips thinned. "Do you happen to know where she went?"

"I'm afraid not, sir." Collins bowed again, stepped back and closed the door, leaving the visitor on the doorstep.

So she wouldn't see him, which struck him as somewhat cowardly and not in the least like Fenella. He was willing to accept that he had allowed his anger free rein, something that he now regretted, but if Fenella hadn't done something so crassly thoughtless, he wouldn't have lost his temper. He had had time to cool down and he had assumed she now realized how far she had overstepped with her interference. He hadn't known exactly what to expect by way of greeting this afternoon, but he had expected her to be here. He looked up and down the street, half-hoping to see her coming toward him, hurrying to their rendezvous. But he knew that wasn't going to happen. She would be with her friends somewhere in the five miles of London inhabited by good Society, but there was no way he could guess at her whereabouts.

So their next meeting would have to be in public, something he would have done anything to avoid. But Fenella had written the scene. He would have to take his cue from her over dinner the following evening.

Edward turned on his heel and set off back to Praed Street. He couldn't believe Fenella was just sulking. It just wasn't in her nature; she was far too straightforward and honest. But why wasn't she prepared to talk it through with him so they could put it behind them? Had he said something unforgivable? It wouldn't be the first time, he acknowledged ruefully. He knew he could be cold, cutting in his anger, and he'd been very angry.

He racked his brain, trying to remember exactly what he'd said to Fenella in the heat of the moment. Unbidden, her face appeared in his mind's eye. Her expression was stricken, raw with pain. He stopped on the pavement as icy remorse seeped into his veins. What exactly had he said to cause that expression?

Chapter Twenty-Four

Fenella was distracted throughout the afternoon and her friends refrained from comment. It was clear to both of them that ignoring Edward Tremayne was no final solution to Fenella's problems and she was obviously trying to decide what step to take next. They dutifully went around the Egyptian exhibition, admiring gold-encased mummies and bejeweled adornments, before taking tea at Fortnum's.

"They do make the most delicious cucumber sandwiches," Petra observed, taking a third from the silver-tiered serving dish in front of her. "You'd think they'd be so simple to make, and yet somehow Fortnum's are better than any you get elsewhere, even at home."

"They use anchovy butter," Diana said. "I asked once. Aren't you eating anything, Fenella? You hardly had any lunch."

"I seem to have lost my appetite," Fenella responded with a shake of her head. "Sorry to be such a misery guts."

"Have you thought of what you're going to do next?" Petra asked directly.

"It rather depends on Edward," her friend said. "I don't want to see him again—I couldn't bear another scene like yesterday's—so I hope he'll take the hint from this afternoon and leave things as they are."

"But what about the play? You still want to play Rose, don't you?"

"Not at this price." Fenella drank her tea, hearing his voice accusing her of viewing his play and her own part in it as no more than a hobby she could indulge because she had the time and the money to do so. She shook her head. "I think my drama fantasy is well and truly over."

"There must be other drama schools," Diana suggested.

"I'm sure there are, but I don't think I'm ready to start looking for one yet." Fenella pushed back her chair. "It's time I went home." She slipped her arms into her coat as she stood up. "You two stay and finish your tea."

"If you need company this evening, just shout," Diana said, kissing her.

"Will do." Fenella smiled a quick farewell and hurried between the tables scattered through the pillared foyer. She found a cab easily enough and sat back, aware of a thumping heart and the absurd urge to bite her nails. Surely Edward would have made his excuses about the dinner party to her mother by now.

She let herself into the house just as Collins

emerged from the drawing room. "Good afternoon, Miss Fenella."

"Did Mr. Tremayne call?"

"Yes, ma'am. At precisely three o'clock. I explained that you were not at home, as you desired."

She began to draw off her gloves. "Did he say anything? Leave a message?"

"No, Miss Fenella. He merely took his leave."

"Have any messages come this afternoon?"

The butler shook his head. "No, Miss Fenella, none whatsoever."

"Not even for Lady Grantley?"

"No, nothing has been delivered. Were you expecting something? Should I send a message of inquiry?"

Fenella quickly shook her head. "No, that won't be necessary. Thank you, Collins." She hurried upstairs. *Now what?*

Her mother knocked at her bedroom door a few minutes later. "Collins said you were home, dear. Where have you been all day?"

"With Diana and Petra. We went to that new Egyptian exhibition at the British Museum." She sat down at the dresser stool to remove the pearl studs from her ears.

"Oh, that sounds nice, dear. I've just finished the seating plan for tomorrow and I have put Mr. Tremayne on your right and dear George on your left. Your father thought it was the right thing to do."

Fenella knew her father well enough to guess that he had come up with this solution to her mother's dilemma about her rival suitors. *Let Fenella seek them out for herself.* It was typical of his method of dealing with situations that didn't interest him particularly, and he had always encouraged Fenella to think for herself.

"That's fine, Mama," she murmured.

Lady Grantley moved back to the door. "Well, I must change for dinner. Are you going out again this evening?"

Fenella shook her head. "No, I'll join you for dinner unless you have other guests and I'll upset the seating."

"We do have guests, but of course you won't disturb anything. You live here, my dear, and your father and I are always more than happy to have your company." On which note, Lady Grantley kissed her daughter and swept from the room, leaving her faint scent of apple blossom on the air.

Fenella stared into the fire, wondering how she had found herself in such an impossible situation. It was time to face the fact head-on. She had fallen in love with an impossible man. But how on earth did one stop oneself from that happening? She hadn't looked for Edward Tremayne. He had just materialized, and from the first moment of their first quarrel, the rest had been inevitable.

Edward tried to work, but his mind would not focus. He kept rising from his table and staring out the window, gazing down on the street as the afternoon slipped into evening. Every cell in his body revolted at the idea of attending Lady Grantley's dinner party the next day. He hated dinner parties at the best of times, but to have to use this occasion to get Fenella to listen to him seemed, at the moment, beyond his imaginative powers. He could already hear the inconsequential chatter from the group of self-absorbed, self-congratulatory guests, braying at each other around the dinner table. But he'd missed his opportunity to make a sudden and impeccable excuse to Lady Grantley that afternoon. And however unfavorable the circumstances, he needed to see Fenella. He couldn't allow the silence to fester.

Surely at some point in the evening there would be an opportunity to get Fenella alone without drawing attention to themselves.

Fenella walked around the beautifully laid dinner table the following evening, reading the place cards, noting the guests close enough to her for any kind of conversation. The Tremayne siblings fortunately were seated well away from her. Shouting across the candles and flower arrangements was frowned upon, and the table was too wide for a subdued personal conversation, but the occasional acknowledging remark was considered unobjectionable. Her attention was chiefly focused on her own place in the middle of one side of the long table and the two cards on either side of her. As Edward was on her right, he would be the one to take her in to dinner, which would put George's nose even further out of joint. She debated switching the cards, but she didn't want to encourage George either.

Lord George could be managed with smiles and

small talk; he would certainly neither do nor say anything to cause a scene. But Edward could not be similarly managed. She wasn't even certain she could manage herself in his company; his sheer physical presence had such an effect on her, however angry and bitterly hurt she was.

Why was he coming? It was perverse, unless he deliberately intended to embarrass her, to make her uncomfortable. But Edward was a man of large emotions; he was not in the least petty.

She turned hastily away from the table with a slightly guilty flush at the sound of the door opening. Lady Grantley came in, the epitome of fashionable elegance in a gown of saffron silk with leg-of-mutton sleeves, topaz earrings and necklace set off by the topaz tiara she wore in her high-piled pompadour.

"I was wondering where you were, Fenella." She examined her daughter with approval. "You were quite right about the dress, darling. It's very dramatic. While young women your age don't wear black as a rule, somehow it seems just right. And those sleeves are so unusual."

Fenella smiled her pleasure. "It is very elegant, isn't it? Thank you for lending me the sapphires; they're a perfect match."

Her mother nodded. "Yes, indeed they are. Again, very dramatic. Almost any gem looks perfect with black, but the fire of the sapphires is so striking."

They would certainly strike Edward, Fenella thought, fingering the rich circlet of stones at her throat. It had been a struggle with herself to wear them as she wondered whether Edward would read some kind of message in the choice, and if so, what kind? But finally, she had decided that whatever he thought about the stones was irrelevant. They were the perfect adjunct to her gown and she was going to look her best.

Lady Grantley walked around the table, her eagle eye catching the position of a fork that needed adjusting, a drooping petal on a low bowl of massed hot house hydrangeas. In the doorway, Collins stood attentively, ready to respond to any word or gesture from her ladyship. But finally, her inspection complete, she said, "Very nice, Collins; as always, you can be trusted to achieve perfection. Come, Fenella, we should be in the drawing room to await our guests."

The doorbell didn't cease its summons for the next half hour. Lord and Lady Grantley stood in front of the fire, welcoming each arrival, Fenella quietly beside them, offering her own greeting. George was among the first to arrive and Fenella braced herself for any spikes. "Good evening, George." She extended her hand with a warm smile. "Long time no see."

"We've been wondering where you've been, George, dear," her mother put in. "Although I don't understand this strange language you young people speak these days, I assume that's what Fenella meant."

George bowed over her hand. "I was obliged to go into the country for a while. My father wanted me to sort out some tenant issues with his agent." He turned to greet his host with another punctilious bow before eventually turning his full attention to Fenella.

"You are looking splendid as always, Fenella." His

eyes searched her face. He looked, she thought, a little wary, as if wondering if she would jump down his throat.

"George. How are you?" She reached up on tiptoe and brushed his cheek with her lips as she naturally would have done. "How was Derbyshire at this time of year? Freezing, I expect."

"I had a couple of good days' shooting," he said, accepting a glass of champagne from a tray offered by a hovering footman. "But the ground's too hard for hunting."

"Relaxing for the foxes, then," Fenella said, then bit back an involuntary laugh as she saw George's expression of pure confusion.

"It's always good to hear of some compassion for our persecuted wildlife," Edward's familiar voice came from behind George.

Fenella's eyes lifted to meet the intense blue gaze and the conspiratorial smile on the mouth she had kissed so many times, the mouth that had kissed every inch of her body, and she felt the ground lurch beneath her.

"Mr. Tremayne, good evening." Her voice was surprisingly steady, her smile bland.

"Miss Grantley." He turned immediately then, to greet his host and hostess with perfect courtesy before extending his hand to George, who still stood beside Fenella. "Lord George, I have had the pleasure, I believe, but some time ago."

"Yes, I believe so, Tremayne." George was curt, his hand merely brushing Edward's.

A rush of new arrivals meant that both George

and Edward were obliged to relinquish their places beside the Grantleys and mingle with the other guests.

Fenella took a breath of relief at the reprieve. From that encounter it rather looked as if George was going to be the sullen and ill-tempered one. But she wouldn't have to worry about him until after the first course was removed when she would be expected to turn her attention to her neighbor on her left.

Edward took his glass of champagne to a book-lined corner of the drawing room and stood with his back to the room, examining the erudite titles, wondering how many of them had actually had their spines cracked in the last decade.

"Oh, these are just for show," a cheerful voice he instantly recognized spoke at his elbow. "The real books that anyone reads are in the library."

"Miss Petra Rutherford." He smiled at her with genuine pleasure. He had liked both of Fenella's closest friends on sight at their horseback meeting in Hyde Park. "I admit I was wondering when they'd last been opened."

"I'm sure they're dusted regularly," Petra responded. "Are you waiting to get Fenella alone?"

"How very direct you are," Edward remarked.

Petra said simply, "It's usually the best way to get an answer."

"So I have always believed," he responded. His eyes were on Fenella.

Petra followed his gaze and before she could change her mind went where angels wouldn't. "Would you be open to a word of advice?"

His eyes narrowed as he looked at her. "Yes. I won't guarantee to take it, though."

"That's your prerogative." She paused, frowning. "I shouldn't be saying anything, but I can't bear to see Fenella so upset. You hurt her most dreadfully. But I think you probably feel for her what she feels for you, so if you're going to talk to her about what happened, don't sound so schoolmasterly." She turned to take a glass of champagne from the footman's tray. "And Fenella doesn't take kindly to being patronized either, and your note was both." She turned away without another glance, leaving Edward both dumbfounded and thoughtful.

On reflection, his exasperated note had been both patronizing and scolding. It was no wonder she hadn't received him that afternoon, on top of whatever dreadful things he had thrown at her outside the theatre. But he had learned the hard way that when he wanted something, he had to go after it. Things would not drop into his lap. Unfortunately, he had fallen in love with a woman who did not react well to bulldozing tactics.

A gong sounded and the room fell quiet, all eyes turning toward the opened double doors where Collins stood holding a sheet of paper as he waited to announce the partnering of the guests as they processed down the staircase to the dining room.

He read out the list of couples, compiled by Lady Grantley, in descending order of importance. "Lord George Headington and Lady Amanda Sinclair," he announced close to the top of the list. George blenched, then flushed before regaining his composure and bowing, offering his arm to his partner. He avoided looking at Fenella, who remained standing calmly by the fire as the list went on.

"The Honorable Miss Grantley and Mr. Edward Tremayne," Collins announced, getting to the bottom of his employer's list.

Edward bowed and offered his arm to Fenella, his face expressionless. She took his arm with the merest nod and allowed him to escort her downstairs and into the dining room. "In the middle on the left side," she murmured as they entered the room, where their fellow guests were taking their seats.

George glared at Edward as they approached their places. Edward ignored him, waiting until Fenella was seated and the footman at her chair had adjusted its position before seating himself on her right.

"What is this, Fenella?" George whispered to Fenella as he sat down. "I always take you in to dinner."

"I know you do, George, but as I said before, Mama thought it was time to change things a little; it's not as if we're engaged. I should sit with other people from time to time. Anyway, you *are* sitting next to me," she pointed out quietly.

George was obliged to accept the explanation and was far too well bred to ignore Miss Sinclair. Fenella took a sip of the white wine in her glass.

"You look magnificent, Fenella, if I'm allowed to say that," Edward said. "And the sapphires are stunning."

"Don't read anything in to them," she returned more sharply than she'd intended. "They simply happen to be the most perfect choice with this gown."

"I wasn't reading anything into anything," he said, taking up his wineglass. "There's no need to go on the offensive when I was merely complimenting you on your appearance."

Fenella was silent for a moment, taking the respite offered by the footman at her elbow as he set a bowl of consommé before her. When he'd moved on, she said, "I didn't mean to go on the offensive."

Edward raised his eyebrows. "I'm glad I misunderstood." He dipped his spoon into the soup.

Fenella bit her lip. This was every bit as bad as she'd feared. "I trust you had a pleasant day, Mr. Tremayne."

"Oh, come now, Miss Grantley, you can do better than that," he chided gently, casting her a quick, almost amused glance.

"My small-talk skills seem to have deserted me," she responded, dabbing her lips with her napkin. "But I'll keep trying. Did you have a *productive* day, Mr. Tremayne?"

"I think you can answer that for yourself," he replied, quietly enough for his voice to blend in with the chink of glass, the clatter of cutlery and the rise and fall of the voices of their fellow diners. "Do you think I had a pleasant and productive day when you refused yesterday even to talk to me?"

"I'm talking to you now," she responded, taking another careful sip of her consommé.

"I have to admit I can't remember everything I said to you about the theatre, but I acknowledge that it was probably very unpleasant, and I'm deeply sorry. I also know the tone of my letter was out of order. But you didn't have to refuse to see me without a word of explanation. I needed to talk to you. You must recognize that."

"It's always about what *you* need, isn't it, Edward," she said, her voice soft but tinged with acid. "Did you think for one minute what *I* might have needed after that appalling scene? But this is not the place for this discussion. Could we keep to small talk, please?"

He was almost prepared to stand up and leave the table, but the only scenes Edward liked were ones written for the stage, and he had no desire to be a part of a social disaster. "Did you go anywhere interesting yesterday afternoon, Miss Grantley?" he inquired in a flat voice.

"The British Museum. There's a fascinating Egyptian exhibition on . . . most informative," she replied, wishing that one of them at least could disappear through the floorboards. How on earth were they to get through the next hour like this?

Silence fell while the soup plates were removed, to be replaced by platters of langoustines, glistening in their shells. Edward deftly removed the head and shell of the large pink object on his place and as deftly switched his plate with Fenella's. "Allow me, Miss Grantley. Those ruffles look to be in imminent danger of a butter bath."

She had been preparing to attack her own shellfish, while wondering how to keep the lace ruffles of her sleeves clear of the buttery emulsion that coated it. There were finger bowls at every place, but nothing with which to pin back the lace. Edward had coolly solved her problem before she had even come to grips with it.

"Thank you," she said. It was the only appropriate response even as she thought she should resent the unilateral action. But then, most men, George included, wouldn't have noticed the problem, let alone offered such swift assistance.

"My pleasure." Edward stripped his own langoustine, before dipping his fingers into the warm, lemon-scented water in the finger bowl.

"It felt like spring was on the way today," Fenella said, spearing a piece of shellfish on her two-pronged fork. "The air felt warmer, I thought."

"I daresay you were wrapped in fur," Edward responded. "It still felt distinctly chilly to me on my walk here."

"I heard the dawn chorus this morning," she persisted. "I've noticed that's usually one of the first signs of spring."

Edward's lips twitched. "I wonder how long we can keep this up. I suppose, after the weather, we could discuss Balfour's latest speech in the Commons, only unfortunately I haven't looked at a newspaper for several days. But perhaps you have another unexceptionable subject we could explore."

"It seems such a pity that we're unable to see any of Mr. Wilde's plays performed again," she said, venturing into socially forbidden territory, hoping that no one but Edward could hear her. "It seems wrong that his work has not been rehabilitated since his death."

"That's not an unexceptionable subject, dear girl.

Certainly not one we can discuss around your mother's table, much as I'd love to." He shook his head. "Let's try something less controversial. Do you have any travel plans for this year? Paris in the spring, perhaps?"

Somehow they limped along until the second course arrived and Fenella was able to turn her attention to George. One look at his hurt and resentful expression told her that this hour was probably not going to be any easier than the last. "Why is that man here?" he demanded sotto voce. "He's a social outcast, Fenella, and you're treating him like an honored guest."

"Edward's not a social outcast, George," she said curtly. "He's a Tremayne, the son of the Earl of Pendleton."

"You should hear how his half brother and sister talk about him," George muttered into his roast beef. "He's persona non grata in the family, you know."

"More fool them," Fenella told him, picking at her beef. "He can't be held responsible for the circumstances of his birth."

"That's not what they object to. At least not the only thing. It's his ingratitude, his bad manners, his refusal to repay any of his family's generosity—"

Fenella interrupted him with an unceremonious gesture. "I refuse to discuss malicious gossip with you, George, about anyone at all. Tell me more about your trip to Derbyshire."

George flushed crimson and took an overly large gulp from the claret in his glass. Fenella pushed his water glass toward him as he struggled to catch his breath, his face buried in his napkin.

"Have a sip of water, George."

"You're so damned patronizing sometimes, Fenella," he stated, his voice muffled in his napkin.

An accusation she had thrown at her other neighbor, Fenella thought wryly. This was proving to be the most disastrous dinner party she had ever attended. But why should she have expected anything else?

It was with supreme relief that she followed her mother's nod and rose to her feet to leave the gentlemen to their port. Edward stood up. "I'll follow you in a few minutes," he said into her ear.

"No, please stay and enjoy the port," she returned. "I'm sure we'll both enjoy different company, and I can vouch for my father's port."

"If you could read my mind at this moment, Fenella, you would be very, very careful what you say next." His piercing gaze held an unmistakable threat and, perversely, she felt her spirits lift at the prospect of a proper quarrel, where they could deal with the misery between them without the fear of being seen or overheard. Clearly, she'd rushed to judgment when she had believed all was over between them.

"Later, perhaps." With a cool nod, she swept gracefully out of the dining room in her mother's wake.

Chapter Twenty-Five

The ballroom in the Warehams' double-fronted mansion in Devonshire Place was illuminated by numerous chandeliers, the highly polished floor gleamed, double doors led into the refreshment room and card rooms. Chairs for the chaperones stood ranged against the pale cream walls.

Fenella walked in with George, who had maneuvered himself into the carriage with her as the procession of vehicles set off from Albemarle Street.

She'd managed to avoid a tête-à-tête with Edward in the drawing room when the gentlemen had finally abandoned the port in the dining room and joined the ladies. She was confused now rather than bitter. It was clear Edward didn't think that what had happened between them over the Music Box constituted the end of anything. He seemed to see it as a mere hiccup for which she was as much at fault as he. Now it seemed the next move was up to her, and she couldn't ignore the inescapable fact that his presence was vital to her happiness, everything about him was necessary, even when he made her furious, when he seemed unkind and unthinking, even then, he was as essential as the air she breathed. She relished the verbal jousting, loved the intimacy of feeling that somehow she belonged to him, as he belonged to her. Could she walk away from that? *Should* she walk away from that?

She lost sight of him in the flurry of departure. It was possible he was in one of the other carriages bound for the ball, but she doubted it. He'd probably simply walked off into the night. She'd get through the evening as best she could and beat an early retreat.

Diana and Rupert were just behind herself and George as they mounted the horseshoe staircase to be greeted by Lord and Lady Wareham, who passed them on to the butler, who announced them to the ballroom at large. Petra, happily engaged in a flirtatious conversation with one of Rupert's fellow officers, entered the ballroom just ahead of them. Fenella adjusted the ribbons that held her silver mask in place over her eyes as she responded to various greetings. As she moved among fellow guests, stopping for a word or two with one group or another, George, in his scarlet mask, stuck by her side, his hand tucked proprietorially beneath her elbow.

"George, please stop steering me around like a ship that's being blown off course," she protested finally, stopping in a quiet corner. She had finally had enough. If he refused to listen to her when she was gentle, it was time to make herself abundantly clear. "You *must* understand that I don't belong to you, whatever you may think."

"You're going to be my wife," he responded with a stubborn twist to his mouth. "You know it and I know it. I know it can't happen until my thirtieth birthday, but we can be affianced and you'll wear my ring. I talked to my father. He likes you, and he said a long engagement was perfectly acceptable—"

"You have no right to talk to your father about me, or to talk in this way at all," Fenella interrupted him in a fierce whisper. "I've told you already that I am not going to become engaged to you. I'm fond of you as a friend, but I wouldn't marry you if you were the last man on earth. I'd make you utterly miserable; you know we won't suit at all. Everything I am, everything I believe in, is anathema to you. How could you possibly have a wife who marched in Parliament Square?"

"You won't do that when you're my wife," he said stubbornly. "I've said before, you'll change. Once you're a mother, it'll be completely different. Even my father says that once you have children you'll stop all this suffrage nonsense and keep to your proper place at home. Now, come and dance. It's a waltz and I love to waltz with you."

Fenella was for a moment too taken aback by his sweeping statements to do anything as he caught her up against him and moved her onto the floor among the waltzing couples. She came to her senses after a shocked minute, finally repeating, "How *dare* you discuss me with your father? Let me go at once, George."

His grip tightened and she could feel the firm imprint of his hand on her back. He was holding her captive and she could see no way to break away without causing a scandalous scene. And then a voice said quietly, "May I cut in?"

She turned her head quickly. Edward, in a black mask, stood just behind her, his hand resting on George's arm. It was all perfectly acceptable behavior and no one took the slightest notice. But George said curtly, "No, you may not. I am dancing with my fiancée and she's dancing with no one else tonight."

Fenella froze where she stood, her complexion ashen. "I am not your fiancée. Let me go, George, *now.*"

Edward's expression remained calm, except for his eyes, which blazed blue fire against the black silk of his mask. "I believe you heard the lady, Lord George."

"She's staying with me," George stated and tried to turn Fenella back into the dance. "My fiancée has no truck with bastards."

His voice had risen just loud enough to be heard by the dancers in their immediate vicinity. Edward was as pale as chalk but his expression remained unmoved. Fenella caught sight of Diana, Rupert and Petra moving through the dancers toward them, their faces filled with alarm.

Edward sighed and shook his head. So much for avoiding scandalous scenes. He raised one hand in an almost leisurely fashion and drove his fist into George's chin. Lord George went down like a stone. People fell back, staring in shock and fascination. This was a scandal to enliven the whole Season when it had barely begun.

Edward took Fenella's hand. "Come along, you. I've had enough of this and we have to talk." He made for the doors to the refreshment room, drawing Fenella against him, easing her through the swiftly gathering crowd.

She went with him perforce, stunned and yet filled with a perverse sense of relief that at last resolution was on the horizon. It would have been better not to have had to leave George unconscious on the floor of a crowded ballroom—that was most unfortunate—but at least it cleared one obstacle off the field.

"In here." Edward opened a door onto a small, windowless room at the back of the refreshment room. It was filled with stacked chairs and folded butler's tray tables, the gas lamp turned low, offering a small, golden pool of light.

In the ballroom, Rupert looked down at George, who was beginning to come around. "I never did see what Fenella saw in him," he muttered to Diana, who, together with Petra, stood beside him. Rupert bent down, caught George's hand and hauled him to his feet with the assistance of several other gentlemen. George stood swaying, one hand on his chin, clearly unsure what had just happened.

"I suggest you make yourself scarce and put your head under a cold tap," Rupert advised.

George blinked, still swaying, still holding his chin, until someone took him by the arm and steered him toward the main doors of the ballroom.

Rupert glanced around at the gaping throng. "Where did Tremayne and Fenella go?"

"I think they went somewhere quiet to talk," Diana said.

"Should we look for them?" asked Petra, glancing around the ballroom. It was abuzz with voices; the orchestra continued to play, but no one was dancing. Small groups gathered across the floor discussing the extraordinary scene they had just witnessed.

"I think Fenella is quite capable of looking after herself," Rupert stated. "I think she and Tremayne probably have some unfinished business and they're better left to get on with it."

"I agree," Diana stated. "Let's go into the supper room, and behave as if nothing untoward has happened."

"You can't address me as *you*; that's so rude, Edward." Fenella took a deep breath, her first since Edward had taken her hand and marched with her out of the ballroom.

"I was extremely anxious to get both of us out of there," he replied. "I wasn't particularly interested in the niceties of social discourse."

"No, you certainly made that clear to the world and his wife. It's not hard to guess what's going to be the main topic of conversation in the drawing rooms of Mayfair for the rest of the Season."

"My gift . . . I hope they enjoy it," Edward responded. He perched on the arm of a discarded dining chair, his black mask dangling from one finger as he regarded Fenella closely. He didn't seem to be in the least out of breath or out of countenance.

"How did you know this room was here?" she asked, aware that she was pointlessly procrastinating.

"I was at school with Freddie Wareham," he said impatiently. "I spent time with him on the holidays and got to know the house. Now, what was all that about your being Lord George's fiancée?"

"It's nonsense; I told you, or rather I told him that. I've been telling him that for weeks." Fenella unfastened her mask, tossing it onto one of the stacked chairs.

Absently, he rubbed his knuckles, frowning at her. "Let's have it, Fenella."

"What do you want me to say?"

"Let your anger out. I need to hear it."

She took a deep breath. "All right. I wanted to give you a present, a surprise. You rejected it in the harshest terms, accusing me of self-interest. Have you never had a gift before?"

"Not since I remember," he replied.

"Never had a surprise?"

"Not a pleasant one . . . plenty of the bad kind."

She gazed at him, stricken. "Not even as a child?"

"Not since I was about seven, when they took me from my mother." He sounded matter-of-fact, but Fenella was filled with horror at everything the plain statement entailed.

"Oh, that's terrible." She gazed at him, her gray eyes filled with compassion. "I'm so sorry, my dear. And now I can't be angry anymore. But . . . but I still don't understand why you hated me so much at that moment."

"No, sweetheart, I didn't hate you. I could never hate you. I love you." He smiled then, holding out his arms. "Come here and let me show you how sorry I am for being such a brute, and then I'll explain why I didn't want that theatre."

She went into his arms without hesitation, resting her head against his chest as he stroked her hair. "You did explain," she murmured. "You didn't want a Society audience. I should have thought of that. I only thought of a big audience applauding, and you receiving the accolades for such an amazing play, and the glowing notices in the papers the next day. I let myself be carried away."

"And I jumped all over you," he said remorsefully. He tipped up her chin with a forefinger. "Can you forgive me, Fenella?"

"If you can forgive me."

"I have nothing to forgive." He lowered his mouth to hers.

After a long moment, he raised his head and looked into her eyes. "Is it over, sweetheart?"

She nodded, then said with a touch of mischief, "Until the next quarrel."

His responding smile was rueful. "That's inevitable, but I will do my utmost to ensure that my part in it remains in touch with the love I have for you."

"I keep crying," Fenella complained, wiping her suddenly moist eyes with a fingertip. "Ever since I met you, tears keep coming out of nowhere for no reason. I hope I'll get over it. It's horribly inconvenient."

Edward handed her his handkerchief. "I don't remember having that effect on any other woman."

"I won't ask how many there have been." She folded her hand over the handkerchief, offering a watery smile.

"So discreet," he returned. "Now, let me tell you what I have decided about the theatre."

"You don't have to decide anything," Fenella said swiftly. "You don't have to use it."

"That would be a terrible waste of money, not to mention a very attractive venue. We'll begin rehearsals there next week, and next month we'll put on a performance for an audience personally invited by me. The people whose opinions matter to me. After that, depending on the response and any criticisms and suggestions, I'll rewrite as necessary. Then we'll continue rehearsing and have a discreet opening for anyone who chooses to attend and is willing to pay for the privilege."

Fenella's eyes widened. "You worked all that out in two days? Did you look at the space?"

"I did, after my wretched tongue had driven you off." His smile was rueful. "I also talked to the manager. There were some adjustments I wanted made to the lighting. You don't mind my putting in an oar?" He raised a questioning eyebrow.

"Of course not. I gave it to you, remember? It's yours to do, whatever you wish." Her eyes were shining now with pleasure.

Edward put a hand inside his coat. "And now, my love, I have something to give you. I've been carrying it around, waiting for the right moment. If this isn't it, then there never will be a right moment." He slid a tissue-wrapped packet from his inner pocket.

Fenella felt a tremor of apprehension as he took her hand and placed the package on her palm, afraid she wouldn't respond as he expected, afraid she would do to him what he had done to her. Her fingers trembled a little as she unwrapped the package.

She gasped at the beautiful object thus revealed. A cuff bracelet, three strands of sapphires, the most unusual stones. She looked at him, speechless.

"Give me your wrist." He took the bracelet from her and clasped it around her wrist.

She held it to the lamplight in wonder as the stones changed from deep blue, to red, to almost black as she twisted her arm in the light. "Color-change sapphires," she said quietly.

"It was my mother's," Edward replied. He was filled with the most serene happiness at her obvious wonderment and delight. "I wish she could have put it on you herself. She would have loved to see you wearing it, particularly with that gown.

"It would look as wonderful if I were dressed in rags," she said.

"And most wonderful if it was all you were wearing," he murmured, his eyes darkening at the image of her naked body, the sapphires against her pale skin.

"That's not fair," she accused, her body responding to the sensual lure of his gaze. "Not here."

He smiled, touching his tongue to his lips. "Don't lose the feeling, my love, but fulfillment must wait for a little. Come." He took her hand. "We must go back to the ballroom."

Fenella resisted. "No, you can't be serious, Edward. We can't go back in there, not after what happened."

"That's exactly why we are going back. I'm not scared of Society's censure, and you certainly have no reason to be. If anyone should be embarrassed, it's that clown Headington. It would have been more convenient to have knocked him down in private, but . . ." He shrugged. "Needs must. Now, we are going back, we will dance one, maybe two, dances and then we will make our formal farewells to our hosts and leave with dignity intact."

"And then?" she asked.

"Use your imagination," he said, pulling her behind him back to the ballroom.

They entered the glittering salon arm in arm. The orchestra was playing a country dance and couples were taking their places on the floor. But there were fewer of them than usual. Around the room, small groups were engaged in animated conversation, and as Edward and Fenella entered the ballroom, conversation seemed to pause, just long enough to be noticeable despite the lively strains of music from the orchestra's dais.

Edward led them into the line of couples, his expression composed. He smiled at his partner as he stepped into place opposite her and the dance began. The precise steps and movements were second nature to Fenella, and she performed her part without conscious thought. Edward seemed as familiar as she, although she couldn't imagine that he'd performed this dance very often.

As they came together and then turned away from each other, she caught sight of Julia Tremayne, and the expression on her face shocked her. The woman was staring at Fenella with undisguised fury. Fenella offered a half-smile and Julia jerked her head sideways. As the dance ended, Fenella saw Julia stalk across the salon and into the card room.

"What's upsetting you?" Edward asked softly, offering her the customary bow as she curtsied. "You look as if you've seen something nasty under the woodpile." He took her arm. "Let's find some champagne."

"It's Julia," she said. "The way she was looking at me, as if she wanted to put a stake through my heart."

"Oh, don't worry about her. She's a malicious creature at the best of times; there's no knowing what sets her off." He raised a hand to a passing footman and took two glasses from his tray. He touched his glass to Fenella's in a silent toast.

"Look, there's Carlton; they're both coming over here," Fenella said, looking toward the card room door. "They look ready to do battle, Edward."

He turned in leisurely fashion just as his half siblings came up to them.

"How dare you bring even more shame on our name?" Carlton demanded loudly, his face red, a pulse beating in his temples. "You cause the worst scandal in years by attacking a good friend—a duke's son, for God's sake—and then you have the brass nerve to walk back in here and behave as if you're an invited guest."

"I am an invited guest," Edward said calmly. "Lord George was causing Miss Grantley considerable distress. When I remonstrated with him, he insulted me unforgivably, loudly and in public. I was, as I'm sure you will appreciate, Brother, obliged to defend both myself and the lady." He took a sip of his champagne. "Not that I owe you any explanations for my conduct, but I prefer to keep the peace." His smile encompassed both Julia and Carlton, and it was a smile that made Fenella shiver.

"And what's that she's wearing?" Julia demanded, her voice almost a shriek, two spots of color burning on her cheekbones. "That bracelet, Miss Grantley, belongs to the family. It's not yours to wear. It's stolen property."

The room seemed to hold its collective breath. Fenella was beginning to feel sick. The vitriol coming from the two Tremaynes was almost palpable. She looked at the bracelet on her wrist, then looked questioningly at Edward. His face was a mask, his lips thin, his eyes blank as stones. He moved an arm and firmly pushed her behind him.

"What a grubby, greedy, spiteful excuse for a human being you are, Julia," he said, so softly it was almost a hiss. "And you, Carlton . . ." He held up an arresting hand to his half brother, "You know perfectly well that the bracelet belonged to my mother. It was a present from my father. You were in the room when he was itemizing the family spoils to be divided between the two of you. The bracelet was the only piece that came to me. Shame on you both."

He spun on his heel, slipping an arm around Fenella's waist, ushering her through the gathering spectators. Suddenly, there were people around them, Petra and her soldier, Rupert and Diana, gathering others like tumbleweeds, moving with them through the crowd. The excited buzz of conversation arose in their wake.

"Dear me," Edward said. "We do seem to have put the cat among the pigeons this evening. I think it's time to make our farewells, with suitable apologies for being the unwitting cause of unpleasantness."

"We'll follow the same path," Rupert said. "And for what it's worth, I must congratulate you, Tremayne, on most successfully routing the enemy. After your intervention, I suspect Headington will be in rustication for the better part of the Season and your half brother and sister might find themselves less welcome in Society's drawing rooms for a while after that unseemly display."

"I can't think what my poor mother's going to say," Fenella groaned. "The doorbell will be ringing with the old cats bringing gossip from dawn tomorrow."

"Oh, we'll be there in support," Petra said. "Probably not at dawn, but we'll come at midmorning, after you've had a chance to prepare Lady Grantley."

Fenella glanced up at Edward, who said smoothly, "You'll be home at dawn."

Epilogue

Three months later

Fenella peeked through the heavy, red velvet curtain looking out over the auditorium. People were still taking their seats and there was an excited edge to the rise and fall of the conversational buzz. She looked for her parents in the seats she had personally picked for them. They were already seated in the center of the third row. She thought her mother looked strained, sitting bolt upright beside Lord Grantley, who, in contrast, was looking around the small theatre with an air of amused curiosity.

"Nervous?"

She stepped away from the curtain, turning to smile somewhat feebly at Edward, who was standing in the wings. "Oddly enough, not as much as I was for the performance in front of your people," she said. "It was so very important that they should like it. Of course, I want it to go over well tonight, but I don't think their reaction is as important to you as the first performance."

"True enough." He shrugged. "Nevertheless, I hope for everyone's sake they don't resort to throwing rotten fruit at the stage."

"They won't do that," she said confidently. "Oh, there'll be some malicious comments—how could there not be, with such an audience—but we have enough friends out there to overcome spiteful jealousy."

"You, my love, certainly have enough friends out there," he said. "Let me look at you." He ran a critical eye over her. She had only two costumes for the play, one white for the pure and gentle Rose, the other a startling crimson and black for the devil Rose. It was simple but effective, and Fenella knew that both styles suited her. The color-change sapphire bracelet never left her wrist.

"Two minutes to curtain up," the stage manager whispered.

Fenella swallowed a momentary flash of panic and hurried into the wings to await her cue.

"I really didn't understand," Lady Grantley said to her husband, while applauding vigorously two hours later. "Did she kill the baby or not?"

Lord Grantley shook his head. "To be honest, I don't think it matters one way or the other. The point is that our daughter revealed a side of herself I didn't know existed."

"She always loved acting in our house party plays," Lady Grantley said, gathering up her stole and gloves.

"This was something quite different." Lord Grantley helped his wife on with her mink coat. "I never expected a daughter of mine to appear on a professional stage, but I have to admire her for it."

"She *was* good," his wife conceded, "but I confess, I cannot like it. It's really not appropriate for someone of Fenella's position in Society to do something so vulgar as to perform on a public stage and charge money for it."

Her husband shook his head and preceded his wife to the aisle.

"Lady Grantley, Lord Grantley, wasn't Fenella *wonderful*?" Diana exclaimed as they made their way to the crowded foyer.

"I knew she would be good, but I didn't realize just *how* good," Petra chimed in. "You must be so proud."

"Well, I don't know about proud, dear," Lady Grantley said. "I hadn't really understood that this was to be a commercial enterprise, money changing hands . . ."

"There are always expenses, my dear," Lord Grantley offered with a soothing smile. "They have to charge something. Just the cost of the theatre must be considerable."

Diana and Petra exchanged glances. "Shall we go backstage and congratulate her?" Diana suggested.

"The door behind the box office leads behind the stage," Rupert said. He made for the inconspicuous door and the rest followed.

They found Fenella's tiny dressing room packed with people and filled with flowers. She turned from the dresser mirror where she was trying to remove her makeup as she saw them struggle to push their way through the throng. "Oh, there you all are." She jumped up. "Please move back, let my parents . . . my friends through . . . I'm sorry this is such a tiny space." She reached a hand for her mother and pulled her forward as the crowd moved back to make room. "Did you like it, Mama?"

"You were very good, dearest," Lady Grantley said. "But I still don't know whether Rose killed the baby or not. Oh, and I wish you hadn't taken people's money to see you."

"Don't mind your mother, Fenella," Lord Grantley said, bending to kiss his daughter's cheek. "I thought it was splendid." He turned back to his wife. "I doubt Fenella has taken any money for herself, my dear."

"No, of course I haven't," Fenella exclaimed.

"Quite the opposite," murmured Diana, sotto voce. "Congratulations, Edward." She greeted the tall figure who had just entered the dressing room.

"Yes, a tour de force, Tremayne." Rupert shook his hand. "And you certainly know how to pick your cast." He kissed Fenella lightly. "An excellent performance, and I'm convinced Rose did kill the baby."

Fenella laughed, shaking her head. "Each to his own opinion, Rupert."

An hour later, she and Edward were finally alone in the dressing room. "We should show our faces at the Shakespeare Head at the party with the cast," Fenella said with a sigh of exhaustion.

"No, there's no need, unless you really want to. I've already made our excuses," Edward said.

"Oh, wonderful. I'm exhausted; I don't know why."

She stood up from the stool and unhooked her coat from the back of the door. "Can we go straight home?"

"That was what I had in mind," Edward responded, taking her coat from her and holding it out so she could thrust her arms into the sleeves. He ushered her out onto the street and into a passing hackney.

She leaned back against the squabs and closed her eyes. "It was a wonderful experience, Edward. Are you pleased with the way it went?"

"How could I not be?" he replied, leaning back with his arms folded, his blue gaze intent upon her. "Sleep for a few minutes."

She dozed, lulled by the clop of the horse's hooves on the cobbles, the slight swaying of the cab until it came to a stop. She opened her eyes. "Are we here?"

"Indeed we are." He jumped out and reached a hand in to help her down.

Fenella stepped onto the cobbles of a narrow street. "Where are we? This isn't Praed Street."

"No, it isn't," Edward said with a smile. "Come with me." He gestured toward a bow-fronted house behind him.

Fenella took a minute to get her bearings. "This is Shepherd Street," she said. "Shepherd Market is just over there. Why are we here? It's not another brothel, is it?"

"Definitely not," he stated. "Come, I have something to show you." He took a key from his pocket and inserted it into the door of the house he had indicated. He flung open the door.

Bemused but curious despite her fatigue, Fenella

followed him into a small square foyer. It was in darkness, but Edward lit a sconce lamp that showed her a narrow staircase and two doors on either side of the front entrance.

"This way." He opened the door to the right, and Fenella stepped past him into a square sitting room. Edward lit the lamp and she looked around. It was a pretty room, pleasantly furnished with an Adams fireplace and a deep bow window overlooking the street.

"What is this house?"

Edward put a match to the fire already laid in the grate before answering her. When the kindling had caught with a comforting crackle, he put a small log on the blaze, then straightened, turning to face her. "Praed Street isn't big enough for two people," he told her, his eyes now dancing. "And I don't think you and Mrs. Hammond would get on too well under the same roof. So . . ." He gestured expansively. "Could you live here, Fenella?"

Comprehension dawned slowly. "You want me to live here . . . with you?"

"I'm tired of getting you home to Albemarle Street by dawn," he responded, his eyes questioning now.

"I can't just move in with you . . . my mother would die of shame."

"I thought to talk to your father as soon as possible."

She stared at him, momentarily speechless until he said, "Fenella, my love, don't keep me in suspense any longer. Will you?"

"Will I what?"

He sighed deeply. "You are not usually this obtuse; marry me, of course."

As proposals went, this was about as unromantic as Fenella could imagine. It was also perfect. "Just so I don't have to go home at dawn every night?" she queried, her own eyes now sparkling.

"You have a wickedly inappropriate sense of humor, Fenella Grantley." He pulled her into his embrace for an emphatic kiss. "Now, give me a proper answer."

"Of course I will," she said, touching her tingling lips with a fingertip. "How could I not? We're like pieces of a jigsaw; we fit together, except sometimes when we seem to be in different puzzles."

"Well, that's part of the fun of it all, isn't it?" Edward said, drawing her into his arms again. "Would you prefer it if we always inhabited the same puzzle?"

She shook her head. "No. I love to quarrel with you almost as much as I love to make love with you. I need the fire. Is that very perverse?"

"Some might say so, but I certainly don't. I need the fire too, my love."

She put her arms around him, pulling down his head so their lips met. "Can we stay here tonight?"

"Everything's ready upstairs. And you'll be happy to know that there's running water, hot and cold, and a water closet. How does that sound?"

"Like a little piece of heaven." She looked around the room, noticing that the bookshelves on either side of the fireplace were already filled. "It's a whole house?"

"A whole house. There's a kitchen, servants'

quarters in the attic and four bedrooms in case we have visitors."

"When can we move in?" Fenella's mind was racing ahead, already making plans for how she would set up her own household.

"I already have done, but I should really talk to your father before you make permanent arrangements," he said.

Fenella shook her head. "My father doesn't really believe in that permission nonsense where I'm concerned."

"What an enlightened man. No wonder he spawned such a wayward daughter."

Fenella reached for his hand. "Let's go upstairs and I will show you exactly how wayward I can be."

"Now, that's a prospect I can't possibly resist."

Don't miss Petra's story in
the next London Jewels romance
by *New York Times* bestselling author Jane Feather . . .

RAVISH ME WITH RUBIES

On sale in early 2021!

Read on for a preview . . .

It was a warm, early June afternoon when Petra Rutherford crossed Parliament Square and approached St. Stephen's Porch at the Palace of Westminster. The police officer on duty in front of the great oak door regarded her with a suspicious frown.

"Can I help you, madam?"

Petra's smile was bland. She was well aware that it was her purple, green, and white silk scarf that drew the man's frown. "I have an appointment to take tea on the terrace with the Right Honorable Mr. Rutherford." She handed the officer her engraved card.

He took it and silently opened the door for her. A liveried officer stepped forward instantly to take the card handed to him by the policeman. "If you would care to follow me, madam."

Petra knew the way well enough but she also understood the rigid, frequently arcane rules and rituals that informed all activities in the Houses of Parliament. She followed the man through St. Stephen's Hall and into the vast, ornate Central

Lobby situated halfway between the House of Commons and the House of Lords.

"If you'll take a seat, Miss Rutherford, I will send a messenger to inform the Honorable Member of your arrival." He gestured to the padded benches around the hall.

"Thank you." Petra glanced around the crowded lobby, looking for anyone she might know. It wouldn't be unusual for a friend or acquaintance to be visiting a member of Parliament at teatime.

"Petra . . ." She turned at her brother's voice. Jonathan hurried across the marble floor towards her. "I was waiting for you on the Terrace." His smile became a frown as he reached her. "Did you have to wear the scarf, Petra? It's a red rag to a bull in here."

"I did have to wear it, Joth, for that very reason. I'm sorry if it sullies the sanctity of these hallowed halls, but you support the cause so you should be proud to acknowledge your sister's participation."

He shook his head. "I don't *not* support women's suffrage, but I dislike drawing attention and making a fuss, and there's someone I most particularly want you to meet and be nice to this afternoon."

"Oh?" She looked at him curiously. "Someone I don't know?"

"Well, you did know him slightly, but a long time ago," her brother said with a vaguely dismissive wave of his hand. "I want to persuade him to support a bill that I'm presenting to Parliament and I need reinforcements. Just offer your sweetest smile and be as charming as you possibly can."

"You mean use my feminine wiles on him, flutter my eyelashes and blind him with flattery?" she asked, half laughing.

"I know better than to expect that from my sister, however helpful it would be. Just be pleasant and charming, I know you can do that much for all your radical inclinations," Jonathan stated. "Let's go for tea. I don't want him to be waiting for us." He offered his arm and Petra allowed him to escort her out of the hall and onto the long terrace overlooking the river.

"Your table is over here, Mr. Rutherford. Good afternoon, madam. How nice to see you again." The rotund figure of the head waiter barreled up to them as soon as they stepped onto the terrace. His eyes flicked to Petra's scarf and then turned aside, his smile of greeting fixed upon his round countenance.

"Good afternoon, Mr. Jackson." Petra greeted him with a warm smile of her own as if she had not noticed that discreetly averted glance. She had known what she was doing, wearing the colors of the Women's Social and Political Union so blatantly in this bastion of male power and privilege, but she was not about to make a scene, her protest was silent and polite. It would still ruffle feathers, though.

She followed the waiter and her brother through the tables where conversation was low-voiced and whose occupants concentrated on the matter in hand, showing no interest in those around them. The table was set for three, she noticed, as she took her seat facing the Thames. Jonathan took the seat opposite, leaving the one next to her free.

"So who is your mysterious guest, Joth?" she inquired, shaking out her napkin and laying it across her lap.

"He's a member of the House of Lords . . ." He broke off as a waiter set a teapot, creamer and sugar bowl on the table, followed by a tray of smoked salmon and cucumber sandwiches, and a cloth-covered basket of warm scones. A dish of clotted cream and a cut-glass jar of raspberry jam followed them.

Petra waited until tea was poured. She reached for the sugar tongs and dropped a lump into her bone china teacup blazoned with the arms of Westminster. "I'm intrigued, Joth." She stirred the sugar into her tea, regarding her brother with an inquiring smile.

Her brother frowned, glancing anxiously around. "Couldn't you put the scarf in your handbag?"

Petra's gaze followed his. "No one seems interested in us, let alone bothered."

"You know full well everyone will have remarked it. *Please* take it off, Petra." His hazel eyes, mirror images of his sister's, pleaded. "This afternoon is important to me."

Petra shrugged and untied the scarf, folding it carefully before sliding it into her handbag.

"Oh, don't take it off on my account." Petra hadn't heard that voice in almost ten years.

She turned her head to the side, feeling the old dislike rising from a deeply mortifying past. "Lord Granville," she said distantly, staring at the man who had been her nemesis in the days when she was just trying her wings in the adult world. He looked older, which was only to be expected, at least ten years older, and there was a hint of silver at his temples. His black hair was as thick as ever, though, and carefully styled, brushed off his broad forehead. His eyebrows, black as pitch, arched above dark brown eyes that if Petra didn't know better could be described as soulful and empathetic. But she did know better. The aquiline nose and well shaped mouth would to most eyes qualify Baron Granville of Ashton as a handsome man. But Petra's eyes in this instance were not *most* people's.

"Lord Granville, I'm so happy you could join us," Jonathan said, half rising from his chair as he indicated the seat next to his sister. "I think you may have met my sister, Petra."

"I have indeed. Although I must say you've grown some, Miss Rutherford, since last we met." His smile, showing even white teeth, was both warm and almost complicit, as if he was sharing an old and happy memory.

Petra met the smile with stony indifference. "It would be strange if I had not, Lord Granville. Ten years is a long time."

He inclined his head in acknowledgment. "Particularly the ten between fourteen and twenty-four. So, tell me what the grown-up Miss Rutherford is doing with her time these days, apart, of course, from making noise with the suffragists."

Petra swallowed hard. Her mind was working

furiously. She had never expected to meet this man in the usual course of everyday life, oh, maybe a fleeting glimpse across a drawing room at a route party or some such, but Guy Granville moved in a very different social set from her own. He was ten years older for one thing. She took a sip of tea and reached for a scone.

"Cat got your tongue, Miss Rutherford?" His tone was gently mocking, his amused gaze watching as she deliberately split the scone and spread clotted cream and raspberry jam on both halves.

Oh, how that tone made her toes curl, that hateful gleam of mockery in his eyes turned her stomach. But she was no longer the naïve unsophisticated girl who had inadvertently given him so much sport ten years ago. Jonathan wanted her to charm Baron Granville of Ashton. She could do that, and she would relish every minute until the moment came to put the knife in.

Petra took a bite of her scone, slowly licking a speck of cream from her lips as she met the baron's gaze. "How wonderful that our paths have crossed again, Lord Granville. Perhaps we can dispense with such formality, though. After all, we were once so very well acquainted." She picked up the platter of sandwiches, the smile of an attentive hostess on her lips. "Do you care for one, Guy. The smoked salmon are particularly good."

She caught the flicker of surprise in his eyes, the instant of quick calculation as he took in her smile and tone, then he reached out an elegant white hand to take a sandwich and she remembered with a jolt those long slender fingers, the beautifully manicured nails.

"Thank you, Petra," he said, his smile neutral although his eyes were sharply assessing.

Connect with Us

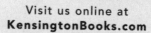

Visit us online at
KensingtonBooks.com
to read more from your favorite authors, see books
by series, view reading group guides, and more.

Join us on social media

for sneak peeks, chances to win books and prize packs,
and to share your thoughts with other readers.

facebook.com/kensingtonpublishing
twitter.com/kensingtonbooks

Tell us what you think!

To share your thoughts, submit a review,
or sign up for our eNewsletters, please visit:
KensingtonBooks.com/TellUs.